# DEEP POWDER

## Dirk Robertson

Published by
The X Press
PO Box 25694
London N17 6FP
Tel: 020 8801 2100
Fax: 020 8885 1322
E-mail: vibes@xpress.co.uk
Website: www.xpress.co.uk

First Edition 2007

Printed by JH Haynes & Co, Yeovil, Somerset BA22 7JJ, England.

Distributed in the UK by Turnaround Distribution
Unit 3, Olympia Trading Estate, Coburg Road, London N22 6TZ
Tel: 020 8829 3000
Fax: 020 8881 5088

Distributed in the U.S. by National Book Network

Author photo (back cover) by Greg Robison

ISBN: 978-1-902934-42-6

For Peter Green

# ONE

Animal's time was running out, but he wasn't to know that. The Double T nightclub was heaving and the music was hard. All the boys were in the house. Wall to wall designer gear sweated style as the DJ pumped up the volume. Tonight everyone was in a friendly mood, but tomorrow it would be a different story.

The lights on the sound system flashed like a million fireflies on speed. Animal danced like a man possessed. He smiled at all the people as they pushed past him. They had to push as he was occupying most of the dance floor. Not a small young man, he was sweating like a bilge pump in his boarding gear. He stunk like a swamp donkey with a body full of pills. Not a good combination by anyone's standard, but Animal danced to a different beat. That was something everyone had come to accept since Animal had first come to Meribel to hone his already considerable boarding skills.

The first season a few of the French had been aggressive towards him. Boarding had not been universally accepted by the winter sports fraternity. They saw the boarders as drop-outs on drugs, and for some, that wouldn't be far from the truth. But they soon learned to leave Animal alone. He had not come by his name by accident; his title was well deserved and was one he had always lived up to. It had been given to him by one of his more imaginative and tolerant girlfriends and it mattered to him; he'd earned the name.

Since then, Animal had not missed a season. Renowned for boarding at night, he used the arc lights to guide his way down the slopes. It was rumoured he had a death wish. But despite his strange and unusual ways, the French had come to put up with him, if not accept him as one of their own.

Somehow Animal managed to recognise some of the faces at the club, which was now crowded well past its safe number. He blinked a few times and waved at the group of Rastas at the corner of the bar. Smiling and relaxed, they were also disliked by the French, not just because they were boarders, but because they too, were a bit different. A couple of them waved back at Animal. Animal waved again, just managing to avoid knocking a drink out of another raver's hand. He grunted an apology as he danced on into the night.

The lights flashed and the music filled his skull. Techno, drum 'n bass, garage or house, it was all the same to him as long as it had a beat to which he could move. He was happier with the younger disc jockeys though. Some of the ageing DJ's with their massive earnings, houses in Buckinghamshire and huge investments, had lost the cutting edge in youth culture. In fact, just before he'd come out to Meribel he'd seen a thirteen year old at a club in deepest Deptford who was scratching with his elbows. Now that was something.

There was a large pool of sweat at his feet, testimony to the copious amounts of liquid which had checked out of his body. Animal was hairy from top to bottom and the heat in the club was almost unbearable. If he didn't get some liquid in his body soon, even Animal's strange metabolism would eventually expire.

He staggered over to the bar just managing to avoid slipping in the watery debris of his over-enthusiastic dancing. A few babes in tight tops and loose bottoms were barged out of the way. They didn't really mind as they were transfixed with the DJ. The Iceman was in the house spinning the tunes; a mixture of new age funk and garage. He was warmly encouraged by whoops of delight and the raising of hands as some of the more flimsy tops threatened to disgorge their fleshy contents.

Animal took a deep breath and tried to feel his way to the bar, being careful not to put his hands on any unsuspecting piece of babe. Eventually he found his way to the bar and the chill-out zone. He inhaled a bottle of water—Evian of course, in deference to his French hosts. It should have made him heave his guts up but it didn't. Animal had the metabolism of something not human. Bald-headed scientists, in their frayed white coats and dry skin would probably have given their right test tube for the opportunity to examine him. Another bottle of water went the same way before Animal had a sudden and uncontrollable urge for fresh air.

# Deep Powder

The Iceman kept the beat coming as the babes continued to move in time to the music. Still perspiring like a hog, Animal left another pool of sweat behind him and made his slow and unsteady way to the dimly lit exit. The door manager, a large Frenchman named Claude, checked Animal for the illuminated stamp on the back of his hand. It was there, clearly visible amongst the short wet hairs which shone like damp porcupine bristles on the back of his hand. The logo of a smiling face beamed back at Claude's torch.

Claude looked at a point somewhere to the left of Animal's ear. He had a stigma in one of his eyes, which was also slightly bigger than the other giving the impression that he was looking out of the bottom of a jam jar. He blinked a few times as Animal staggered past him. English bastard, he thought to himself.

The cold hit Animal like a runaway train. He held onto an icy concrete pillar to steady himself, breathed in the night air through his hairy nostrils and stretched his neck. The stiffness seemed to ease a bit, he must get a massage from Leather Hand Lil, the resort's top masseuse he reminded himself. Animal took that part of his physical health very seriously, besides she did a nice line in extras which you wouldn't find in the Meribel guide book.

Something off to his right attracted his attention. There was noise in the shadows. Animal blinked. He could just make out some human shapes in the darkness. He squinted, then smiled in recognition and waved; rays from the light overhead danced off the cheap watch on his damp wrist. Grunts of acknowledgement were returned. A more astute individual would have known that his presence was not welcome, the grunts were not those of welcome but of people angry and deeply irritated at having been spotted.

With a rather unpleasant noise, Animal sucked air deep into his lungs. He choked and spluttered, which brought more disturbed activity from the shadows. Animal sniffed and wiped a half-frozen stream of snot from his nose. He munched it, as it probably contained traces of drugs, like the rest of his body. Shame to waste it. He looked up at the night stars in wonderment. He had never grasped the rudiments of the galaxy at school, something which he suspected he shared with ninety-five per cent of the adult population.

Animal hitched up his trousers and reached into his cavernous pockets for a packet of Lucky Strikes. He'd always smoked, ever since seeing an advertisement on a billboard outside York station years ago. Suddenly hit by a surge of health consciousness, he looked at the smokes in his hand, pursed his lips, thought better of it, returned the ciggies to his pocket and turned to go back into the club. As the door banged behind him, a huge mound of snow and ice crashed from the roof. Animal looked back through the window at the debris on the ground. Dangerous, he thought to himself, someone could have been hurt. The hidden figures watched from the shadows, then vanished.

Back inside the club, Animal nodded to Claude who gave a sick little smile back. "English bastard", Claude whispered to himself. French twat, Animal thought, as he pushed his way through the dancers, snoggers and druggies. His unopened packet of Lucky Strikes banged against his knee as he walked slowly back to his spot on the dance floor. A few people nodded to him but this time he didn't respond. Animal wasn't really the sociable type; he'd come to Meribel to board and to do a few drugs, though nothing heavy. He hadn't come to make friends or influence people.

# TWO

Animal would be dead soon, but he didn't know that. He adjusted his boots, clipped them into the bindings, flexed his neck muscles and twisted his hips so that his legs were parallel to the slope, he flipped his body to a standing position and then put his headphones on. Time for some drum 'n bass.

The night air made him feel high, as though pure alcohol had been injected into his bloodstream. The Alps looked sweet tonight. After his exertions at the night-club he'd slept the day away and now the adrenaline pumped through his heart like a storm surge. The lights were still on, illuminating most of the mountain runs. Not for Animal's sake, but to light the work being done to prepare the piste for tomorrow's revellers. Giant machines were cutting slabs out from the mountainside to reduce the risk of avalanches; tidal waves of snow were bad for business.

All the other winter sportsters had long since headed to the bars to drift into drink induced consciousness prior to hurried, mean, neanderthal sex in someone else's chalet. Animal had taken a snowmobile, noisy though it was, up to his favourite black run. He chuckled to himself. He would have asked the owner's permission but when he had come to the area where he knew the snowmobile was parked, he hadn't been able to find them. He took a deep sniff of the scent of the mountain, waited a few moments then looked up at the sky where the last sliver of daylight had been sucked into space. He pulled up the sleeves of his Chromaphobia jacket. It wasn't really his; most of Animal's gear was either borrowed or stolen, apart from his Grenade Gloves. They were his. He never left home without them. Once the jacket was sorted to his satisfaction, he produced a roach and lit it. Inhaling good and deep, the smoke caught his lungs like a Venus fly trap and curled down into his soul. He felt sweet tonight and ready to do some stuff.

Animal loved his night runs. Most folks knew about them, but no one had ever tried to stop him; it was almost a local tradition. Besides, it was his risk and he never hurt himself; how could he, he was doing something he loved. In Animal's view people only screwed up when they had poor karma. Bad blood produced bad results. As far as Animal was concerned, he was where he should be that night, doing what had to be done. There was no right or wrong about it.

Time to rumble. Animal put out the roach in the snow and licked his lips. This was like sex; no, it was better. He threw his head back and gave a maniacal laugh as he pushed himself off into the night. Shadows threw themselves off his back as he carved a deep wake through the snow. He hit a ridge at full pelt, but it didn't matter, he'd been expecting it; he knew it was there. Animal flew into the air like a bullet and with a whoop of delight did a 'Stale Fish', using his back hand to grab his heel edge as he boned his rear leg. His 'Airwalk Match' cut through the air like piano wire. He loved this board; he rode 'fakie' and it favoured this style of riding with his board backward and gave him an excellent centered stance. He stuck it and felt like he was going to come in his pants. It just didn't get any better.

Animal carved a deep trough and felt himself pick up even more speed as he flashed past the pine trees, which stood to attention like some guard of honour. He half expected them to scream encouragement at him, like enthusiastic spectators. Lowering his stance, his hands millimetres away from the ground, he linked his turns and flashed through the snow like a chemically enhanced razor blade. He was in his element now. There was another ledge just around the next group of trees. He was as low as he could be for this one, screaming round the bend, the board at its very limit. He hit the ledge and took off like a Lear jet, sticking a Frontside 180 as he spun to the left and flew through the air. He hit the ground like a fat man on a Northern night out. Low centre of gravity and plenty of wobble. He managed to stay upright, just.

His heart was pumping overtime as he came to the next section of the run. Around the turn there was a long smooth section besides a line of trees. He had to come really close to the wood, otherwise he would miss the turn and go off the side. It was a steep drop and that wasn't something you wanted to do if you were looking for long term health. Animal knew this, tucked in really close and brought his speed down. Pity. If he hadn't come so near to the wood and slowed down, he would probably have lived.

Animal wasn't the only one on the mountain that night who

knew there was only one proper route into that turn. The two men in their black outfits were almost invisible against the night sky. Animal, mind focused and body in line with his board, had his eyes fixed straight ahead; he was in another zone. He never saw the men or the massive forked branch held just in Animal's path but close to the ground. The branch couldn't have been placed better if it had been computer controlled and laser guided.

On cue, the man holding the piece of tree raised it shoulder height and Animal hit it full on, his neck travelling up the middle of the fork. His windpipe shattered as his neck snapped like a dry twiglet underfoot on a cold wet dawn. Animal twitched in a macabre dance of death, his eyes rolling in their sockets as he struggled for breath. When the other man was sure Animal had exited this world, only then did he signal for his mate to lower the branch. This was done slowly, almost respectfully.

Animal's broken and twisted body dropped to the ground. A packet of Lucky Strikes lay in the snow. Bubbles of blood on his now pale lips told their own grim tale of now useless lungs. The taller man, who had given the signal, stood over Animal and grinned like a deranged artist contemplating his handiwork.

"Nice threads, boy," he hissed as he watched the young man die.

∞∞∞∞

"Papers are for rolling, man," the hat said. Somewhere underneath the thick woolly mound a human form dwelt but Finlay couldn't be sure. He smiled and put the newspaper down on the bench. Finlay had finished with it and even though the young assistant in the ski hire shop had made it clear it was of no interest to him, he thought someone else might like to read it later. Finlay hated to waste things; he believed everything had a useful life.

The assistant scratched his goatee then laid the board out on the bench in front of him. Finlay checked it over. It was as aerodynamic as a tractor, but there was nothing he could do under the circumstances. Outside, the French Alps boomed their cold winter's welcome. Figures on their snowboard, skis and backsides were just visible through the ice-covered window. Despite the early hour, the massive network of lifts connecting the Three Valleys ski resort were already in action, heaving a sweaty mass of living ski suits and baggy outfits up and down the slopes. Snow-burnt faces sweating out the excesses of alcohol, shone like sprinklers on bonfire night.

Finlay smiled again, as he caught sight of his reflection in the mirror on the wall. His hazel eyes were clear and bright, testimony to his fitness and his disinterest in booze. His skin was smooth and a light coffee colour. He checked his hair, he'd had it done before setting off on his travels. He was pleased with the result. Strong, even teeth gleamed back at him. Sugar was something which he stayed as far away from as possible; it had paid off.

Finlay picked the board up, turned it, put it back on the bench and looked at the assistant. He reached inside his jacket to produce his wallet. Unusually, it was full, thanks to a recent win. The accumulation of more points meant that the sponsors had been generous. The cash had been most welcome and had come just in time. Finlay, Monday and Wot had been broke and hungry figures, but now things were looking up.

"How much for the week?" Finlay pulled some euros out of the well-used leather money holder and started to count them off. The boots were soft, just how he liked them but they were by no means perfect; after all, they weren't his. All three had their own equipment but the airline had decided to hang onto the gear and fly it around Europe a few times before giving it up, whenever that was going to be. The official explanation was incorrect labelling on transit to Heathrow; how the bags turned up on a flight to Venice is anyone's guess.

Hat looked at the money Finlay held out in front of him. A look of horror spread across his face; he recoiled, his nose turning up as though there was something nasty on his top lip.

"No money, man. It just gets sucked up into the fat cat's multinational capitalist system. This one's on me." His accent, was a cocktail of French and cockney English,

"Why?" Finlay was appreciative but taken aback.

"I saw you win the comp, last season. You're the bomb, man. Cool, no worries. Buy me a beer or twenty, when you get the chance."

"What about your boss?" Finlay put his money back inside his jacket. He wasn't too sure about this. He didn't want the generous young assistant to pay with his job. That would have been a bit much even though the savings might come in handy.

"No problem; he won't worry. What he doesn't know, doesn't touch him. He'd be cool anyway." The last bit was optimistic but he waved Finlay away. There was obviously going to be no more discussion about it.

"Thanks," Finlay said as he walked outside to join the others.

"No problem dude, Give my love to the Tuesday girl. She's well sweet!" he shouted after Finlay's disappearing form.

"It's Monday," Finlay said without turning around.

"Whatever, man."

The good-natured reply was lost on Finlay as he stepped outside. Hat turned back to the computer to enter the details of his moneyless transaction onto the floppy. He frowned and reached out to take a swig of the Michelob sitting invitingly amongst a pile of old boarding trousers. He took a deep swallow, enjoying the feeling of the cold beer against the back of his throat. It was early in the morning but no matter, he liked his beer better than the full English breakfast.

Finlay joined Monday and Wot who were already kitted out with their stuff and in place at the cafe, drinking creamy hot chocolates. Neither of them shared the young assistant's liking for beer early in the morning. Meribel was buzzing and the snow looked hot. Finlay was looking forward to the day. He was going to pay for all three of them. That was how it was. One looked after the other two. It had been that way since they first met at a competition in the freezing hell of the Scottish mountains.

None of them could wait to get away from that place. It has a bone cracking temperature which cannot be replicated anywhere in the world. Even the temps at the North Pole would have a job equalling it. Something to do with the wind chill factor and the speed of the rain. It's surprising anyone could survive in the Cairngorms for very long when the weather was in it one of its moods.

Three individuals from quite different backgrounds, the three shouldn't really have had anything in common. But they did, the love of boarding, which seemed to touch each of their spirits in a very personal way. That seemed to be the bond, but they had far more in common than they realised. A high-class shrink, after a few hours of billable time, would eventually have arrived at the conclusion that all three of them were really outsiders, that they didn't actually know how to function completely on their own and they were intertwined, like strands of rope.

Monday sipped her hot chocolate and smiled at Finlay. "How

much did he take off you?"

Her voice was soft and definitely middle England. Testimony to her time spent in red brick university land. A place she had spent every waking moment rebelling against. She'd completed her degree in American studies, but only just. Her time spent drinking, drugging and shagging made sure that she just scraped by with a second class degree. Scraped is the right word for someone who could have strutted her stuff at Cambridge. A certificate of attendance her bitter father had called it. Her parents had never really gotten over the disappointment and it increased the tension in their already shaky and fraught relationship. Her dropout life as a boarder, as they saw it, was not guaranteed to build bridges between them, not now anyway.

Monday and Wot couldn't have been further apart on the parent front. His elderly mum and dad thought his bohemian life was something which they also should have done, in their younger days. Rich, they sent envelopes of cash to Wot. That is, whenever they managed to track him down. They meant well, but it didn't help his quest to appear like a man of the people.

"Wouldn't take any dosh," Finlay sniffed in reply as he sat down. The pants were a bit too tight for comfort. He missed his own stuff and hoped it wouldn't be too long before the airline reunited them with their gear. Wot didn't really care as he threw on any old stuff, but Finlay and Monday were a bit more attentive to things sartorial.

"Why?" asked Wot beneath a cream moustache. The topping from the hot chocolate couldn't muffle his cut-glass accent which sounded a bit strange because of his valiant but unsuccessful attempt to mask it. It was awful, but he wouldn't listen.

Finlay stretched and yawned. The sun flashed off the slopes like quicksilver. "Said something about not wanting to contribute to big business; fat cat's and all that," replied Finlay in a mixed accent of Scots, Jamaican and Nottingham.

"Irie, Finlay. I an' I are please to see unu." The big smiling face grinned as he spread his arms wide toward Finlay, Wot and Monday. Finlay jumped to his feet and laughed as he hugged the large figure tightly. "Pon my soul, batti!" Nyaman whistled through his teeth at the disappearing form of a tight young backside with spray-on ski pants.

Finlay laughed as he stepped back. "You could spot a backside from a hundred yards." Finlay looked at the bottom as it stepped into a ski lift. It certainly was a generous spread.

"I an I have no kass kass on that, me man."

Nyaman threw his locks back and picked up his smart smooth board. It didn't take Sherlock Holmes to work out where he was going next. The slopes and the bottom beckoned. He smiled at Monday and Wot and broke into perfect English as he always did when addressing them. He enjoyed doing it simply because it was the last thing a lot of people expected of him.

"People, how goes it?" Nyaman's teeth reflected the sun back onto the slopes; they were perfect and he showed them off at every opportunity. He was very proud of them and of his naturally athletic build which had helped him master a number of sports before being lured to the slopes. His three Rasta friends: Donny, Pattu and Menelik, were already high up on the black run, almost out of view. Unlike Nyaman, who loved his sleep, they couldn't wait for the break of day and the adventures it would bring.

The four were the only group of Rasta boarders. Sponsorship had not been a problem as they had style, attitude and that indefinable X factor. They were not great competition winners; their only victory was a third won by Donny in an international competition. But what they had was edge, feel and a presence which could only be good for a sport which had grown faster than a mushroom in a pile of shit.

"Can't stay here chatting all day. I'm off to join my maroon brothers. See you later," he said in an almost old English accent. He smiled at Wot and Monday. "Gone, bredrin."

He touched fists with Finlay and was off, board under one arm and his big woolly hat under the other. He wouldn't put it on till he was up on the slopes and needed his hands for balance. He liked to let his locks flow. Even in today's changing times, a locksman on the slopes of the fancy winter resort was not a common sight. Sure, there were a few people with their hair done this way and that, but Nyaman and his three friends saw themselves as modern day nyabhingi, people determined to end domination by white folks one way, or another. The original group were said to be led by Haile Selassie and did their thing their way. In modern life, the slopes was as good a place to start as any.

## Deep Powder

Nyaman jumped up onto the chairlift, showing his pass to the attendant as he did so. The fit, tanned young man looked like something from the Hitler youth, so Nyaman expected to be given extra attention. He was right, but it didn't bother him. The day he would start to worry was when people ignored him. Then he would know he was doing something wrong.

Another pair of tight ski-pants passed by; Nyaman licked his lips. Everything was looking sweet and nice. Something nagged at the back of his mind as he absent-mindedly swung his Scott board underneath him. Now what was it? Then he remembered. He had forgotten to ask Finlay whether he's heard about Animal. He shook his head. How could he forget something as important as that. He kissed his teeth, annoyed with himself. Then he relaxed. He'd see Finlay again, later. He could tell him then. He looked down at his board and thought about Scott's merchandising motto: 'Tomorrow is today.' Yah man. He smiled ruefully to himself. Animal's death had underlined that for him.

"Why does he call them maroon?" Wot blinked against the strong sun and drained the last of his hot chocolate. His blond wavy hair fell to one side. Finlay looked at him for a while then smiled before he spoke. He ran his hand over the hire board. It was cheap, rough and nasty, like a boar's tongue.

"What do you mean?" Finlay knew what Wot was getting at but it did him good to learn to be specific, particularly on matters of skin.

Monday flicked her hair out of her eye as she looked at Finlay. Her hair was blonde but not as bright as Wot's. Finlay could string Wot along something wicked when he wanted. She also wanted to know the answer as it had been puzzling her for a while.

"Well?" Wot hesitated.

Finlay was usually fine on such things, but sometimes he could get on his high horse a bit, which would see Wot's confidence wobble a bit. Wot didn't want to upset the applecart as things had been going so well between them. Even the mix-up with their gear not arriving at the same time as them, hadn't caused much strife. The chemistry was good but that could change like the wind blowing in from the mountain tops.

"They're not like, well...you know...actually maroon in colour." There, he spat it out. Things didn't seem too bad as Finlay was smiling and seemed relaxed. That wasn't always a good sign as he could fly off the handle at a second's notice when he felt like it. That didn't appear as though it was going to happen today, much to Wot's relief.

Finlay sniffed, like an elderly Cambridge Don about to explain the obvious."Well, you see Wot, they're not actually referring to their colour. It goes way back." He was sitting directly opposite Wot now, looking even more like a highbrow professor, albeit one in boarding gear. Times are changing after all.

Monday smiled in a kind of benevolent way. She shouldn't have though as she didn't have a clue why they called themselves maroon.

"It actually comes from the Spanish word cimmaron, which means untamed or wild. There was a group of black people in the eighteenth century who actively rejected British oppression and domination. They called themselves 'Maroon.'" He pointed up at the slopes where he imagined the boys were doing their stuff. "They feel the same, so they adopted the name."

Finlay sat back, just like an academic would, after having enlightened a group of students with his superior knowledge. There was something about Finlay's manner though, which robbed it of any offence. Basically, he was too fond of Monday and Wot to really rub their noses in any of that stuff. He tried to go gently with it, after all, they were his friends. But sometimes being the educator and supplier of basic information on all things racial was tiring. Not that the story about the Maroons was basic in any way.

Monday had finished her hot chocolate. "Let's ride," she said with the unbridled enthusiasm of a five year old who has just discovered that she is going to sleep over at her granny's place.

# THREE

Monday, Finlay and Wot grabbed their cheap and nasty gear and marched to the lifts. The queue was moving quickly, so they didn't have long to wait. With Finlay's cash, Monday had already sorted the passes. Finlay's recent competition wins and sponsorship had kept them on the slopes and their bellies full. Other times, Monday would get work as a chalet girl. She hated it, but she had to pull her weight when it was required. A stunning looking girl with long, flowing, naturally blonde hair, the description 'perfect skin' could have been coined just for her. Piercing, blue eyes and elfin-like ears all worked beautifully with an hourglass figure which most men and boys - as well as a few women - couldn't keep their eyes or hands off. Her real name was Tamara. She'd had a bit of a shagfest at university, but then something happened.

One grope too many, one drunken fiddle too much, and the effect had been profound. She woke up one morning and realised that on the whole she had come to despise men. She was sick of them. Maybe it came back to her dominating and controlling father. Who knows? The fact was that she'd had enough of them. One of the guys she had a fling with didn't like Mondays, so Tamara became Monday.

Like it was yesterday, Monday could still remember the first time she met Finlay and Wot. Since that day the friendship had grown. It took her a few seasons to really trust them, but they had never shit on her and she knew that they never would. Their bond had come to be the most important thing in Monday's life.

Neither Monday nor Wot could board well enough to create income from the slopes. Though they were far from beginners, Finlay was the only one who could produce dosh on the back of a well waxed board. Monday was cool with the chalet work but it was a hard grind sometimes. The over-oiled accountants from Croydon who thought she would put her ankles up around her ears for two and half minutes of poking and fumbling, more than tried her patience. They had as much sex appeal as Vietnamese pot-bellied pigs, even the good looking ones. Of course, they never took the hint until she gave them a good slap.

Nyaman, in his more generous moments, had passed on a few

tips from his wide range of martial arts knowledge. He would only give a few though. Monday thought it may have had something to do with male ego. She always felt alright with Nyaman and despite his awesome reputation, he had never tried it on with her. It was almost as though he knew it was a real issue. He had never laid any childish lezzie jokes on her either; he must have taken his lead from Finlay.

Wot and Finlay shared a lift. Monday found herself next to some guy from Birmingham. Friendly enough, he chatted away in that strange, high-pitched, nasal twang, then he hit on her. The lift deposited them at the top. She gave her usual clear response.

"Fuck off, six chins." She was polite as always. Finlay smiled as he and Wot waited for her to join them.

"Making more friends, I see."

"Whatever."

Monday put her board down and adjusted her pants which had ridden up a bit on the lift; a result of edging further and further away from the corpulent one.

"I think it was more like seven, to be honest." Finlay blinked in the fierce sunlight.

"Sorry?" Monday was ready to go and slipped past them as she spoke.

"Chins. I think there were seven, not six," Finlay said with a twinkle in his eye.

She paused, then sniffed before answering. "I didn't read maths at university, you know that." With that she was gone, curving a deep line in the snow.

Finlay took off behind her and Wot made up the trio. There was a big mixture on the slopes that day. French, Spanish, American and English accents could be heard, left, right and centre. Finlay quickly overtook Monday without trying. His line and speed was better, even on a board which had as much style as one of his Mum's old tea trays. In fact, a tea tray would probably have done better.

Wot had a style which was different. It looked like a drunk, who thought he was sober, trying to stay on his feet. But he was better than he looked. He was tall, and quite thin; his drunken appearance was more to do with the way he crouched into his stance, lowering the centre of gravity. He always looked awkward doing this but it worked. The wild flop of blonde hair and the kind of vacant look also contributed to his less than athletic appearance, but his style worked for him and that was what mattered. Like Monday, he couldn't hold a candle to Finlay when it came to the fine art of boarding, but he enjoyed himself and this life was just right for him.

Finlay was just a distant speck now, flying like the wind. He always seemed like he had the devil hanging off his back when he was in full flight. There was little to touch him. He made sure he took a line which did not bring him into contact with others on the run. He knew, in a Zen-like way, exactly where anyone was going to be before he actually got to that point. This meant, as he carved his way through the fine white stuff, he could avoid everyone and they didn't interrupt his intense concentration.

As he approached a series of ridges and deep concealed bumps, he got down low. Others would not have known they were there, but Finlay knew this area better than most of the French instructors and mountain guides. This was always a source of frustration and irritation with the locals at Meribel. They did not like British expertise or knowledge when it came to what they saw as 'their mountains.'

Finlay started to take off and pulled his front leg up into his chest and using the tail of his board, popped the 'ollie'. He did it sweet. His back leg was kept tight and his weight was perfectly balanced in the centre of the board. As he landed with a whoosh, he kept his legs bent to absorb the impact. It was special but he made it look as simple as catching the bus. It was just his way. The best always made it look so easy. You would have thought your granny could have done it, with or without the kit.

The cobwebs were well and truly blown away now and he was going at a fair old speed. He licked his lips and checked the front of his board as it cut through the snow with minimum drag. He was skilled in making tiny movements with his body, almost like an aircraft sorting its trim and adjusting the yaw, the bit on the back of the plane just above the rudder which stops it from flapping all over the place. He ollied off the lip of the next ridge, bringing his knees into his chest and grabbed the toe-edge of his board with his leading hand, spotting his landing at the same time. His speed increased. There were a few skiers and boarders off to his right who couldn't help taking notice. He was that good; you just couldn't ignore him.

# Deep Powder

He slapped a landing with a slight wobble, but didn't lose his balance. He carved a few turns, then came to a relaxed and confident halt not far away from the mountain cafe. It was always open first thing in the morning and he could see Nyaman and the boys chatting as they rested up. He looked behind him, Monday and Wot were still a long way back. They seemed happy enough. He'd slow down on the next section. After all, they'd come to enjoy themselves together, for the first few days anyway. There was a competition, but not just yet.

Nyaman was smiling as Finlay unclipped his board and ambled over to the assembled throng.

"I know. I wobbled," he said grinning.

Donny, Pattu and Menelik were leaning against the wooden bar nursing a variety of drinks. Donny and Menelik were all smiles as they greeted Finlay. They liked this young man and his boarding was awesome. Pattu, however, gave Finlay a begrudging nod. He was a different story. He and Finlay had already been around the block a few times and there was little love lost between them. Finlay prided himself on being reasonable and pretty switched on when it came to matters of culture. For Pattu, Finlay was a coconut– a closet white man. Pattu was not very forgiving and considered himself a radical on all things black. Finlay felt that Pattu lived up to his name, a bird of bad omen. But then that was why Pattu had changed his name from plain old Gregory. He wanted to feel that he was something special on the roots and culture front and as far as he was concerned he was.

Finlay sighed as Pattu's ice-cold welcome was plain for all to see. Nyaman kissed his teeth. He didn't like the tension between the bredrin. Not good for the blood as far as he was concerned. He gave Finlay the news.

"Yah hear about Animal?" He looked all around as he was talking. Nothing to do with interest in the surroundings, it was more to do with his upbringing on the streets of Peckham. People who didn't keep alert whilst talking or mixing with others didn't last long. South London was not a place to lose your wits. Things like that do not leave you.

No, what about him?" Finlay was completely ignoring Pattu who was shooting him some vexed looks.

"Dead." Nyaman was to the point.

"What happened?" Finlay felt the cold prick his skin. He'd never made up with his father and his dad's early death left him with a strange response to the issue.

Nyaman shrugged his shoulders. "Me nah know, yah know. Got a turn wrong. Him neck broke."

"I heard he liked going out late, on his own. Was it at night?"

"Yeah." It was Donny who spoke, his hair was in dreads, all tied up at the back. His real name was Donald but he liked the shortening of it to someone he had always admired: Donny Yuen, a kung-fu star of the Chinese cinema.

∞∞∞∞

Finlay bent down to adjust the bindings on his board. He tightened them, checked them, then pulled them until they were just how he liked them, nice and snug with just enough movement for tight turns but not so loose that control would be difficult. Nyaman smiled at Finlay then crouched down next to him. That's when he saw the frown spread across Finlay's fine smooth features.

"Somet'ing wrong, bredrin?" He put his gloved hand on top of Finlay's.

The lighter skinned man sighed and stood up brushing excess snow off his jacket as he did so. "It's Animal. He took lots of wrong turns in life, but not on a board. It's kind of weird."

"Me know that, man," Nyaman said quietly.

"I mean, death is not welcome anytime. I hear Animal didn't endear himself to the locals so there's probably not much mourning going on." Finlay blinked in the fierce sun.

"That's for sure." It was Donny who spoke. Light green eyes and eyebrows to die for, he always had a smile on his face, even in the coldest winters.

Pattu was still standing there with a hard look on his face. Menelik tapped him lightly on the arm but he ignored him. Finlay knew Pattu couldn't stand him but this was heavy. Pattu had it all over his face: Finlay the coconut. He might as well have been wearing a sandwich board emblazoned with the name. Pattu was a good boarder, but if he spent less time dissing other people and more energy on his sport he could be very good indeed, Finlay thought to himself. Pattu's eye narrowed as these thoughts went through Finlay's mind. Pattu kissed his teeth and sniffed.

Nyaman reached out and put his hand on Pattu's shoulder, like

Menelik had done a few moments before. Pattu looked back at him, his eyes deep and intense. He opened his mouth as though he were smiling, but he wasn't. There was a gap in the top row of teeth, where there used to be a gold molar. It had lost an uneven battle with a rocky outcrop last season when Pattu had been overly ambitious with a 560 and had caught an edge on a black run.

Pattu breathed slowly out and the tension in the group went down a few decibels. Pattu would not mess with Nyaman but he couldn't stand Finlay with his fine British manners and perfect skin. He blinked a few times, glanced down at his bindings, then set off down the mountain without a backward glance, narrowly missing a couple of French day-trippers.

"Merde!" one of them in a skintight ski outfit shouted. The one giant eyebrow, which at one time used to be two, knitted in fury as he shook his equally hairy fist at Pattu. The disappearing figure was oblivious to the anger, as he glided down the mountain, linking turns smoother than a glass of cognac. His locks blew in the wind like streamers.

One of the irate French men tripped on his oversized hire skis. They were so chipped, uneven and awkward it had only been a matter of time before an edge was caught, which is exactly what happened. Another profanity split the air like an ice axe, though this time it was not directed at Pattu. As the Frenchman fell he dragged his countryman to the ground with him. The scream, along with the ripping of an overpriced ski suit, was clearly heard by everyone.

Pattu was now a distant figure on the snowline. If he was aware of the commotion behind him, he didn't show it. He was just a small human blip on the white frozen landscape, off piste and out there, on his own.

"He's got a real problem, your boy there." Finlay squatted, his eyes shielded from the strong sun by a fancy pair of Bolle sunglasses. Had they been in his luggage they would have gone the same way as the rest of his stuff. The sunlight reflected off the runs like a light show. Finlay was looking in the direction in which Pattu had gone, though he was no longer visible.

"Him nat mah bwoy, yah know." Nyaman's voice was still friendly but there was a chill in the tone. Finlay was aware of it as he scratched his head. The china bumps were still tight on his skull; instant facelift Monday called them. His mate, Little Youth had done it for him. Strange, as he was neither young nor little, but that was the only name people knew him by. A trained car mechanic, he made more money doing peoples' hair as his skill was known London wide.

Nyaman shuffled up close to Finlay, his board cutting little ridges in the snow as Donny and Menelik looked on. "Relax Finlay, 'pon mi word, 'tis no big deal. Every man here has his own way." He pulled a lock out of his face which the now piercing wind had blown there.

Finlay's voice held a chill of its own which he did not try to disguise. "I've got my way but I don't bother others,"

Monday and Wot had carved a route down towards them. Menelik reached into his jacket and produced a spliff, the answer to all problems or at least some of them.

"Brother, man, have a smoke." He lit it inhaling deeply, the pleasure spreading across his face like sunrise in the morning. He handed it to Finlay who refused it politely but firmly, "No thanks."

"What dis, yah na smoke? Yah Jamaican?" Menelik meant no offence, he was just taken aback at the refusal. It was good stuff too. The smoke swirled about his head filling the mountain air with its sweet pungent essence. Donny took it eagerly when it was offered to him. He wasn't sure if his Kung-Fu heroes smoked but he was sure that they would have if given the chance. He took a good deep drag and smiled when it hit the back of his lungs. Menelik looked directly at Finlay who smiled back at him, then positioned his board down the mountain, dropped his hips, flexed his ankles and set off just as Monday and Wot joined them.

"Real Jamaicans don't smoke, my friend," Finlay said as he sped away, his word mixing with a slurry of snow.

Monday and Wot watched Finlay's disappearing form. He was flying, it was unlikely either of them would be able to keep up with him. Monday stood with her hands on her hips as Wot sniffed the air. There was a fragrance he recognised and a knowing smile spread across his face. Menelik held his clenched fist out.

"Touch me nah." Wot touched fists with Menelik and greedily accepted the spliff. Menelik was the least adept at boarding but the most able when it came to getting dope from local sources. The look on Menelik's face told Wot that he'd held the spliff more than long enough; he coughed a bit as he handed it back. Menelik took it and the smile returned to his usually calm and placid face.

Wot turned his board down the slope and started to feel the pull of gravity. He exhaled the smoke and pushed off.

"Later, Menelik!" Wot shouted.

"Yah, man." Menelik smiled and delicately held the remainder of the spliff between his finger and thumb, as though it was a piece of ancient art. His gaze was intense; he'd come across a very fine specimen indeed. He offered it to Monday who waved it away.

"Some things I don't do up here. That's one of them," she responded and followed Wot down the mountain, almost in his tracks although she didn't mean to. She took a couple of deep swinging corners, gathering speed. The snow flashed up around her shoulders as she shifted her weight from foot to foot, feeling the curves through her thighs and hamstrings. Sometimes she could even feel the sensations in other more intimate parts of her body. The boys said they never felt like that although they did admit to feeling spiritually connected to the white stuff. Monday felt it had more to with practicalities; boarding with a hard-on was not cool. But as the mental imagery came to mind, she thought it could be kind of sexy.

Menelik watched her departing bottom with more than a passing interest. It was tasty. "Is she Finlay's?" he said to no one in particular.

"Nah." The voice was Donny's.

"She's her own girl, that one."

∞∞∞∞

Finlay was well ahead of the others, as he carved his way through the powder. He stopped and looked behind him but they were distant figures. He took the t-bar, put part of it between his legs and relaxed as it tugged him up the slope. It was quiet where he was going. Most of the people on the mountain that day were strictly funsters. The majority of the serious boys and girls were having some shut-eye before the comp tomorrow.

As he went higher, he took in the scenery, the board bumping and sliding up the track. T-bars were not easy. There was a saying, 'Next time take the chair.' Even some top boarders took a long time to master it and some never did. Anyway, the real fun was in coming down.

The mountain range looked like a bunch of icy old men gathered round a domino game, some with long beards hanging round their necks. Finlay could never get over the way the mountains were such equalisers. The whole environment was guaranteed to either calm you down or bring you up, depending on your personality.

Finlay had been a bit of a rebel. He didn't or rather couldn't concentrate at school; he got into trouble. Things got worse when he moved to Nottingham though his mum reckoned things would be better there. She obviously hadn't done her homework; things don't get better in the Meadows. Finlay ended up in care. A medium sized local authority home in Bulwell. Looked like it had been built by someone from the sixties, on speed, with a burning hatred of kids. The majority of the staff fitted that description as well. Finlay had not settled in. He had a chip on both shoulders and a rage against the world he could taste in his mouth.

There was a group at the time, which thought that getting troublesome kids out of the city environment and into the wild was the answer. It worked well for a while and it certainly did wonders for Finlay. He found that in nature there was nothing to rage at or to throw stones at. The mountain environment was bigger than everything or anyone that had ever come into its life. The programme ended after it turned out that some of the group leaders had strange ideas about what bonding with teenage girls actually meant. A few knickers round the ankles too many, meant they were suspended and there were a few red cheeks around County Hall for a while. But it was too late for Finlay; he was hooked.

One way or another he got himself up to Aviemore every season and learned everything he could, not just about winter sports, but about the mountains themselves. He was good on the survival front. Learned everything he knew from Neil, a wiry Scotsman of few words, who'd fled to Glen Nevis from a dead marriage and a couple of kids who hated him. There had been precious little which he had not passed on to Finlay about the ways of the wild.

The flutter of some brightly coloured ribbon brought Finlay's thoughts back to the present. He skipped off the t-bar and glided over to the group of trees where two sections merged. Clearly this must have been the spot where Animal had breathed his last.

The sharp wind chill made Finlay draw his breath in as he came closer to the trees which looked like a macabre bunch of giant pipe cleaners, all twisted in a tuneless dance. There were tracks all over the place which Finlay correctly deduced had been left by the police. He shuffled around for a while not really knowing what he was doing or why, then something caught his eye. He knew that he had found something very interesting. He leant under the trees and looked up to where the branch had snapped off. The one which had brought about Animal's demise.

Finlay licked his lips as he stood deep in thought. He was not aware of the shapely skier who had stopped some way behind him. She lifted her sunglasses and squinted at Finlay. Body like an hourglass, perfect olive skin and two clear blue eyes oozing self-confidence. Her shiny thick hair was tied high in a bun with a few strands hanging down at the nape of her neck. She stood at an awkward angle, so she adjusted her position, her shapely bottom wiggling seductively under the tight fitting suit. It was the same rear which Nyaman had admired from afar earlier that day. She licked her top lip, smiled to herself, then she was gone.

A flurry of snow blew in Finlay's face. The wind was whipping up now and the slopes were not such an inviting place to be. He put something in his pocket, turned, and then headed back down the mountain. At the bottom there was much activity as others had also wisely decided to call it a day. The wind was howling fiercely now and it would only be a matter of time before the piste was closed. Finlay hoped conditions would not persist and ruin the next day's competition. He met Monday and Wot at the bottom of the lift.

"Where did you get to?" Monday asked.

"I got caught up at the spot where Animal died."

"Gross," Monday said as Wot pulled a face. He was a bit sensitive.

"Were you looking for it?" Monday had a strange look on her face.

"No," Finlay answered defensively. He hadn't meant to be, it had just come out that way. Wot smiled, hoping this conversation would come to a close; discussions of death were not his cup of tea. Neither was it Finlay's, but his curiosity and natural prying instincts had been awakened by what he'd found up the mountain.

Monday and Wot hurried off. They were getting cold and Wot was looking forward to listening to some trance, namely Paul Van Dyk's 'Out There and Back.' When Wot had music on his mind there was little else which would get in the way.

Finlay sorted his gear out then started to follow them. He didn't get very far. A soft hand came to rest on the elbow of Finlay's thick padded jacket; slight, feminine and connected to one of the most attractive young women Finlay had set eyes on for a long time. Bright, even teeth flashed the brightest of smiles which, even through the heavy fall of snow, seemed to light up the spot. Golden blonde hair, and sparkling eyes and skin shouted good health from every pore.

"Hi, I'm Roisin," she introduced, extending her hand which had now left its resting place on Finlay's elbow.

Her voice was like velvet on silk and a rush of lust flooded his well-padded loins. Finlay smiled and swallowed at the same, making a strange kind of gurgle, like a frog. Finlay felt his skin start to warm up, like a teenager getting his first glimpse of a bra strap. He swallowed again, which made him sound even more like a pond dweller.

"Are you alright?"

"I'm sorry, I was miles away. Yeah, I'm fine." He smiled and held his hand out.

"My name's Finlay." His confidence was coming back like a dry river, swelling after a summer of drought.

"I saw you up there, by the trees. Couldn't help noticing you." She nodded in the direction of where Finlay had inspected the trees. A whisp of hair hung attractively over her left eye. She brushed it to one side, which only served to increase the flow of blood to Finlay's trousers.

"I didn't see you." Finlay was nearly shouting now as the wind was getting louder and fiercer by the minute.

"I know," Roisin shouted back. She touched Finlay's arm again and drew closer. "I'm here with some friends. Where are you staying?"

Finlay licked his lips before answering. His mouth was dry despite the swirling snow. He was concerned, in case it made him look like a lech. If Roisin noticed, she did not give anything away.

"In the chalet at the top of the street. The last one on the right." He pointed at the street which went sharply up and away from

Meribel's town centre. Roisin smiled and nodded.

"I've got to go now, but maybe we could meet up, if you like." She smiled and flashed her eyes at him. Finlay smiled and nodded.

"That would be great." He picked his board up and slung it over his shoulder. He'd been intending to walk with her, but she was already on her way.

"I'll catch you later then."

With that, she was gone. Finlay stood there for a few moments to gather his thoughts. Thunderbolt, the Sicilians call it when you are struck by a woman in that way. Finlay couldn't remember the last time it had happened. But one thing was for certain; there, in the car park in Meribel, he'd felt it.

Finlay checked his pocket as he walked up the road to the chalet. Satisfied the contents were safe, he bowed his head in the prevailing wind which was now so loud he hardly heard the car come up behind him. A smiling Nyaman was at the wheel of the multi purpose vehicle with a relaxed looking Menelik next to him. Donny was in the back seat, looking like he was ready for his bed. He lacked the stamina of the others when it came matters of the mountains. Pattu stood out like a sore on a bride's lip. He wore a scowl on his face whenever Finlay was around. Finlay didn't even bother acknowledging him, it was getting out of hand. The joke was that they hardly knew each other. Donny dug Pattu in the ribs which just made him roll his eyes and kiss his teeth, like a stroppy teenager mainlining on attitude.

"Hi," Finlay said as he leant forward and put his head just inside Nyaman's open window. He grinned from ear to ear.

"What are you so happy about?" Nyaman asked as the chairlift groaned above them. The wind was now too high for it to operate safely and the metal creaked and groaned like a group outing from an old peoples' home.

Nyaman stroked the soft leather of the custom built ride. He'd hired it from a specialist firm in Lyon. He had a few pounds thanks to his internet travel company, Rasta.com. It specialised in cut-price holidays to the Caribbean. Nyaman was a wizard of the cyberworld. A new world which, unlike the old, did not have the same hang-ups about race, class or colour. The others had chipped in for the car as well. It wasn't too pricey, as business was slow in the upper end of the French luxury car hire market.

"Saw you check the gyal," Nyaman said with a wink. The way he stroked the wheel was positively rude.

"*She* spoke to *me*." Finlay couldn't believe how defensive he sounded.

"Whatever."

Nyaman selected a gear and after a few seconds the tyres bit and the motor was on its way with a hand waving goodbye out of the window. Finlay could see it was Menelik's. He was sure it wouldn't have been Pattu's.

The snow was now flying about like debris from a giant with a serious case of dandruff. Time for Finlay to get back to the chalet to join Wot and Monday. He licked his lips. If he was lucky Wot may have some scoff on the go. He was quite nifty when it came to producing something from the kitchen. Finlay walked up the steep road, carefully watching his step as he went. It was seriously icy.

# FOUR

The music was thumping when Finlay opened the chalet door. Any louder and he could have sold tickets. Monday was on the sofa, busy doing her nails. It was good to see her do girly things. Sometimes Finlay worried that she was not in touch enough with that side of things. Looking at her deeply engrossed in her two-tone nail polish, he needn't have worried. He walked through to the equipment section which was next to the garage, it was warm, cosy and dry enough to sort your gear out in next to no time. He waved at Monday who smiled back as he made his way to the kitchen where something smelt good.

Van Dyk's 'Alive' was pumping from the sound system. Not bad for someone who hails from East Germany and used to be a Smiths' fan, thought Finlay as he sought out Wot in the steamy kitchen. The window was open and the cold air from outside, combined with the hot air inside, produced an effect not unlike a sauna. Wot was in the corner poised over the cooker producing some mouth watering roti. Even Pattu would have had to acknowledge the skill. He turned and handed Finlay a plate of one of his creations. Finlay promptly found a place for it in his mouth. The business. If he closed his eyes he could have been back at Mad Errol's in Nottingham, the finest place for roti and saltfish in the Midlands.

Wot liked his food and had no problem stuffing it away. But looking at him you would not have realised it. The fattest thing on him was his hair. A thought flashed in Wot's mind and he walked past Finlay, munching the remainder of his roti, and went over to the sound system and punched a button. The machine made a whirring noise and he removed Van Dyk's offering. He rummaged around in his bag which never left his side. If it had then it would have been off on the same travels as the rest of their belongings, which were now God knows where.

"What do you fancy? he mumbled, his mouth full of roti.

"Not bothered. You're the music man. Finlay wiped some crumbs from his mouth and removed his jumper; the sweat was dripping off him.

"How about this?" Wot asked in that way which people do when they have already made up their minds. He turned like a magician pulling a white rabbit from a hat and plonked a cd into the system. 'Smash the Gnat' from Hardfloor filled the kitchen and Finlay's senses.

"You like the German boys, don't you?" Finlay had to shout to be heard above the music. Wot grinned at him then they both realised that something was up. Thick, black smoke was pumping out of the cooker. They leapt to the oven doors. Wot was just ahead of Finlay, and was confronted by a row of blackened roti. Overdone was an understatement.

"What's dying?" Monday had been alerted to trouble in the kitchen by the smell. She was standing, half in, half out of the door with a smile on her face, the one which people wear when they already know the answer to their question.

"Wot's roti," Finlay replied like a funeral announcement. Hardfloor provided the memorial music in the background.

"I've not even had any." Monday's voice had a mock tone to it.

"I can make some more!" Wot shouted above the music. Strangely, the rhythm of Hardfloor's sounds were in complete timing with their respective statements.

Monday shook her head and hands at the same time, indicating that for her, the moment had passed. She ducked back out of the kitchen door.

Finlay smiled at Wot. He gestured at the sad remains in the oven as plumes of smoke danced out through the doors. "Do you want a hand cleaning that up?" The smoke alarm had been set off but they had not heard it over the music. A kitchen remix. Wot had things under control so Finlay left him to it and went through to the front room to join Monday who was shaking her hands in the air to dry her nails. Finlay slumped down next to her.

"Why did you bother doing that?" he asked though secretly pleased that she was doing something for her femininity.

She nodded to the window, completely covered in ice and snow. "Well, we're not going out again, are we? Not in that." It was more of a statement than a question.

"Yeah, you're right." Finlay stood up and went over to his jacket. He felt in his pocket, pulled something out, and put it in his trousers. He came back and sat down again. Monday's nails appeared to have dried, she was playing with the television remote control. She hadn't noticed Finlay's coming and going.

The phone rang. Finlay picked it up.

"Yeah?"

"Finlay?" the disembodied voice enquired.

"Yes, who is it?" Finlay was always a bit disconcerted when people phoned him to ask who *he* was. After all, they were phoning him, *he* should be the one doing the asking. It was Donny.

"Any sign of your gear, man?"

"Nah. I hope it comes before the comp though. Haven't a chance if I have to take part without my stuff."

"Yeah, right. Me and the boys were just wondering, you know, concerned about what was going on with your gear and all that." Donny's voice had a sympathetic tone.

"You mean you and the two others." Finlay looked down at his socks. One was badly in need of darning. There was a pause at the other end of the phone.

"You don't want to take any notice of Pattu, man. He just has his ways. You know that." Donny paused before continuing. "What's that music in the background?"

"Oh that. It's Wot's. Hardfloor. They're a German outfit."

"Oh yeah. I know them. Bald-headed geezers." Donny was impressed.

"Are they?" This was news to Finlay.

"Yeah. Not a hair amongst them." Donny was pleased that subject had moved from Pattu. He was not comfortable trying to excuse Pattu's behaviour. Being an apologist for others wasn't his scene.

"Later." Finlay voice was quiet.

"Yeah." Donny replied.

Finlay gently replaced the receiver.

∞∞∞∞∞

"I think there may be more to Animal's death than meets the eye." Despite the fact that he wasn't looking at her, Monday had to assume that Finlay was speaking to her. She was the only other person in the room; Wot was busy getting rid of the remains of his cremated roti.

"What makes you think that?"

Monday stopped fiddling with the remote, largely because she was only getting old re-runs of Ivanhoe and some French news channels.

"I found something up the mountain which just makes me wonder," Finlay said quietly.

"What?"

"Well, I'm not sure. I'll tell you when I'm more certain."

"Finlay!" Monday threw a cushion at him as well as an irritated look.

"What?" He caught it.

"I hate it when people do that. Tell me" She was exasperated

"No, not till I have something proper to say. I've just got a hunch, that's all. It may be nothing."

"If it was nothing you wouldn't be dwelling on it." Monday sighed.

"Just wait. I'll tell you the minute I arrive at some reasonable conclusion."

"Oh bollocks." She threw another cushion at him. He didn't bother trying to catch this one and let it just bounce off his head. Monday disappeared off to her room. Finlay was getting on her nerves with his half-baked information.

Wot stuck his head out of the kitchen."Where's Monday?"

"Gone upstairs." Finlay arched his back and shoulders; he had a slight twinge in his spine.

"She alright?"

"Yeah. She was just a bit pissed off with me." Finlay felt something start to give in his back, so he wisely stopped pulling his body in that direction.

"Why?"

"Just something I was playing around with. She wanted to know more, but I'm not sure about what it is yet."

Wot didn't understand a word of that, but he was less curious than Monday so he went back into the kitchen, letting the fancy alpine doors swing behind him. Finlay lay back in the sofa and took an item from his pocket. It was a small piece of branch, still wet from the mountain snow. He turned it in his hands looking at it deeply, like a philosopher considering his latest social theory. It immediately made him think of his father.

As a young man, Finlay's dad was a good looking seaman in the merchant navy. His travels took him to the port of Leith where he met Mairi, who worked in one of the dockside cafes which catered to the thirsty, hungry men. She fell in love. They moved into a cramped one bedroomed place in Stockbridge. That may be one of the fancier addresses in Edinburgh now, with the Scottish parliament and all that, but then it definitely was not. There were not many black people in the Edinburgh of yesteryear and Mairi found herself completely estranged from her family, who were horrified at the idea that she was with a black man. It would have been worth it if the man had been worth it.

In and out of fights when he wasn't nose deep in a whisky bottle, he could have been forgiven in some way; life was not easy. The locals could, and did, get Finlay's dad to fight over a number of things. Matters were made worse when he beat them all. There was his reputation to protect, which he did with great enthusiasm. He won scars, like badges of courage, all worn with pride on his previously unmarked face. This was not conducive to good family life. Even if all that was excusable for Finlay's dad, then being someone who was determined to sample all fine Celtic pussy was not. Women in every port; one in every street more like it. It had gotten to the stage where it was impossible to tell whether Finlay's father was being provoked because of his reputation as a fighter or because he had slept with yet another man's wife.

Local kids tried and succeeded, to find all sorts of names to describe Finlay but sadly, 'person of mixed parentage' was not one of them. And unfortunately, Finlay had not inherited his father's combat skills. In fact, there was precious little that Finlay inherited from this man - with one exception. Despite his toughness, his father had a love and a knowledge of plants and trees which was unbelievable. That was the one legacy he had passed on to Finlay but it had never occurred to him that this would ever come in useful. Until now.

Finlay was tired. He hadn't felt settled since he'd arrived. He knew it would be better once his gear joined him. Wot and Monday didn't seem so bothered about having to wait for their stuff, but it was getting on his nerves. He'd slept for a short while and dreamt of his childhood, and of his relationship with his mother in particular. He had not had a good relationship with his mother but she was always on his mind, especially now that she was unwell. They'd found a shadow on her lung which turned out to be the dreaded cancer. She had been responding to treatment, but she wasn't young and her nerves had never been that good. She wasn't dealing with it all very well.

# Deep Powder

Twisting the cap off with his finger and thumb, Finlay opened a bottle of Lucozade. He held the top in his hand as he put the bottle to his lips and took a deep swig of the liquid which he had grown to like so much. A while ago they'd sponsored a competition which he'd won. They'd treated him like a Greek god and he'd been taken with the brew ever since. He felt the cold liquid cascade down his throat as he went over to open the window again. He needed some fresh air. The heating, designed to combat the freezing mountain air was too strong. The top slipped out of his grasp, wet with the moisture from the fridge-fresh bottle. It hit the floor and slipped away under the sofa. Finlay sighed as he bent down to pick it up. He hated untidiness; a trait which was to save his life.

Something meant for his neck flashed past like a laser. It missed him by a fraction of a millimetre, grazing the tender skin just under his chin. It travelled at many miles an hour, coming to rest with a thump in the solid oak beam at the entrance to the sitting room. Finlay stayed low for a moment. It seemed like an age, but it wasn't. A near miss; his life flashed before him. He had a choice: to stand up or drop to the floor. The thing, whatever it was, had meant to check Finlay out of this life and into the next. It had not come from below him, so he allowed his knees to buckle and he slid with grace and speed to the highly polished chalet floor. Wood had never felt so good.

Finlay lay on the floor for what seemed like forever but was, in fact, only a few moments. There was little incentive to leap to his feet in case there was more metal flying about at God knows what speed. Surely it was his imagination, but he could almost hear the beam still reverberating from the impact.

Wot appeared as if from nowhere; it was actually from the kitchen.

"Get down!" Finlay hissed. Wot obliged and hit the deck like a beached whale; less than graceful, but fully in accordance with Finlay's wise and assertive instruction. Something in his tone told Wot this was not a time for discussion.

"What is it?" Wot whispered back.

The smell of burnt-out roti drifted through to the front room. Finlay crawled on his stomach across the wooden floor. He glided over its mirror smooth finish. At that moment, Monday appeared at the top of the stairs. She'd heard something and her curiosity had gotten the better of her despite her desire to remain sulking in her bedroom. She could get moods going with the best of them. From the floor Finlay gestured at her to get back in her room, which she did; he was obviously not playing around.

By this time Finlay had joined Wot by the kitchen door. There was milk all over the floor, spilt from the glass which Wot had been carrying when he'd come out of the kitchen. Some of it had soiled Wot's clothes but he was not overly concerned about that as he followed the direction of Finlay's finger. He was pointing at the beam and giving him something more important to worry about. There was a thick bolt of metal sticking out of the wooden plank. Attached to the end were some small tidy feathers; an arrow of some kind. Whatever it was, good and kind intentions were obviously not the message it had been intended to convey.

Slowly Finlay brought himself to his feet, craning his neck towards the balcony where he believed the shot to have originated. There was no sign of any activity. He stood there for a few minutes then eventually nodded to Wot who was now rising to his feet. Monday was nowhere to be seen. Finlay walked over to the balcony. He could see nothing, just two footprints in the snow. No-one else had been on the balcony since they had arrived so it seemed reasonable to presume that they belonged to whoever had tried to plug him. Wot craned his neck to get a look. Footsteps descending the stairs told them they would soon be joined by Monday. Dumfounded, the three of them stood looking at the spot where someone had tried to introduce Finlay to a premature and untimely death.

# FIVE

The police came quickly. There were three of them: a sharp looking plain clothes and two uniformed plods. Had Finlay not warned them, all three would have impaled themselves on the beam. The uniforms were grateful, but the dark suited detective barely grumbled a thanks. His name was Picot and he was feeling mean and nursing a giant hangover thanks to an all-nighter the previous evening in Albertville. It had been a party in honour of the local policemen but by some stupidity the two uniforms were not invited. Despite being local, they and a lot of the other uniformed officers from the immediate vicinity, were not considered senior enough to grace the proceedings.

It wasn't Picot's fault and to tell the truth he was uncomfortable about the whole shambles. Mind you, it had been a gigantic piss-up; hence the headache. On top of all this, he'd now been summoned to this chalet because someone had tried to plug an English snowboarder. Now that was something. The list of suspects would be long. He didn't know anyone who liked English boarders apart from themselves. He sniffed. He had to keep up appearances, but he was truly irritated by the whole thing. First Animal's accident which was a king-sized pain with all the paperwork and now this.

He didn't say a word as he examined the beam with the bolt sticking out of it. He did not touch it as the forensics were on their way; he did not want to make enemies of them. Rumour had it that if you got on the wrong side of them they had a thousand ways to spike your lunch. Picot's delicate stomach heaved at the thought; he did not have a very strong constitution at the best of times. Medium build, dark brown hair and a ruddy appearance, he had a thickening waistline which he hated. It made him look more like a farmer than a razor-minded policeman. That was the main reason he wore a suit, despite the ridicule of his colleagues.

Picot went out to the balcony whilst the two uniforms stood next to the beam. One of them smiled at Monday. She was most definitely not in the mood for male attention and he realised his mistake as soon as he'd made it. Returning from the balcony, Picot came to his rescue. Just like his favourite film stars when they were about to solve a crime, he pursed his lips and stood there with his hands on his hips, jacket spread wide.

"Crossbow bolt. Came from the balcony." The first bit was news the second part was pretty obvious.

"Any reason why someone would want to kill you? Picot did not look at Finlay as he spoke.

Finlay shook his head but did not speak, partly so Picot would be forced to make eye contact. Finlay thought for a few moments then reached into his pocket and produced the small piece of branch.

"What's that?" Picot's eye narrowed.

"A piece of the tree up where Animal died."

"Oh." Picot came over to Finlay and took it off him. It looked ordinary, like any piece of tree Picot had seen before. He dropped his head and looked sideways at Finlay, just like one of his favourite film stars. He'd picked that look up from Kojak but would never admit it.

"What's this got to do with anything?"

"I'm not sure, but there's something strange about that piece."

There was a knock at the door. Picot nodded at one of the plods, who went to the heavy wooden door and opened it. Quite an effort, the door, like the chalet, was very well built and meant to last. There were two men at the door, a third was getting some stuff out of a large van behind them. Plod stepped back and let in the forensic boys who had come to dust and do whatever else they did. He never could quite grasp how they worked. They never seemed to actually find anything but they always seemed to come up with results. They did on the movies anyway.

The plod went back into the dining room where Picot was showing one of the forensics the beam. He turned back to Finlay who was standing by the balcony door, flanked by Monday and Wot. They had no reason to, but they felt a bit guilty. Something to do with the way Picot looked at them.

"That piece of branch from the tree Animal hit is really worth looking at," Finlay said quietly.

Picot sniffed. "Why?"

"It looks as though it was broken off before Animal came on the scene," said Finlay.

"You shouldn't have been up there." Picot was visibly annoyed.

Finlay shrugged his shoulders."I was passing." The sarcasm was lost on the Frenchman.

"What are you trying to say?" He was visibly irritated.

"Just that the tree shows signs of having a branch broken off a couple of days before the actual event. I can tell by the drying of the fluid and some other stuff." Finlay felt tense.

"How do you know so much?" Picot pursed his lips.

"His dad taught him," interrupted Wot.

"How nice." Picot was learning sarcasm fast. He handed the twig to one of the forensics."You don't mind?" he said to Finlay. His tone did not sound as though he was expecting an answer. Finlay arched his back. The tension was really hurting now.

"Do you think this may be connected to what happened today?" Picot wandered over to the kitchen door and pushed it open. The smell which greeted him made him go no further.

"I don't know. I've not spoken to anyone about it, except you." Finlay answered. He sounded guarded, though he didn't mean to.

"Are you certain?"

"Of course." Finlay sighed.

"Alright. I may need to speak with you further. What are your plans?"

"We're not going anywhere," Finlay answered for all three. Picot nodded and left with one of the plods. The other one stayed behind with the forensic boys. They were quick and efficient with the beam and the crossbow bolt, but there was little that could be done for Wot's roti.

∞∞∞∞

Finlay stood for a while, deep in thought. It was not every day that you came so close to death. He surprised himself with his relative calmness, he expected to feel more. Maybe that would come later. You know, like a bereavement. No tears come for six months then one day you're reaching for the butter, or margarine or whatever you spread on your toast in the morning and bang......it comes. The floodgates open when you least expect it. Just as long as it wasn't when he was on the halfpipe; that would take some living down.

The phone sliced through his thoughts. It was Mick the Trick, the sponsors rep. The 'Trick' part of his name came from his uncanny ability to get himself out of tricky situations. The problem was that he also had an unfortunate trait of getting himself into them. Finlay checked his stylish but inexpensive watch. A watch strap was the first thing to go on a tumble on the slopes so there was no point in having a nice one.

"Yol, Finlay." Mick was white but he spoke like he thought he was black. It was a shame as Mick had many endearing qualities but this was not one of them. Many of his mates had told him this, but he didn't listen.

"Yeah, Mick, how's it going?" Finlay rubbed his neck.

"Irie Finlay, everyt'ing cool, man."

Finlay gritted his teeth. His fake black accent seemed to have thickened since the last time they spoke.

"What can I do for you?" Finlay smiled at Monday who was looking a bit pale. It looked like she was feeling the effect of recent events more than Finlay.

"Not'ing man. It's cool. I was just ringing to say your gear's come in from the airport. You and the other two cats."

Mick talked like a black man from the 70's blaxploitation films.

"Good." He paused. "How come the stuff came to you?"

"They weren't sure which chalet you were in and your bags are covered with the firm's stickers so they just brought them to me. They knew where to find me, man." His speech was actually slipping back to normal. The black talk was difficult to keep up.

"Alright. I'll come down in a bit," Finlay said.

"Nah, you don't have to. Some of the boys will drop your stuff off, OK?" Mick said. .

"In fact," he continued, Finlay knew what was coming next, "...I'll come up myself. Give me a chance to see y'all."

Finlay groaned, his last word was all the way back to black.

"Yeah, alright." Finlay put the phone down and went into the dining room. Wot had joined Monday and they were watching re-runs of Ab Fab.

Plod one was looking over Wot's shoulder, trying to make something out of Ab Fab. There was a quizzical look on his youthful features which suggested he was not having much luck. The forensics finished up, mumbled something to the plod, then quietly let themselves out. Finlay went over to the window and watched them pack their gear into the car. Their outfits gave them a surreal look, like vacuum cleaning demonstrators from the late sixties. He looked back at the policemen, who looked all of twelve years old. At least it wasn't only the Brit police who were recruiting from nurseries these days. Finlay's mother had some crazy notion once that he should become a policeman. He shuddered at the memory. It probably had something to do with the fantasy that the police were able to control everything. People always thought that if you became one then you would learn to control yourself.

Finlay caught the policeman's eye. Wot and Monday turned around to look as well. It suddenly dawned on the man that his work was finished; there was no reason for him to be there. He smiled, then nodded at them all and turned to leave but cracked his head hard on the solid beam. Everyone grimaced in sympathy. He held his head for a few seconds and did a strange little dance.

"You alright mate?" Finlay couldn't help himself. He wasn't keen on uniforms but this man had done him no harm. The sound his head had made when it cracked against the beam had been sickening. Eventually the uniformed adolescent nodded slowly as though the signals to his brain had been affected by the blow. He made his unsteady way to the front door. A gust of wind blew in as he opened it. He limped out and closed it behind him with a bang.

Finlay waved at the closed door. He didn't know why he did that. It was a habit from his childhood. He tried to resist it, but always failed. When a door closed in front of him he would wave at it. What would a psychiatrist make of that?

Finlay sat down on the sofa, squeezing uninvited between Wot and Monday.

"I'm scared." Monday said without a trace of drama. It had a chilling effect precisely because of that. She might as well have been asking for another bowl of cereal, her tone was so matter of fact. She was looking straight at the television screen, but did not appear to actually be watching it.

"So am I." It was Wot this time. He actually did appear to be watching the television.

That just left Finlay. He didn't say he was scared, but he was. But that didn't stop his mind racing.

"That Joanna Lumley's a bit of alright, you know," Wot said without a trace of irony. Finlay and Monday looked at each other in horror. Further conversation on the subject was cut short by a new arrival. It was Mick the Trick. Suddenly, as though he'd come from nowhere, he was standing behind them with a big smile on his large face. He hadn't bothered knocking. Mick never knocked. It was a habit he had. Unlike most people, he'd avoided knocking his head on the beam, which would surely have announced his arrival.

"Hey dudes and dudess. Wha'appen?" Monday cringed at the sight and sound of Mick. Medium height, snow bleached hair with a mass of freckles. There was a baseball cap turned backwards sitting on his head and a pair of Oakleys perched on his slightly greasy nose. The sunglasses were held in place by two large pimples which kept them from sliding. The diamond studs, one in each ear, would have made Elizabeth Taylor proud. A gold tooth, completed the look.

Baggy jeans with too much room at the crotch and the box fresh trainers, looked liked they had cost more than the defence budget of a medium sized third world country. Bad enough he introduced himself like he was black, but the crowning sourness of the man was the fact he had kissed goodbye to forty many moons ago. All in all, not a pretty sight.

"Your gear's outside."

The three of them got up, as one, to retrieve their long overdue property. As Finlay walked past Mick, the ageing funkster touched him on the arm.

"Everyt'ing OK? I saw the filth leaving when we pulled up."

Finlay hesitated before he answered. "Not really. Someone tried to plug me." He pointed at the hole where the crossbow bolt had been. There was a neat chalk mark around it.

Mick the Trick nodded as though he saw this kind of thing every day. "Most uncool, man," he said. If he had been challenging for the kingdom of understatement, he would have been king without hesitation. He smiled ruefully, the golden tooth glinting ridiculously in the light. Wot was temporarily blinded by the light which only subsided when Mick turned his head to inspect the hole in the beam.

"Yah know," he said.

"What?" Finlay was standing behind him as he probed the hole.

"Me wonder what the job's like?"

"Job?" Finlay thought the Trick was losing his marbles.

"The one where you draw the chalk mark around the body." There was no trace of humour in Mick's voice.

Finlay took a deep breath and pushed past him. "There is no

body." The irritation in his voice was sharp and clear.

Mick looked at Finlay's disappearing form with a puzzled look on his face. Outside Monday and Wot were unloading their gear from the van. There were a couple of pasty-faced men in the front of the vehicle. They did not get out to help. They didn't like English people with their stupid clothes, dirty fingernails and rotten teeth. Mick didn't count as they'd never been able to work out what he was anyway. They were not alone. Finlay helped Monday and Wot finish unloading the van.

Mick pointed at the two scowling faces sitting in the front. "I see you've met Tasty and Morsel. They're brothers. I gave them the nicknames." The last bit of his sentence may have meant to explain their stupid names but it didn't.

Mick looked proud as he opened the door and got in, closing it behind him with a satisfying thunk. It sounded so good he was tempted to open it and do it again. He wound down the window as Wot retrieved the last of the bags out of the back and closed the large rear door with the same expensive sound.

"Yol, catch you later dudes."

With a flurry of snow and ice the people carrier rolled into the cold night with its cargo of two scowling French brothers and a rather strange English hybrid. Finlay, Wot and Monday looked at all the bags in the driveway. It was good to be reunited with their stuff. In celebration, Wot went inside, put on some more music and started doing one of his strange dances to the strains of Shakir's Da Sampla. It helped to ease the tension.

∞∞∞∞

The next morning was perfect for the halfpipe. There was hardly any wind and even the coldest heart could not be warmed by the sun's rays licking across the mountains. Monday was competing in the women's section and Finlay, obviously, was in the men's. Wot wasn't taking part; he was feeling rusty and of the three, he was having the greatest difficulty in keeping the attempt on Finlay's life, to the back of his mind. The music was pumping out a combination of beats. Over and above it, a French MC was chattering away ten to the dozen.

A sudden chilly gust caught Finlay in the back of the throat; it was like a breath of a god. On a day like this, Finlay felt he could live forever. He paused as he remembered that someone in the

44

Alps had other ideas about that. As the heaving throng made its way to and fro– strains of all European languages drifting across the snow, Finlay checked his board. Above the din, he could hear Mick the Trick's strange white-black talk; Finlay knew the man was near. Sure enough, through the teeming crowd, he saw Mick emerge with another man walking just behind him. He was a bit taller than Mick; lean and wiry, with a tough weather beaten face with skin like leather. He had dull blue eyes which told the tale of prolonged low-grade substance abuse. The toxins had most likely left his body via the bald patch just visible at the top of the neatly tied ponytail. A gold ring nestled in his left ear lobe, but there was no ring in the right one as there was only half an ear remaining.

"Finlay, guy, this is Old Man." Mick gestured to the aging hippy at his side. "Old Man runs a new shop here. Great gear, totally rad man." He did a shuffle of satisfaction in the snow as he completed his introduction.

"Old Man?" Finlay held his hand out.

"Yeah, that's my name. Least ways that's what everyone calls me." His tone was friendly but sharp. This was a man who had been around and survived to tell the tale.

"Good to meet you," Finlay said as he offered his hand. It was a strong firm grip which was at odds with the distant, dull expression.

"Sorry?" Old Man hadn't heard what Finlay had said.

Mick laughed. "You have to speak up Finlay. Old Man's hard of hearing. Been that way." He pointed at the piece of twisted flesh which was the remains of Old Man's right ear. "Ever since an angel from hell discharged a shotgun in his ear."

"It was both barrels," added Old Man.

He blinked in time to his sniff, at least one eye did as the other looked like it was slightly behind. The contents of a gun whistling round your head could do that.

"Good luck," Mick said as he slapped Finlay on the back.

"Come into my shop, man, we're open all hours." Old Man sniffed again as he and Mick walked away.

Finlay thought that along with the residue of shotgun powder, there might be traces of the white lady's legacy in Old Man's system. He was about to say something, but the two were already gone, swallowed up like a couple of pilot fish in the belly of the masses cavorting over the mountain. Finlay shrugged and resumed checking his gear. He didn't have very long to himself before he was interrupted again.

"Nice board, man."

The voice was deep and booming. Not European. Finlay looked up. Blocking the sunlight was a large, blonde and very wide figure. The face was square and the jaw looked like it was hewn from solid granite. A mass of muscle. Finlay shielded his eyes from the sun which came briefly into view as the massive shape shifted position slightly. A far lovelier, more welcome sight stood behind the large shape.

"Roisin," Finlay blurted out. Most uncool, but he was very pleased to see her.

"Finlay."

Her voice was like liquid hot chocolate being poured all over his body. Finlay's thoughts immediately went from focused and sporty to wide ranging and most definitely carnal.

"I see you've met Rocky." Roisin gestured to the piece of human meat which smiled back at him.

"Yeah." There was little trace of enthusiasm in his voice. Most unwelcoming in fact. Not really called for but there was something about the man mountain which did not warm the cockles of Finlay's heart. Rocky reached out and touched Finlay's board like a chef feeling a particularly fine piece of cheese.

"P-lex 4000 Electra; stone ground, sintered base. Neat, very neat. Doesn't matter what the conditions are, this baby can snooze right through it." The accent was North American, or somewhere round there. Rocky knew what Finlay was thinking.

"Canadian, man. Best country in the world."

"Yeah." Finlay wasn't really listening, his attention was fixed on Rocky's board which was slung over his shoulder.

"Winterstick, Dimitrize Milovich's company. Nice board." Finlay eyed it up and down as Rocky quivered with pleasure.

"166. I'm a big guy."

Finlay looked again. The board size made sense, but the demonic look in Rocky's eyes suggested the one should be replaced by a six.

"See you later, man. Good luck in the comp."

Rocky was gone, leaving Finlay with the delectable Roisin. Finlay came to the conclusion that he liked Rocky's back view better than his front. That was for sure. Roisin rested her hand gently on Finlay's arm as Nyaman and Donny were getting ready, far up on the ridge just above where Roisin and Finlay were standing.

The atmosphere was alive with excitement and there was a taste in the air which you could cut with a knife. A kind of choose life thing. The women's event was first and Monday was in good form. After the first run she was in second place to a fresh faced Norwegian girl with an unpronounceable name. Despite Monday's best efforts that position didn't improve and in fact, a boarder from Lake Tahoe sneaked into second place with some stylish tricks, which meant Monday at the end of her section, took the bronze. That was fine with her. She collected the medal then came up to Finlay's side as he was loosening up and getting ready for the men's event that was announced in the usual kind of distracted way over a crackly microphone.

"Good luck," Monday said as Finlay walked away. Break a leg is not a term which was encouraged on the mountains. Calling it tempting fate would be an understatement.

"Thanks," he said as he stopped and turned.

This gave Roisin the perfect opportunity. She walked up to him and planted a kiss on his cheek, then looked directly at Monday. Finlay was taken aback but very pleased at this turn of events. He introduced the two but didn't detect the frostiness in Monday's response. He was far too busy getting his mind ready for the next event. Monday, however, knew that it had not been lost on Roisin. She had taken an instant dislike to the girl, but it bothered her that she hadn't been able to control her feelings. After all, Finlay was like a brother to her, wasn't he? So why was she reacting in such a strange way to Roisin who, after all, had every right to take an interest in a healthy good-looking young man.

Finlay stood at the top waiting for his turn to drop in. Stretched in front of him 450 was feet of halfpipe. The walls were 20 feet high and beautifully prepared. There was a young spotty kid in front of him. He looked nervous and uncomfortable with red eyes and blotchy skin and looked distinctly unhappy. After a few moments they were ready for the spotty youth. Just before he pushed off, Finlay heard him mutter under his breath, "For Animal." The accent was French. Then, he was gone. He stuck a couple of good tricks but his concentration went and he failed to deliver, kissing the snow like a rodeo rider bucked by two tons of angry prime beef. He'd tried a 900 but it was just too ambitious.

Finlay was up next. A hand fell like a meat splicer upon his shoulder. It was Rocky.

"You haven't a chance with me in the competition." His smile was like a mountain weasel's, displaying less than the usual good spirit associated with such events on the circuit. Rocky had obviously tried to whisper, but his massive chest meant that every sound echoed round the covered area where they were standing.

Finlay looked him straight in the eye and smiled with equally little warmth. "That's where you're wrong," he paused before continuing, "I've got two chances."

He did not elaborate as he pushed off with a little smile on his face. Rocky stood there, unsure of what to make of what he'd heard. He shook his head and made some last minute adjustments to his equipment. Finlay went straight into a kicker. Air whooshed past his body. He was travelling fast and sweet. He remembered a racing driver on the telly saying that when he was moving at two hundred miles per hour everything seemed to stand still. He'd said he could see the flowers by the side of the racetrack and that the smell of new cut grass would assault his senses so strongly that it was the only thing he was aware of. Finlay couldn't quite recollect the driver 's full name, but he was called Jackie and he was Scots. He knew that tartan figured somewhere along the line.

Finlay didn't smell new cut grass now but he did see Pattu's scowling face as he flashed through the air. Didn't he ever let up? It wasn't as though he'd actually done anything to him. What a difference. Jackie the racing driver king gets new cut grass; Finlay gets Pattu. He was also aware of the commentators words shooting forth machine-gun style. According to the man on the mike, Finlay was a big-air expert. He was in a backflip almost without knowing it. There was a little hand touch which he knew would lose points but despite that, it felt good. Looking up, his chest heaving from the exertion, eyes blinking in the sun, he read the score. Not bad.

A couple of other riders came after him. They were good and stuck some neat tricks but they didn't have Finlay's poise and balance. His biggest strength was his low centre of gravity. Despite being quite tall, he could get right down with his hips. He had flexible ankles and legs like tree trunks. Came from his dad.

Apart from the knowledge about plants and trees it was probably the only good thing that he had inherited from him. There may have been others but Finlay would probably be a good deal older before that sunk in.

Rocky was next and he came out like an express train on speed: the crystal variety. A slick switch 540 saw him edge just in front of Finlay. He was wise, keeping it relatively simple, with a stale fish grab. There was no disguising the look of triumph and pleasure on his face. That was enough to clinch it if the positions remained the same after the second run. They did. Finlay went up to congratulate him but was not prepared for the reaction. Rocky gave him a look which could have frozen a Mississippi swamp.

"Some of us are winners." He pushed past Finlay then stopped as though something had just occurred to him. He turned round. "What did you mean by two chances?"

Finlay shrugged his shoulders and gave Rocky a rueful smile."Two chances. No chance and a dog's. The important thing is to know which is which."

Finlay walked back to the car park managing to keep his distance from Mick the Trick who was going to do a high five but changed his mind when he saw the look on Finlay's face. He managed to slap him on the back, but only just. He then touched fists with Nyaman which saw a look of horror cross Pattu's face, like he'd swallowed a liver sandwich, complete with some anchovies well past their sell-by date.

# SIX

"**W**hat do your friends think of the fact someone is trying to kill you?" Picot came straight to the point. A Southern man, he had no time for Parisian bullshit. He liked order, neatness and things in their place. A look round his office told you that. The whole place looked like it had just been taken out of bubblewrap. You could eat your breakfast off the skirting board and the carpets creaked with shampoo and freshener which stunk of vanilla. The walls ,like the carpet, were cream. There were pictures of Picot graduating from his police academy on the wall behind his large Gallic head. A shiny drinks cabinet squatted underneath the window overlooking the nursery slopes. It was highly polished with big, bold, brass handles. Picot had paid a considerable percentage of his annual salary when he had bought it from a fancy antiques dealer in an over-priced shop in Paris. It was old, imposing and expensive.

"I've not broadcast it."

"Any particular reason?"

"Maybe. I'm not sure who my friends are?"

"You don't look like a young man who spends much time alone."

Picot's comment was supposed to sound profound, an example of his hard earned certificate in the human psychology of the criminal mind which he had earned as a part-timer more years ago than he cared, or was able, to remember. But in truth, it sounded like a clumsy pick-up line. Finlay leaned forward and put his hands on Picot's spotless desk. He could not have committed a worse sin if he had painted a moustache on the graduation photo. The older man grimaced at having his meticulous work area disturbed. Precision was his middle name.

"The others with you. The girl and the boy; friends?"

"So?" Finlay wasn't sure where this was going, but he was feeling distinctly unhappy. Picot's small, sharp, blue eyes didn't help either. It was obvious that it wasn't only French lorry drivers and farmers who liked to control everything and everybody around them.

"Well, maybe they know something."

"They don't know any more than me."

50

Finlay looked out of the window at the Alps. They were like a bunch of old men at a bus stop, some high and mighty, others more stooped and wide at the hip.

Picot pursed his lips and held his hands to his furrowed brow. "People often know more than you think."

Finlay thought about this for a moment as he looked out of the window. Dark shadows were spreading across the mountains. The weather was so unpredictable in this area, it could change without any warning. If you were someone who had moods affected by the weather, you were in for some serious multiple personality issues in the Alps.

"Like I said, Wot and Monday don't know any more than I do about who would try to kill me."

Blinking, almost in time with his thoughts, Picot sighed deeply. He was in line for promotion and he knew that his superiors were not all rooting for him, particularly the Chief of Police in Albertville who had a face like a mountain goat and a beard and breath to match. He could not afford to have all this going on unsolved in Meribel. It could cost him his future. None of this was welcome at all, not at all. The press were already sniffing around trying to find out more about Animal's death and to top it all the tourist numbers were down this year, thanks to last season's higher than usual avalanche deaths.

Picot probed a space in his teeth where a filling had jumped ship during the consumption of a particularly tasty baguette. It was time for a visit to Phillippe, his younger brother. Instead of following Picot into the police force, he had forged a different and more lucrative career as a dentist. They'd always managed to get on well, avoiding the usual pitfalls of sibling rivalry. He didn't live far from Meribel. Picot would call him as soon as he had bade farewell to this strange young Brit.

"Well, if anything should come to mind, you come straight here and tell me. Meanwhile…"

"-Don't go anywhere. Sure. Don't worry, I wasn't planning to flee the Alps," Finlay completed.

His sarcasm was not lost on Picot.

As Finlay was being shown the door he turned towards the older man. "Remember one thing."

"What's that?"

"It was me who was almost killed. I haven't done anything

wrong."

Picot said nothing as he ushered Finlay out and quietly closed the door behind him. A sharp piercing pain shot through his mouth. He went straight to the phone, picked up the receiver and dialled Phillippe's number.

∞∞∞

The air was sharp and sweet as Finlay made his way back to the chalet from Picot's office. A fine sheet of light snow was falling. Any thicker and Finlay would probably have missed the figure darting across the street. Thin, wiry and wearing gear which Finlay instantly recognised, it was the red-faced boy from the mountain. He darted up a lane as Finlay ran across the street. There were some questions he wanted to ask him about Animal. He got there just in time to see the youth disappear into the front door of one the cheaper looking chalets in Meribel. Finlay didn't get any further as a hand descended on his shoulder.

"Fin, my man." It was Old Man, the ageing hippy Mick had introduced him to. This time Finlay got a better look at what was left of his ear. Not a pretty sight. The flesh was gnarled and malformed. There was a hint of blue-grey in what was left of it. Gunpowder, how delightful. Old Man touched it when he realised Finlay was looking.

He licked his lips as he spoke."It's called living, man, Hell's Angel style." He laughed. Spots of spittle flew into his greying beard as he gleefully threw his head back.

"More like nearly dying," Finlay said.

He stopped laughing as though someone had just flicked a switch, then just as quickly the smile came back.

"Yeah, I suppose that's one way of looking at it." He paused then said, " You said you'd come to my shop."

"I will."

"Well, there's no time like the present, is there man?"

"I don't know." Finlay hesitated. He wanted to catch up with the spotty youth.

"What's there to know?" Old Man took him by the arm and guided him up the stairs to the upper level of shops. The bars and restaurants there faced out towards the nursery slopes and the giant wooden building which housed the mechanics of the ski-lift. Finlay didn't bother resisting. He'd made a note of the chalet the youth had gone into. It could wait till later.

Old Man's shop was certainly something. There was every conceivable item of clothing and boarding equipment you could possibly want and some hot skiing stuff as well. But it was obviously the boarding which formed the backbone of his interest.

"This is my first season here. It's going to be a good start for me." Old Man stroked his beard.

"I hope so. Finlay didn't know what else to say. Old Man's eyes narrowed as he answered.

"Ain't nothin' to do with hope, man. It's to do with enterprise." There was something in the way he pronounced the last word which seemed strange.

"Where are you from?" Finlay's curiosity was aroused. Old Man turned and looked at him as he felt the edge of a board which was suspended from the roof; the cost of which would not have left change out of five hundred quid, not euros.

"Why?"

"Just wondering, that's all."

"I'm from everywhere."

"No, I mean originally."

He hesitated, then shrugged his shoulders. "New Cross."

"I knew you were a Londoner."

"What's the big deal?"

"Your accent sounds American."

"Yeah, well, like I said, I'm from everywhere. Sides, a Yankee accent's good for business." Old Man's eyes narrowed in a knowing way.

"Not in Iran."

Finlay had a point.

"They don't board in Iran." He was not smiling. There was tension in the air. Then, with no warning, Old Man slapped him on the back.

"Not yet anyway." He laughed then looked Finlay straight in the eye. It reminded him of a snake from a wildlife programme.

"I like you Finlay. You got something, man."

"Thanks." Finlay coughed a bit. Old Man was a lot stronger that he looked and he took a step back in case he tried to repeat the back slapping. Old Man didn't move. It was safe on that front. Finlay walked round the store examining the goods. Most had a logo on them. A small smiling face, with one ear. No need to ask where the inspiration for that had come from.

"You like the logo?" Old Man was still stroking his beard as though he would discover some hidden treasure secreted in the hairy tresses.

"Yeah, it's clever. Not much of a likeness though, apart from the ear." Finlay smiled to avoid any offence.

Old Man smiled but said nothing as he carried on stroking.

There was certainly some prime gear on show. Something caught his eye. The gloves made by Grenade. Animal's favourite. He sighed. Memories of Animals's free spirit came flooding back. The boards were fantastic. Finlay ran his hand up and down the models hanging from the ceiling. Impressive alright and unusual. There was something in particular which made them stand out; he couldn't put his finger on it, but now was not the time to bring it up. He had other things on his mind and though the shop had a warm and homey feel, it was now time for him to go.

"I'll catch you later," said Finlay.

"Yeah, right," was Old Man's weak reply. He looked distracted, almost disinterested in Finlay. Then suddenly he looked as though a thought had come to him. His eyes lit up as he stood up from the stool where he had been sitting with one arm resting on a newly waxed board.

"Drop by any time, man." He smiled and his eyes turned a deeper shade of blue. They were obviously young once, a long time ago, but they had seen too much since then.

Finlay closed the front door behind him and stepped out onto the balcony overlooking the promenade below him. From the Swiss chalet type restaurant to his right, a strong smell of coffee wafted towards him. Below, some guys from good old Britain were getting as much lager as they could down their gullets. He smiled. Christ, the Brits loved their booze. It was a miracle they ever got any work done. Finlay walked towards the chalet he was sharing with Wot and Monday, then stopped. He still wanted to have a word with the spotty youth and there was no time like the present.

Finlay stood in the sidestreet where the he'd seen the youth disappear into the chalet. It was deserted except for a sweet wrapper blowing in the wind and a couple of empty cans of cheap imported beer, probably purchased at an overpriced French supermarket by a short-sighted lout of English origin. They get everywhere, thought Finlay to himself as he walked up the street, kicking one of the empty cans to one side. It was like a scene from High Noon.

Finlay pulled the collar of his jacket up around his ears. The cold was really penetrating his bones. The wind howled as it blew in from over the mountains. He stood outside the solid oak door, the second to last on the street. A pretty alpine balcony creaked above his head. Finlay knew he was at the right door as he recognised the sign nailed to the side pointing the way to extra parking. He pushed the brass bell, there was no answer. He waited a few moments before trying the door handle, expecting to find it locked. To his surprise it was open. Another surprise waited inside the dimly lit hallway. The sight froze him like a banshee's breath.

The spotty youth was unlikely to enlighten Finlay on anything. In fact, he was not going to speak, ever again; the thin rope secured viciously around his neck would see to that. He was suspended from a hook high in the ceiling. His feet banged against the wall some four feet above the ground. Finlay went over to him but he knew that any help was futile. His bulging eyes, the froth gathered on his purple blue lips and his ghostly pallor indicated that it was far too late to save him.

Finlay was no coroner, but instinctively he knew that this had been no suicide. He touched the exposed flesh of the corpse, just above the ankle where the sock had slipped down. The youth was not wearing any shoes, although he still had his boarding gear on. The jacket had a small logo on the sleeve; a smiling face with one ear. Finlay had not expected to see that logo so soon, and certainly not under such unpleasant circumstances. Any further thought was driven from Finlay's mind as a noise above him brought him swiftly back to the here and now.

Someone was in the room above him. He grabbed a table lamp, ripping the flex from the wall as he bounded up the steps two by two, just in time to see a figure disappearing onto the alpine balcony. It was like something out of Murder on the Rue Morgue, as the shape bounded over the balcony wall onto the street below. Finlay ran outside to see the intruder run down the street in a cloud of snow and sleet. The weather had gotten worse over the last few minutes. If it hadn't been for that, Finlay might have gotten a better look at the fleeing person. He stood there for a few moments holding the lamp with the flex trailing in the wind. He went inside and called the police, by now he was familiar with the number. Not that he'd planned to be so closely associated with officers of the law..

# SEVEN

Picot didn't speak for a while as the forensic people dusted the place for prints and other stuff. When he did eventually speak it was none too friendly.

"You are making a habit of this," he said gesturing to the figure still swinging gently above them. The unfortunate youth had not yet been cut down from his final resting place.

"What do you mean, habit?" replied Finlay defensively.

"Death seems to be following you around."

A touch dramatic but Picot had a point. Further conversation was interrupted by one of the policemen who touched Picot on the shoulder.

Someone was on the end of the policeman's walkie talkie. He handed it to Picot, who put it to his ear. He nodded and mumbled a few words which Finlay could not make out. Picot was pleased. It was his secretary. An appointment had been made to see Phillippe, tomorrow morning, to sort out his tooth. Not before time, as it was sending a constant searing pain up through his jaw. He was finding it increasingly difficult to concentrate on his work and this was not a time to be distracted.

Finlay gave his statement to one of the plods as Picot wandered around the chalet. It would appear, despite the three bedrooms, that the spotty youth had been staying there on his own. Only one of the rooms had any possessions in it. It did not take a rocket scientist to work out that they were the worldly belongings of the poor soul who by now had been cut down and was now the contents of a body bag.

A nod from Picot told Finlay that he was free to go. It seemed unnecessary to give Finlay the spiel about not leaving and all of that, but Picot did it anyway, he was that type of man. It did, however, lack a certain gravity thanks to the swelling in his upper gum. A policeman accompanied Finlay back to his chalet but it was not concern for *his* welfare which was at the root of this gesture.

The next morning, Finlay stretched and yawned as light streamed through his window. Picot was on the way to visit his brother for some serious pain relief, whilst his juniors filled out the copious amounts of paperwork which represented the lives, deaths and non-existent futures of Animal and spotty youth. There was a knock at Finlay's door. It was Monday and Wot. Monday came in first with a worried look on her pretty snow-tanned face, followed by a sheepish looking Wot. He was carrying a tray. Finlay knew what that meant.

"I've made some breakfast to cheer you up." There was a basket of croissants which had been given the Wot treatment in the oven. A plate of dead animals, which were now bacon and eggs sat in the middle of the tray. There was a glass of freezing orange juice, which looked most promising. Finlay took hold of it as Wot placed the tray in front of him.

Monday plonked down on his bed. "What's going on?" Monday was to the point as the cold orange juice hit the back of Finlay's throat. He stretched and accidentally hit Monday on the thigh.

"Sorry."

"It's OK." She rubbed her leg pretending mock injury.

"I don't really know, but there's stuff stinking to high heaven and…"

"-we better watch our arses." You could tell Wot had been to public school the way bottoms figured so much in his language. Wasn't his fault, it was just the way it was.

Finlay sighed and nodded. Any further conversation was cut short by an urgent knocking at the door. Finlay's eyebrows knitted together with concern.

"It's alright. There's a policeman outside. Been there all night. Probably wants another cup of cocoa, bless him."

Monday got up and left the room, heading for the front door. She returned, grim faced. A man Finlay did not recognise walked into the room behind her.

∞∞∞∞∞

The snow was piled high by the side of the road. There was little wind and the roads were relatively free of ice. Picot made good time to the little village nestled between Meribel and Albertville. The big machines employed to grit the roads and blow away the snow with their giant suckers had done their job smoothly. Just as well, as Picot was feeling homicidal with the pain from his tooth. A car - a big four wheel drive - was pulling out of Phillippe's driveway as Picot turned into the smart little street where his brother's practice was located. Dentistry obviously paid well as he also had a smart pad in Paris.

Phillipe was standing in the doorway of his house, the sleeves of his smart casual shirt rolled up. Old-fashioned, gold elasticated bands were around each arm just above the elbow. His small gold-framed glasses and tidy precise features, topped off by a mass of thick, luxurious, Liberace-type hair, gave him an almost academic air were it not for the fact that underneath his shirt was a solid pack of muscle.

Phillippe worked out seriously. The bulging belly and sagging skin of a man who couldn't care less about his appearance were not for him. That would have been as nasty as having bad breath; business suicide for a French dentist. He would have had to work in Britain. They seemed to care less about personal hygiene there, as far as Phillippe could tell on his one and only trip. He couldn't wait to leave the ghastly place with its sick little people with their yellow teeth.

His face lit up when he saw Picot, then he frowned. "You're early. I wasn't expecting you for another thirty minutes."

Picot gestured to his mouth as he got out of the car. It's killing me, besides the road was quiet."

Phillippe looked up the valley and nodded in agreement. "Yes, I can see that."

"Who was that just leaving?" Picot asked as he walked beside Phillippe towards the front door.

"Oh, just another satisfied customer."

Picot nodded at the brand new AMG Mercedes poking out of the garage. It's sleek, black paint, low profile tyres and state of the art wheels made it look like it was going fast even when it was standing still. Stylish and head-turning, it must have cost more than a few years of Picot's state controlled wages.

"I see you've got a new one. Things are going well," admired Picot. He laughed and patted his brother on the back.

"Yeah, happy customers pay well." His brother smiled back and guided Picot into the house where some muchs needed relief was waiting for the policeman.

∞∞∞∞

Wot, Monday and Finlay sat on the sofa looking at the sobbing man in front of them. Immaculately dressed in an Armani suit, his

Saville Row overcoat was draped casually over the side of the chair. The efficient alpine heating system in the chalet had seen him dispense with its expensive service almost immediately. He had manicured hands which would not have looked out of place on the cover of a woman's fashion magazine. But then that was hardly surprising, as he was a client of one of the most exclusive salons in Paris, next door to the George V hotel— fingernail heaven as it was known amongst the smart Parisian set. His face was finely boned and tanned with a real tan, the kind you can only get from Antibes, Cannes, St Vincent or wherever, not the fake type from a catalogue sunbed with dodgy electronics. A pinkie ring with Tanzanite and diamonds glinted in the sunlight streaming through the window; its cost would have made the hardest gold card squeak.

No one said anything as the man sat there sobbing like a baby. Not surprising, he had just come from identifying his only son's body; cold, lonely and blue on a marble slab. There wasn't a lot to be said. Parents should not bury their children. Everyone knows it should be other way round.

Eventually, he took his hands away from his face. His eyes were a deep blue and his smooth skin made him look much younger than his years. Even though he had been crying, his eyes were still clear and striking. He sniffed and wiped his tears with a handkerchief which probably cost more than a week in the chalet. He took a deep breath before speaking.

"You found him?" He looked at Finlay, who hesitated before answering softly.

"Yeah."

"Did he say anything?"

"He was dead, sir." Finlay did not make a habit of calling anyone sir but somehow the circumstances demanded an exception. More tears welled up in the eyes before slowly rolling down the cheeks to be caught in the folds of the soft handkerchief.

"He was not always a good boy, but....he was my son." He shook his head as he looked out of the chalet window at nothing in particular.

"Who would have done this to him?" He looked at all three of them.

Monday answered. "We don't know. How old was he?"

"Nineteen." His head bowed and his shoulders arched with sheer physical pain. Then as though a switch had been flicked, he sat bolt upright and put the handkerchief in his pocket. He looked out of the window, paused then turned towards Finlay.

"Walk with me." It was not a request. He stood up, put his coat on, then turned and left, nodding to Monday and Wot as he did so. Monday didn't react but Wot nodded back. Mister Le Blanc did not see this as he was already out of the chalet door. Finlay sighed and put his jacket on.

"Won't be long." He went outside to join Le Blanc and the policeman who was still standing guard.

"We take the lift up." Le Blanc spoke quietly as they walked along the road. A cable car, full of enthusiastic sportsters, hummed above their heads. Le Blanc didn't speak again until they were inside one of the metal and plastic bubbles.

"You don't know what happened, but I want you to find out." The people below them scurried around like little ants round a pile of sugar.

"I'm not a private detective." Finlay was taken aback by the request.
Le Blanc fixed him with steely blue eyes. He was a man who was not used to the word 'no'. The strong wind buffeted the cable car as it headed for the first stop on the mountain.

"I know," his voice sounded a million miles away, "but I also know you care."

All this killing was getting to Finlay. This was not what he had come to the mountains for. He almost felt violated with all the doom. The Alps were a place for healing and growing, not meeting an untimely death, unless it was avalanche related. The man was right; Finlay did care and the youth's death and like Animal's, it upset him deeply. There was no getting away from it.

The wind was fiercer now as the plastic bubble stopped at the first station. Le Blanc produced a fancy looking card from his pocket. Finlay took it, immediately noticing the quality of the high grade paper upon which were printed the words: Le Blanc. The letters stood out so proud of the card it could almost have been a braille version. He flipped it over; there was a phone number and an e-mail address. Simple and to the point. Finlay liked a lot of white on paper. Not too many words and the message gets across.

"You need anything, get in touch." Le Blanc slipped on the uneven slope but quickly regained his balance. Le Blanc walked along the narrow little path covered in matting which led to the waiting plane. The pilot turned the engine over and the propeller spun round, catching the light like a thousand fire flies. It was a smart and very expensive hunk of machinery. Le Blanc did not look like the type of character who went shopping at Budget Bill's.

A couple of women in three grand worth of clothing sipped their hot chocolates as they sat on the veranda of the exclusive mountain hotel which owned the landing strip. Their clientele did not come in by snowmobile, that was for the less well-off further down the slopes. The women blinked, almost in unison, as the light glinted off of the plane. They looked like a pair of cats in the tomb of Seti the First, Finlay thought to himself as he looked at them and then back at Le Blanc who was seated behind the pilot. As the plane moved slowly off, whipping up the snow around it like an angry child in a day nursery and lurching towards the edge of the mountain, Le Blanc looked back over his shoulder at Finlay. There was an empty blank expression on his face. "Poor sod," Finlay said to himself.

The engine noise increased rapidly as the plane lurched off the edge. Like a stone, it dropped out of sight and whined like an angry hornet. The sound echoed throughout the valley. The pitch of the engine changed slightly and the plane rose back into sight, banked to the left to avoid a particularly nasty outcrop, and then dipped again, disappearing from view. Finlay knew that would not be the last he would see of Le Blanc. This was not a man who would take the death of his son quietly or with resignation.

Finlay ran his tongue around the inside of his mouth. It was dry and sticky. He was dehydrated; he needed some fluid inside him, pretty sharpish. The ladies raised their steaming glasses of hot chocolate in greeting to him as he made his way back to the bubble. They liked what they saw of the young man and were not afraid to acknowledge their approval. Finlay stopped and smiled. They beckoned him over. He was tired and not in the mood for socialising but the better part of his nature cut in. They were only being friendly, so what harm could it do.

"Hi, couldn't help noticing you when you said goodbye to your friend," said one of the women as she stood up to greet him and kissed him gently on the cheek.

Finlay was taken aback by the gesture and her fruity smell. It was a combination of fresh morning dew and pure sex. He could not avoid seeing the tanned smooth skin of her cleavage as she'd leant forward. Hardly surprising, as she had lowered the zip for exactly that reason. She was in her mid to late thirties with green eyes; long, dark, hair and skin which had probably spent a little too long in the sun. She had a pair of hips which matched her top half and a slim slender waist. Finlay turned to look at the other woman who by now had stood up. The material of her ski-suit was thin and her nipples stuck out in such a way that he could not miss them. They were as thick as a child's thumb.

"We couldn't help noticing you over there by your plane." She smiled a warm, wicked, smile that is often the preserve of people who feel completely in control.

"Oh, I'm, Mariel and this Lisa." She offered her hand with a glint in her eye which suggested there was a whole lot more on offer than just a handshake. Her hand was warm and moist with a softness like a butterfly's wing.

"It's not my plane," he laughed.

"Oh, is it your butler's?" Mariel giggled.

"I haven't got a butler."

Finlay smiled and let go of the hand which he had held a little too long.

"Nice hands." It was Lisa who spoke this time. She had the same soft lilting French accent as Mariel.

"Where do you come from? You don't look English." Mariel gently stroked Finlay's collar. There was some serious flirting going on.

"Scotland." Finlay's voice was husky.

"Scotland. Isn't it cold there?"

"Yeah, but my Dad was Jamaican. Bit warmer there."

Finlay licked his lips. These two women were delightful and he had a rough idea where all this was going. He was up for it too.

"Which bit of you is Jamaican?" Mariel smiled as she and Lisa shared a knowing look between them.

"Quite a big bit of me," he replied sweaty with anticipation.

Mariel stepped back and to one side, gesturing to the building behind them. Like the walkway they were standing on, it was a solid wood construction. It was also one of the fancier places in Meribel. Finlay had never actually been inside but he knew that was about to change.

"We're staying here." She shivered and put her arms around

herself. "It's cold. Why don't you come up to our room and warm up?"

Lisa smiled, which told Finlay all he needed to know about whether or not she was in agreement. He nodded.

On the way up to their room Finlay found out that they were joint partners in a fashion design house in Paris. One of the smaller ones but successful nevertheless. And like successful people everywhere, they basically did as they pleased, which in their case was sex and lots of it. Finlay could think of worse things to do for recreational pleasure.

Once they were in the hotel room there was no more small talk. Mariel leaned against the wall and looked Finlay directly in the eye. It was time to see these breasts in all their glory. Finlay slowly and deliberately pulled Mariel's zip down. Even the noise was erotic. Two large, perfectly formed, brown breasts bobbed into view. They were encased in a low cut lacy bra which barely contained them. Finlay pulled one of the bra straps down in an almost lazy fashion and a nipple sprung out, thick and erect. He lowered his head and gently took it in his mouth and began to suck as she stroked the back of his neck.

Meanwhile Lisa had unzipped Finlay's trousers and took his stiffening penis in her hand. With her other hand she cupped his balls softly. She licked her lips and then lowered her head and took his member in her mouth. Finlay let out a long, deep groan. He could not remember the last time he had felt so good. She whispered, "Is that all for us?" That statement alone leant another inch and a half to his already impressive erection. She sucked his penis all the way down the shaft then looked up as she paused. "How did you know I liked my meat salty? Finlay tried to sound manly but his voice was a strangled groan. "I kind of guessed."

Lisa reached up and pulled the remainder of Mariel's zip down and then pulled her damp panties to one side and caressed her vulva. Mariel's moans were clearly ones of approval as with her other hand Lisa guided Finlay's penis into her friend and then rubbed his balls as he moved in and out of her wet and eager pussy. After he had come, Lisa and Mariel changed places. It did not take a brain surgeon to work out that Finlay was expected to perform with Lisa in the same way he had with Mariel. He managed it, but only just. It was great fun but Lisa and Mariel hardly noticed him as they finished off with each other what he had started. He let himself out of the room. He would shower back at the chalet.

As he closed the door he saw a small card on the desk by the window. It was advertising Old Man's shop. Meribel was a small place, in more ways than one.

# EIGHT

Finlay did not try to explain what had happened when he returned to the chalet. Wot would have been jealous and Monday, well, they didn't tend to share these kind of details. This trip was not turning out the way Finlay had expected. He always associated Meribel with fun and good times. Up till now, death had not been part of the equation. The season should not have started like this. The two ladies he had just encountered were the only good thing that had happened so far, apart from Roisin. In fact Roisin had not been far from his mind when he'd been enjoying himself in the hotel room. He went to the kitchen and took a jug from the fridge. Finlay looked approvingly at the cranberry juice. He had long abandoned alcohol. Childhood memories of his father's love of the stuff meant he had gone the other way. Any juice, so long as it was clean. Neat and sweet, that was his motto.

Finlay poured the juice into a smart looking tumbler. The light from the kitchen ceiling danced fairy-like through the crystal. He took a drink and savoured the cool, crisp taste. It hit the back of his throat like an ocean liner. He ran his tongue over his teeth, savouring its aftertaste. The aggressive attack of carbonated drinks was definitely not for him. From the window he gazed out at the fresh layer of snow. A figure scurried across the path. There was no mistaking Pattu. Even if the fur lined, full-length designer coat hadn't been a clue, the two diamond earrings and the mane of dreadlocks would have given the game away.

Fresh snow was falling and the wind whipped the white powder into a cold curtain of icy fingers. Pattu stopped, looked around, blinked, then frowned as a worried look spread across his face. Finlay stepped back from the window. This was one dude he did not want to make any more waves with.

There was something strange about the way Pattu was behaving. Why was he scurrying around like that? There was no reason why he should not go where he pleased, so why all the spy stuff, Finlay thought to himself. He looked back through the window. Pattu was gone. Finlay was puzzled and disturbed by what he had seen, given all that had gone on recently.

# Deep Powder

Finlay poured himself more juice and looked out of the window again. The snowfall had become a blizzard and any sign of Pattu was long gone. The look that had been on Pattu's face took Finlay's thoughts far away, to another time; another place.....

The room was familiar. It was dark and warm. He was six years old again and in bed, surrounded by the few toys his mother could afford. Dad worked, but little money ever found its way past the till of the local pub. Finlay remembered that night. It was close to Christmas and the snow lay on the ground, smooth and crisp and even. Street lights flickered through the cheap, thin curtains. A noise startled him and he got out of bed and padded to the bedroom door.

He adjusted his eyesight. His mother was standing there looking at his drunk father, who was only just managing to stay on his feet. Even from his bedroom, the odour of what Finlay would come to know only too well as whisky, assaulted his young nostrils. He grimaced and took a step back, knocking against the door as he did so. The noise made his mother look in his direction. He did not know why, but guilt sped through his little body like an electric shock and a look of shame covered his face like moss on a hillside. He closed the door and crept back to bed, catching sight of his reflection in the mirror. The look on his face was the same as the one Pattu had worn, a short while ago on the windswept path.

Finlay took one last swig of his cranberry juice, put the glass down and closed the kitchen door on his memories. Forty press-ups were the next thing on the agenda. Despite the sexual Olympics, he still found the energy to do his press-ups nice and slow. They're not much use any other way. A quick shower washed the sweat off, not to mention the juices which Lisa and Mariel had so generously slathered him with. He smiled to himself, salty meat indeed. The sex had cheered him up. It was nice to meet some people who wanted to ride him rather than kill him.

Wot and Monday were lounging around, taking it easy. Finlay decided to lie down. He wasn't going to rest very long, just enough to recover from his exertions with Lisa and Mariel. It only seemed like a short nap, but by the time he awoke it was late afternoon with just enough time to get a few runs in before the evening set in. He went into the bathroom, filled the basin with water, then plunged his face into the cool liquid. He never used soap on his face if he could avoid it; bad for the skin. Finlay liked to keep his skin in the best possible condition. Exposure to elements on the mountains, took quite a toll. You could see it on people who did not look after their skin. Some just looked a bit patchy whilst others looked seriously unwell.

∞∞∞∞

The slopes were quiet. Finlay jumped into the lift; he was looking forward to a few peaceful runs. There was a lot on his mind.

"Hi."

It was a silky female voice. He recognised it straight away. He didn't mind this interruption at all, it was Roisin and she was alone. Finlay tried not to make his enthusiasm too obvious.

"You alright?" he asked cooly.

"You don't sound too pleased to see me." There was a trace of hurt in her voice. She flicked her head to one side. A wisp of blonde hair fell in front of her eyes. It was one of her favourite techniques for making herself look sexy. It worked well because she had practised it time and time again.

Finlay bent down and strapped himself into his board. He didn't mind not having much time or space to think now. He was looking forward to this, especially as it looked like he had some welcome company now. He stood up and dusted the snow off his backside. Roisin smiled at him. He smiled back.

"Where's man mountain today?"

She squinted with a puzzled look, as she didn't know what he meant at first. Then it dawned on her.

"Rocky?"

"Yeah. Is that his real name?"

"He's sleeping off his hangover..... and it is, in fact."

"Figures, you couldn't make one like that up."

Roisin smiled. It was pretty obvious that Finlay had not warmed to the granite jawed one. If her instinct was correct, and it was rarely wrong, then he may even have been a little bit jealous. That pleased her. Roisin liked to be in control and jealousy was one of the best ways of keeping men exactly where she liked them, at the end of her whims. She was good though, as she did not make it too obvious that she had picked up on it. People are manipulated best when they don't know exactly what's happening to them. However, Finlay was different to a lot of men she had met in the past. He had that laid back casual feel of a man who was not too bothered about most things. But if there was one thing he did not look like, it was a fool.

Finlay stood up. "It feels good. You joining me?" He turned to Roisin as he flipped his board downhill and allowed the momentum to take him away from her.

"Why not?" she shouted as she turned her skis and thrust herself forward. The steep slope meant that she was soon moving at a rate of knots, parallel with Finlay as he carved his way down the mountain. She had a low centre of gravity and a smooth easy motion. Finlay thought from the way she moved from side to side like a fish whipping through water that she must have been a dancer, at some point in her life. Any bumps or moguls were taken without a moment's hesitation as she pulled in front of Finlay who by now was finding it increasingly difficult to take his eyes off her and it was not just her prowess on the slopes which kept his attention. Finlay stuck a few tricks; he couldn't resist showing off.

One trick too many - his concentration was not really what it should have been - and he was flying through the air like a cannon ball. Luck was on his side, the snow where he fell was soft and deep. His board flew quite a distance, as he hadn't bothered to tether the strap to his ankle. Doing such a serious flyer hadn't really been his intention; his aim had been to impress Roisin. Somehow he knew - as he spat bits of the mountain out of his mouth - that he had probably fallen somewhat short of that mark.

She skied up to him as he clambered to his feet. "How long did it take you to learn that?" A small smile started at the side of her mouth and spread across the rest of her face.

"It just comes naturally," he replied smiling in embarrassment. Finlay felt like a fool— not just because he fell, but because he had been unable to resist the temptation to impress her in the first place.

She reached out and dusted some of the snow off him. "Come on, let's forget this and go for a drink." She gestured with one of her ski poles at the small but inviting mountain lodge which had only recently been converted into a coffee and snack bar. Finlay smiled. He felt more at ease now that his ego had started to calm down a bit.

"Yeah, let's go." He didn't suggest that they race there.

∞∞∞

The place was not very busy and there was some old rock and roll blasting out on the sound system as they went in. It was Eddie Cochrane. He recognised it, as his dad had liked all that sort of stuff like: Gene Vincent, Vince Taylor, Screaming Lord Sutch; along with reggae, calypso, and jazz. Finlay felt the memory of his father wash over him as he walked up to the bar, slightly behind Roisin, who looked over her shoulder at him.

"You alright?" she asked as bars of 'C'mon Everybody' filled the room.

"Yeah, just the music; it reminded me of someone."

"What, this old stuff?" She eased her rump onto a stool and smiled at the bald-headed barman. It was his tape. He'd been brought up on rock and roll in the suburbs of Marseilles and played his music at every opportunity. He hated all the drum 'n bass shit.

"It's an old man it reminded me of," said Finlay as he smiled at the barman when he placed two menus in front of them both.

"Which old man?" Roisin scanned the list of munchies and drinks.

"Mine." Finlay said quietly.

"Where is he?" Roisin flicked her hair to one side.

Finlay felt his memories judder and fade as though an old black and white projector had stuttered to a halt.

"Don't ask." Finlay's tone was a cold as the weather.

"Ouch." Roisin leant forward and gently touched his hand.

"Sorry. Some things make me less than jolly."

"You shouldn't worry about things like that."

"Like that?" Finlay squinted at her.

"Family. Remember, you don't choose your family."

"But you can choose your friends, eh," said Finlay sarcastically.

"Can I get you folks something?"

The barman with the shiny head had a perfect American accent despite coming from the south of France. He'd wanted to get into the movies ever since he was a kid. Everyone in the flicks seemed to have American accent, so he had perfected his over the years. He had practised it at every opportunity. So far he had only managed a couple of days extra work on a low budget Brit flick which had been shooting in Paris for a few rainy days. It had pissed him off; he thought his part was bigger than the split second of screen time he'd ended up with. He had even considered porn but wasn't sure how to get started; he heard the money was good.

"I'll have a coke," Roisin said. Her accent was mid-Atlantic, posh, and Swiss finishing school all rolled into one.

"Me too." Finlay adjusted his position. The seat was not quite big enough.

Baldy barman went off for a few moments then reappeared with a couple of fizzy cokes, ice and a slice of lemon in each. Finlay reached into his pocket then realised to his shame that he had come out without any money. He felt the embarrassment rise in his face. Roisin didn't bat an eyelid.

"Ronnie, I'll sort it later." She looked the barman in the eye and smiled. He smiled back.

"No worries, Roisin." He liked to throw a little bit of Australian into his conversation as well. After all, they made films there as well .

"You know him?" Finlay took a swig from his coke.

"I know a lot of people." Roisin's eyes narrowed a bit.
Finlay felt she was looking a bit defensive. The smile returned to her face.

"I've been coming here for quite a few seasons. Good business."
"What is your business?"
Finlay drank the rest of his coke. He'd tried to take it easy but he was terrible. As soon as he had any kind of drink he had to finish it quick. It was good he didn't drink alcohol; if he did he would have sucked it down fast and probably all of the time. Then surely he would have ended up like his dad– the one thing in life which frightened him more than anything else.

"Bit of this, bit of that, but I'm not sure if it is any of your business," she said, keeping the smile on her face so he wouldn't take it the wrong way.

"When does it become mine?"
"Once we've shagged."
Roisin licked her lips, the enjoyment dancing in her eyes. She liked throwing people a curve.

"Two more cokes." Ronnie slammed them down with a flourish and a smile; on cue like in a film.

"Thanks, Ronnie."

Roisin did not take her eyes off Finlay as she picked up her coke and took a deep sip of the ice cold drink. She licked her lips. It tasted good; she might even have another. There would be plenty time for some of the hard stuff later; first she wanted to get off the mountain with everything intact. She didn't mind taking risks but not pointless ones which might endanger herself; she was much too fond of herself for that. Roisin also liked to be in control at all times. In control of her environment and the people around her. If she wasn't in charge, she wasn't interested.

"About that shag?" Finlay tried to sound relaxed. He took a sip of his coke after he spoke.

"What shag?" She did not smile, her features were cold like the Northern wind. She loved playing games.

Finlay tilted his head slightly to one side. She was a teaser alright. It ought to have made him mad but it just made her all the more desirable. It was lucky for her he had been given a good seeing to by Lisa and Mariel, otherwise he would probably have been trying a little too hard to get inside her ski suit. As it was, he was probably being a bit too obvious for any chance of success at the moment. He knew that, but he also knew that Roisin was not a woman he could read like a book, not unless he could see inside covers.

Roisin changed the subject. "Tell me about Monday and Wot."

Finlay went with it. He wanted this to be a worthwhile chase. It was going to be fun. No need to spoil it by being too pushy, even if he was finding it hard to control his lust.

"Not much to tell really, they're my mates."

"I know that," Roisin said a little testily.

"How did you meet them and where?"

"Well, I met Monday at a comp. She was doing promotions for a drinks company. We hit it off straight away and have been friends ever since."

"Friends?" Her eyes danced with mischief.

"Yeah, It wouldn't work otherwise. Sex always seems to take the edge off friendship."

"Depends who your friends are." She enjoyed being difficult when she had conversations like these.

"If she's not with you, who does she see?"

"Well, she's not too keen on a lot of guys. Thinks they are just after one thing."

"And what's that?" Rosin asked as if she didn't know.

"You know what I mean."

"Yeah, I know what you mean. Is she a muff diver?" Roisin was genuinely interested as she did not mind a bit of three way action if it ever came up. Monday was not bad looking either, in a kind of downbeat sort of way.

"A what?" Finlay squinted at her. She had so many strange turns of phrases. He realised what she meant just before she answered.

"A girl lover, a lezzie."

"No, she likes guys."

"How do you know?"

"She's my friend."

"Oh, yeah, of course, you said." She changed tack.

"And Wot. *What* about him?" She smiled at her own joke. She always enjoyed her own sense of humour.

"He's from a good background. His parents don't understand him but they love him and are dead generous to him."

"How do you mean generous?"

Well, whenever they find out which place we're staying at they send money, to help him out."

"What about you, does it help you out?" She was searching now.

"Whatever money we bring in, we share."

"Like a commune?"

Finlay laughed. That was probably a fair description.

"Yeah something like that," he said as Ronnie put on Howling Wolf.


Ronnie liked the blues as well as rock and roll. The deep gravely voice cut through the air like a baling hook; he loved this music and felt contented as he washed a couple of glasses, watching Roisin out of the corner of his eye. She was a one alright and what a looker. Played men like fish on a hook. He'd seen her here for a couple of seasons now. She was a big player and a cock teaser. Ronnie knew. When he'd responded she'd made him look like a complete dick last year. But he'd get his own back sometime soon. Of that he was in no doubt. The cockteasing little hussy would get to know all about why they called him Rock Hard Ronnie.

Finlay caught him looking at them. He smiled quickly and Finlay smiled back. Ronnie was good at switching the smiles; he had to be in this game. If people knew what he really thought of them then he would lose business. Of course if they knew what he did to their drinks and food sometimes, not only would he lose business, he would get more than a visit from the health standards agency.

Again, he looked up at Finlay and Roisin, especially Roisin. Stuck up bitch. He couldn't wait to get at her. He bit his lip at the thought of wiping that smart upper class smile off her face as he had his wicked way with her. A plan began to hatch in his hot, dirty, little mind. He'd score a few drugs later, then he would see about making that girl pant for him. It would be good to ride a woman who wasn't made of plastic, didn't let off air when he bit her and didn't have made in Germany stamped on her arse.

Ronnie approached them. "Can I freshen up your drinks?"

"Nah, you're alright, Ronnie."

Roisin didn't look at him this time. But then why would she, he thought to himself. He was only a hired help, a doormat which she could walk over. He wisely kept his thoughts to himself as he looked at Finlay.

"No, you're alright; no more for me."

Roisin pulled a plastic card out from nowhere and gave it to Ronnie to settle the bill. The gold flashed in the light. Finlay never minded when other people paid– men or women.

"Aren't you even going to offer?" Roisin said with a playful lilt in her voice; she knew his pockets were empty.

"I never argue about money."

"Not a bad policy. I'll remember that one when I'm out with you next time."

Without looking up, she signed the slip which Ronnie had put in front of her. She was relaxed and poised. Finlay looked at her hands. They had never done a day's work in their life, at least not of the type which required sweat and tears. There was, however, a rock on her finger which had the sweat and tears of *other* people written all over it. She saw him looking at it as she handed the pen back to Ronnie, who by now could barely conceal his thoughts about Roisin. If either one of them had looked at him they would probably have sussed that something was up.

"You like it?" She held it up in the mountain light. Rays of yellow, gold and silver shot out at all different angles. It was pure white, not a hint of yellow, emerald cut and bloody rare. That much Finlay could tell. He hadn't done a course at Christie's gem

74

department but he knew a thing or two. Four carats, if not more. It was so big, he was surprised her finger was strong enough to carry it.

"Yeah, it's alright, if you like that kind of thing," he said quietly.

She shot him a look of disapproval. "What's wrong? I thought you liked things of quality.

He tried to save the situation and almost succeeded. "I like what's inside it." He held her hand; she did not take it away.

"I like fine things, the more expensive the better." She turned the ring and her eyes glittered like the diamond. "You like fine things?" She blinked a few times.

"Yeah, but expensive doesn't always mean good. Tell me about Rocky." Roisin was not the only one who could switch subjects without warning.

She was taken aback but it was fair enough. She'd quizzed him about his friends. "As drag coefficients go, he's not bad."

"Drag what?" Finlay didn't have a clue what she was on about.

"Drag coefficients. It's what I call relationships or friendships. They can drag you down and hold you back if you're not careful."

"So does Rocky do either?"

"Nah, he works for me. I found him under a rock in a ski resort, hence his name. He was mixing drinks for corporate fat cats and rich bitches with necks like turkeys. He's my personal assistant which basically means he does anything I tell him."

"Sounds a bit clinical to me," Finlay said gently. He didn't want to fall out with her but it was a bit extreme.

"Fair point, I suppose."

Suddenly Roisin put her hand down and got up from the seat; her mood was suddenly warmer. "Come on let's go; I've had enough of this place." She took him by the hand and led him back to where their equipment was stacked up outside. Ronnie looked at the departing pair and sucked his bottom lip. I'll see you later Miss tight knickers, he thought to himself as he dried a glass with a dish towel advertising the delights of the French Alps.

# NINE

Outside, the temperature had dropped considerably. Roisin and Finlay stepped back into their gear. Finlay stretched a bit; he had stiffened up during the time in the bar.

"Do you think you can manage to stay on your feet this time?" Roisin shot him a sly grin as she pushed off down the mountain.

"Yeah, I never do the same thing twice!" he shouted after her disappearing form.

He wasn't trying so hard now so there was less chance of him falling over. He pulled a few tricks and glided nice and easy down the mountain. At the bottom, Roisin took off her skis and leant against them, only slightly out of breath.

"That was fun. I'll see you later."

"Where are you staying?" Finlay brushed some of the sweat off his face. He always leaked a bit when he exerted himself. Roisin pointed up at one of the fanciest chalets in the middle of town, if not *the* fanciest.

"There. Come up and see me sometime." She blew him a kiss and walked away.

"I will!" he shouted, then under his breath he whispered to himself, "I most certainly will." He turned and almost knocked over Donny.

"Yol, man what's the hurry?" He playfully punched Finlay on the arm.

"Hey Donny. how's it going? I was just saying goodbye to..." He didn't get the rest out as Donny interrupted him.

"-the lady, yeah, I saw her man. She's quite somet'ing. What was you up to?" He raised his eyebrows in a mock cynical smile.

"We were just chewing the fat and I was busy falling over." Finlay fiddled with the strap on his board as he spoke.

"Ain't like you." He was genuinely surprised.

Finlay shrugged, there was not much he could say. Donny stepped back and gave Finlay a small wave.

"Catch you later, dude."

"Yeah, later, man." Finlay picked up his board and made his way back to the chalet. He felt unsettled, but he wasn't quite sure why. The last few days had not been pretty with death visiting the Three Valleys, but that wasn't it. Something else was gnawing at his insides and he couldn't put his finger on it.

∞∞∞∞

From the chair lift station, where he had disembarked not long after Roisin and Finlay, Ronnie watched him disappear. He also had something gnawing at his insides and it was stretching his trousers big-time. It was still too light outside for what he had in mind; it would have to wait till later. Time for a few beers and some drugs to make him feel sweet before he did a fishmonger on Roisin. He giggled to himself. She was a piece of fish and he was going to fill it. The giggling turned to a maniac laugh as he sniffed in air through his nose. Cocaine had not done his septum many favours but there was plenty to be had in the resort now. It was awash with it.

∞∞∞∞

Finlay arrived back at the chalet to find Monday and Wot watching the telly. He padded in his socks over to the sofa and threw himself down, landing with a scrunch on a pile of newspapers. He picked them up and was about to throw them on the floor when something caught his eye. It was in French but there was nothing wrong with his grasp of all things Gallic. The story featured a photograph of Old Man clutching a snowboard with his logo - in gleaming colour - all over it. He was grinning at the camera like a Cheshire cat. It had been taken in front of the shop. He read the small piece of text below the photo which informed him that it had been snapped at the opening of Old Man's new venture a few weeks ago. It wasn't a bad photo. He had snow bum written all over his face, a kind of look which was bound to attract fresh customers.

Something else caught his eye. In the background, with that jaw like a ski-jump, was Rocky. Nothing unusual in that, but there was a look in Rocky's face which made him stand out from the rest and it wasn't just his rugged looks. Whilst everyone else was cheery and bright with that lovely glow you can only get from snow, he looked like he had swallowed a razor blade which had found its way to his major intestine. Finlay whistled softly to himself.

"What is it?"

# Deep Powder

Monday raised her arm, put it behind her neck and stretched an old injury she had sustained a few years ago when she had been overambitious on the trampoline. Finlay handed her the paper. She took it lazily with her free hand and scoped the picture. She shrugged.

"What about it?" Monday felt she may be slow on the uptake but she wasn't getting this.

She heard a little crack as she stretched a bit too far. Wot, standing by the window, squirmed. He had a thing about backs and knees– the popping noise ran through him like someone scratching a blackboard and they always seemed to pop when he was around.

Finlay pointed at the figure of Rocky. "He just looks a little out of place, don't you think?"

"Finlay, this is a winter sports place. That's what he does. How can he look out of place?"

Finlay stretched out on the sofa and felt something hard dig into his backside. It was the remote control of the telly. "It's not the fact he's there, it's just the way he looks." He retrieved the remote from somewhere near the crack of his backside and pointed it at the telly. The room filled with CNN and the continued search for the world's terrorists. Unfortunately, to anyone but a trained observer, that would seem to cover anyone who did not appear to agree with the majority of the Western governments.

Monday continued looking at the photo, while Wot cringed in the corner at the thought of back, bones and knees. He shook his head and shivered.

"You alright?" Finlay asked him, pressing another button on the remote. Some mild porn came up. After a few moans he switched channels again. It was a documentary about the U-boat during the war, with some old retired Nazis sitting on the balconies of their expensive apartments in Anytown Germany. They were pontificating about how they were only doing their duty when they went to war, it was nothing personal.

"Yeah, I'm OK, just the sound of Monday's back clicking made me go funny."

"It's strange when you see this…" Wot came over, pushed Finlay's feet out of the way and sat down on the sofa, sliding back on the shiny leather.

"What's strange?" Finlay asked as Monday put down the paper and went into the kitchen. They heard the noise of the kettle being heated.

"Make mine a tea!" Finlay shouted and looked at Wot who nodded. "Same for Wot!"

"What do you mean, what's strange?" Finlay asked again.

"Well, if you believe all this, none of the Nazis were interested in world domination, they were just career soldiers. But look at their eyes." Wot pointed at the telly.

"What about their eyes?" Finlay looked back at the television.

"They're all the same colour and they are as cold as the inside of a deep freeze. What a bunch of shits." He leaned back, pleased with his assessment of the situation.

"What made you think I was going into the kitchen to make tea?" Monday interrupted the conversation, hands on hips.

"That's your job, you're a woman," Wot said, not taking his eyes off the telly. If he had he would have seen the dishcloth which was coming flying towards him like an Excocet. It hit him full in the face. He flinched and smiled at her.

"I take it you've resigned?"

"No, I'll make you one this time. But you're no better than these Fascists on the telly." She went back into the kitchen which had steamed up a bit from the kettle.

Finlay stirred as Monday came back through with a cup of tea. The music from the telly, which was some nasty German marching stuff, sounded like someone had recorded stamping jackboots overdubbed with some old fool on the spoons.

"Ta," Finlay said as he took the cup of steaming hot liquid off Monday who put the other one, meant for Wot, on the small Alpine table by the side of the sofa, where she had also put the paper with Rocky's picture in it.

"Mention it," Monday said, her dry wit intact and functioning on full horsepower. Finlay had to think for a bit before he knew what she was talking about. Wot didn't say anything, he was complete absorbed in the documentary.

"So, how was your little session?"

"OK. I met Roisin. She joined me and I took a tumble."

"You met her on your own?" Monday did not bother to try to hide the sarcasm in her voice.

Finlay looked sideways at her. He knew she was joking but there was some venom in her voice. "You don't like her, do you?"

"It's not a question of that. It's just that with everything else going on, like people trying to kill you, or us, and all that heavy shit, I just thought..."

"You thought what?" Finlay said quietly.

"I just thought you would have other things on your mind than what's cooking in beaver country."

Wot choked on his tea.

"Monday. You can be pretty crude when you want to be," Finlay whispered.

"You taught me well, master," Monday said, the sarcasm dripping off her voice like fat from a cheap fish supper.

Finlay had to accept that she had a point, both about the pussy hunting and the tutoring he had given her in the art of crudity.

Monday stood up and changed the subject. "You're right, you know. There is something strange about that look in Rocky's face."

Finlay dipped his head to one side."And?" he scratched his chin.

"It looks like he's seen something which has pissed him off, big time."

"Yeah. Roisin with Finlay," Wot laughed.

"The picture was taken a few weeks before we met, clever arse," said Finlay dryly.

"Oh...yeah." It dawned on Wot that his grasp of timing and dates could have been better.

Monday went back into the kitchen. Before she'd been interrupted to make tea, she had meant to be taking in the view. In the kitchen was a clear glass skylight through which you could get the best nighttime view of Meribel and see the stars. Seeing stars at night always reminded her of being a child and waiting for her dad to come into the bedroom to kiss her goodnight and speed her on to the land of nod.

She was close to both her parents, who had been less than thrilled when she'd dropped out of university to pursue life as a snow person. They loved her the most but they did not love her lifestyle choice. The argument that she could always go back to university at some point in the future when it actually meant something to her, had not fallen on very fertile ground.

Monday looked up at the stars to try to find the one her dad had named after her. She knew it was up there somewhere, she just hadn't been able to find it since she'd been a little kid. Tonight she wanted to see if she was going to get lucky and see it again for the first time since it was christened all those years ago, on the occasion of her sixth birthday.

# TEN

Ronnie slapped some oil on his bald head, winked at his reflection in the mirror, then noticed something odd. He peered closer then, like a hunter in a rain forest. He snatched at the offending articles: several long black hairs sprouting out of his nose like a newly sprayed crop. At first he was unsuccessful, then after a more concerted effort, the offending strands were held aloft as he triumphantly inspected his trophies. He examined his nasal passages again, but to his relief there were no more.

Satisfied with his efforts he sprayed some Kenzo aftershave on his face and head. He winced as it stung the raw, newly shaved skin. The smell completely filled the bathroom, reaching every crevice and space. Previous girlfriends had always complained about his obsession with aftershave - the ones who actually hung around long enough to get to know him better, that is. Ronnie had been able to sustain a few short term relationships, but they always ended abruptly when the unfortunate young women - they were invariably blonde - realised the depths of Ronnie's sexual excesses. He was not a man you took home to mother; in fact, he was not a man you would allow anywhere near people you remotely cared about.

Ronnie had occupied a succession of bar jobs, moving from resort to resort. This meant no one really got to know him, which suited him just fine. The only way he wanted someone close was if they were female and spread-eagled under him. He felt good tonight; he always felt good when he made decisions. Tonight he'd made a good one: Roisin was going to get sorted. He was convinced, in his rather strange and simplistic way, that Roisin would probably enjoy what he had in store for her. After the bruises had healed, he was sure that there would be no repercussions.

He reached into the cupboard and retrieved a pair of nail scissors. They had seen better days as there was a bit of rust on one of the blades. Ronnie ignored it as he peered at the mirror once more. He pursed his lips trying to focus his eyes on the job in hand. After a few moments, he located what he was looking for– thin, fair, hairs which were growing unevenly out of his eyebrows. Ronnie, like many of the pathologically disturbed, liked to have things kept in their place and in an orderly fashion. It bugged the hell out of him when he had long eyebrow hairs growing like antennae. He snipped each one in turn, then washed the corpses down the plug hole. After putting the scissors back in their rightful place, he switched off the light, then went back into the sitting room of the small chalet supplied by his job.

Now dressed, Ronnie went into the room where he kept the goodies he would need for the task tonight. In each carefully arranged drawer of the smooth wooden chest were the required items: thin silken cords, a couple of sets of handcuffs, and a solid supply of knock-out drops. He wouldn't need the handcuffs tonight, he thought to himself. Roisin was a silken cord type of girly. He felt a hard-on grow in his trousers as he held the soft but immensely strong cord to his face. Ronnie liked to smell things; that was his passion. In another time and place he could have been a successful tea blender, but life does not always run smoothly. Ronnie was a serial rapist. That was his job. The employment in the bars was just to pay his bills and to give him an excuse to indulge his real passion, hurting women. Tonight, he felt that he was going to exceed himself.

There was a soft flurry of snow falling as he let himself out of the apartment. He knew exactly where to go; it had not taken any real detective work to realise that Roisin would be staying in the most expensive place in Meribel. Ronnie had seen her going into the fancy chalet. He waited for an hour or so to see if she would go out. She didn't, so he presumed that she was not coming out again that night. He went down to the bar in the centre of town, careful to avoid any drunken Brit tourists. He had no desire to draw any attention to himself, tonight. As an added measure of security, he even had a condom along with his ski mask. That DNA business was a right pain in the arse.

After indulging in quite a few beers, he walked away from the centre and away from the chalet. When he was sure no one was looking, he doubled back and walked along the small forest track just on the edge of town, which he knew led to the rear of Roisin's chalet where he could gain entry through the service door which had a faulty lock. Ronnie knew the lock was broken because the locksmith, who he had served at the bar many times, always seemed happy to chat about the details of his business once supplied with copious amounts of alcohol.

The noise from the town was just a distant buzz as he fiddled with the lock a few times, then quietly and gently let himself in. There was no sound in the chalet as he paused amongst a pile of drying skis and equipment. He reached into his bag and pulled on his ski mask. It was difficult to walk properly, as his erection kept rubbing against his trousers. Never mind, he thought, we'll soon have you out and up to no good.

A small drip of saliva formed and then dropped from his mouth, wetting the inside of his ski mask; that always happened when he was excited. He made his way up to the top of the stairs and waited, as his eyes adjusted to the darkness. Then he saw her coming out of the bedroom, putting on her dressing gown. He licked his lips; he could already feel himself inside her . She walked past him and after she had gone a few paces, he stepped out and punched her in the back of the head. The plan was to knock her to the ground, tie her up, rip off her panties then ride her like a horse. Plans do not always work out.

The blow did not fully connect as it glanced off the side of her head. It was not enough to knock her out or daze her, but it was certainly enough to tell her that someone was in her chalet and they did not have her well-being in mind. She went with it and rolled forward, twisting midway so that she was able to spring to her feet, her dressing gown falling open as she did so. It was the nearest Ronnie was ever going to get to her.

She stepped forward, spun on the ball of her front foot, and threw her whole weight into a spinning back kick which connected, sweet as a ribbon, into the would-be rapists stomach. He didn't have time to be surprised as he vomited even before he hit the floor. Ronnie was not used to fighting women, only beating them up and screwing them. Roisin was a fighter, a very good one in fact. She was used to scrapping and was only interested in winning.

Ronnie reached out with one of his hands to grab on to her. He found a piece of her but could not hold on. She raised her foot and stamped on his hand, breaking two of the fingers clean, like dry summer twigs. He let out a scream of pain and anger as he tried to get to his feet. This was not going as he had eagerly anticipated and it was going to get worse. She slammed the heel of her hand into his face, shattering his nose. He needn't have bothered pulling all these nasal hairs out. As he crouched there, blinking through the blood, his erection a shadow of its former self, she ripped the mask off, not unlike the way he'd been planning to tear off her panties.

"You!" she gasped.

Ronnie tried to speak as he rose to his feet but blood was blocking most of his mouth so he just managed a kind of burble, before she dropped her weight onto one foot and with a loud scream side-kicked the man full in the groin. He flew back through the window and over the balcony dropping a few metres onto the soft snow. He managed to get up and with blood streaming from his wounds, beat a retreat. Roisin stood on the balcony, bosom heaving and sweat dripping off her brow, but not for any of the reasons Ronnie had hoped for.

∞∞∞∞

Finlay was asleep when he got the call from Roisin. He threw some clothes on and was over there faster than he could have imagined possible. Picot was already there with some of his uniforms, looking none too pleased. Attacks like this on rich young tourists were as bad for business as the soaring murder rate. If this hit the papers then the whole season would be a disaster.

Roisin had a blanket around her as Finlay bounded up the chalet stairs two at a time.

"You OK?" He was breathing heavily as he approached her.

"Yeah, I'm alright. Lucky for me he wasn't up to much."

"Who was he?" Finlay nodded to Picot who nodded back. They were both getting to know each other far better than either would have liked.

"Ronnie, the barman from the mountain cafe." It was Picot who spoke through gritted teeth.

"What was he after?" Finlay realised the answer to the question almost before he'd asked it.

"Well, he didn't get it," she said with a steely look in her eyes.

"Madame is an accomplished fighter, which stood her well tonight," Picot remarked with admiration, running his fingers through his hair

"Fighter?" Finlay thought she was just good at skiing.

"Yeah, karate. I do a bit," she said quietly.

"More than a bit. Madame is an expert of international merit," Picot hastened to add.

"Where did he go?"

Finlay touched Roisin on the arm. She smiled, his concern was obvious.

"Out and over the balcony, but not voluntarily," she said with some accuracy.

"He won't have gotten far; my men will pick him up soon." Picot gestured to the balcony where Ronnie had made his speedy, involuntary exit.

At Roisin's request, Finlay stayed with her for the rest of the night. He slept on the sofa with one eye open while Picot's uniformed boys stayed on guard outside. Mind you he had to admit, once he had heard how Roisin had defended herself against Ronnie, it sounded as though he was not there in a body guarding capacity.

Finlay was glad his time in Meribel was coming to an end. There would be a few days in London, then Whistler. He was looking forward to Canada; the French Alps and the high body count was enough to last him for quite a while.

∞∞∞∞

Picot was right on one score but wrong on the other. It didn't take his men long to find Ronnie but it did take a while to pick him all up. It looked like he had been run over by a herd of elephants. Dead was an understatement; his body had been taken to the morgue in more than two bags. It would be a while before everything about the cause of death was clear, but whoever had done the job on Ronnie had excelled themselves.

∞∞∞∞

The wind whistled through the corridors of the morgue. Dr Piaf winced as he walked down the corridor. His back was killing him. Like many medical people he wasn't too hot when it came to looking after himself. His wife often said it seemed as though he forgot everything he knew when it came to his own well-being, but he was an expert when it came to others.

The wind whistled through the morgue's ill fitted windows; the doctor had never bothered to fix them. The residents of the morgue rarely complained; they grumbled sometimes, but that was a different kind of wind, he mused to himself and then laughed at his own wit. If he hadn't been a doctor, he might have chanced his arm on the stage. He could have tried his act out on the people laying on the slabs. Again, he smiled at his own humour, then turned the corner to find Picot and one of the uniforms waiting for him.

They didn't look too cheery, but then Dr Piaf often forgot that this wasn't a very happy place.

"Good morning. Gentlemen."

"Morning." Picot smiled back at him as he stood to one side to allow him to move into the room where Ronnie's remains awaited.

Pierre, the uniform, tried to smile but it came out like a kind of rictus grin. He breathed out slowly. He did not feel at all well. This was his first time in a place like this, it had not featured much in his training. Reluctantly he followed the other two into the room. Then the next thing he remembered was waking up to Picot slapping him in the face. After the first couple of slaps it dawned on him that the good Inspector was not hitting him so much as to revive him but was really expressing the irritation written all over his face.

Pierre had collapsed at the first sign of what used to be Ronnie. He had been taken to another room by one of the assistants and had missed what had had been relayed to the others– every cold and gory detail. Apparently Ronnie's demise had been at the end of a machete. Someone had diced him to bits with more efficiency than a combine harvester.

∞∞∞∞

Geneva airport was heaving with people. They'd checked their stuff in a good hour ago and Monday and Wot had wandered off to check out the shops for some useless items. Wot liked to gather at least one useless item from every airport they visited and Monday had gone with him to make sure that whatever he had in mind was not too trashy. Finlay stayed behind and rested, leaning against his bag.

In the distance, by the British Airways check-in, Finlay saw a familiar figure. It was Roisin. If the events of the last few days had taken their toll, it did not show. She was talking to two men. Finlay was surprised, they were Old Man and Mick the Trick. Roisin saw Finlay and waved. She turned back to the other two, said something, then gathered up her belongings and walked over to Finlay. She looked radiant.

"Wow, you look good," Finlay whispered as he kissed her on the cheek.

"Thanks for being there for me, when I needed you," she said as she brushed her lips gently across his ear.

"You're welcome," replied Finlay as he smiled to himself. He sounded like a waiter.

"It meant a lot to me, you know." She paused for a few seconds then looked around, almost as though she was making sure no one else was listening to her.

"It had a big effect on me." Finlay nodded.

"You look good though, relaxed," he added.

"Yeah, well, I'm good at putting things behind me," she said.

"Strange about Ronnie, wasn't it?" Finlay bent down as he noticed one of his shoe laces had come undone.

"Yes, it was. Can't say I'm overwhelmed with grief, but it was spooky." Roisin shivered her shoulders.

"You can say dat again, man!" Finlay stood up as they were joined by Mick the Trick. He was grinning from ear to ear as he extended his hand.

"Gimme five, Clive."

Finlay wanted to say his name wasn't Clive but the Trick didn't mean any harm, so he playfully hit the hand. Mick pretended to be hurt.

"Ouch. Mind the meat," he laughed before continuing,"I was just saying to Roisin here that I wondered if you was fleeing the scene after making mincemeat of dirty Ronnie." Mick did a little shuffle in his expensive trainers.

Finlay bit his lip. He didn't think it was very funny. Mick could see by his reaction that he was not happy.

"Here, sorry man. You're doing a Victoria. No offence, blood, it was a joke."

Finlay smiled, it was difficult to stay irritated with this guy. "Victoria?"

"Yeah. One is not amused." Mick grinned at the depth of his own humour.

"Very good, Mick, very good." Finlay nodded in approval.

# Deep Powder

Mick smiled, and kissed Roisin on the cheek. "Catch you later. See you in Whistler, dude." He smiled at Finlay then shouted, as he was now some yards away, "Sorry, once again, blood!"

Finlay waved him away, to show he wasn't worried. He turned to Roisin, "I didn't know you knew Mick and the Old Man."

"Yeah, why shouldn't I?" She sounded a bit frosty.

"I just didn't realise." Finlay backed off a bit.

"Some of my business involves sports promotions. I know them through that." Some of the warmth returned to her smile.

Finlay realised that in all that had gone on, he had not actually enquired as to what she did; so that was one question answered. Any further probing was put to one side by the arrival of Old Man who looked a bit out of breath.

"Yeah, Finlay. Glad to see you. Why haven't you come by the shop to check me out? I was waiting for you."

"I've been kind of busy, Old Man. I was going to pop in when I came back after the competition in Whistler," Finlay said.

"No worries. Look, I had something for you. Thought you may be interested. I was going to let you try it out when you came by."

"What?" Finlay was curious.

"A new board I've been working on. Look, it's in the van, why not take it to Whistler, give it a go, see what you think. No obligations." He scratched his good ear with a long fingernail. The golden ear ring glistened in the terminal building light.

Finlay shifted uncomfortably from foot to foot and looked about a bit before answering. "I'm not being funny, Old Man, but I've got sponsorship and all that. I can't be riding other peoples' boards. It's not right." He rubbed his eyes; he hadn't really caught up on the sleep he had lost during the night he'd stayed over at Roisin's, after Ronnie's unsuccessful rape attempt.

"I understand, but I'm not asking you to ride it in the comp. Not realistic anyway, not until you've tried it out and all that. Just give it a go when you have a spare moment. You won't regret it. I mean it." Old Man's voice was quiet and rhythmic; he had a certain persuasive air about him.

"OK," Finlay sighed.

"Great, Just wait there for a moment. I'll go and get it from the van."

Old Man was off before Finlay had a change of heart. He wasn't

88

too sure about this. For one thing, it was too late to get it in the hold of the aircraft; it would have to travel on board with him. He turned to Roisin. "Are you going to London on the B.A. flight?"

"I was, but I've a few things I'd like to do here, so I think I'll change it to a later one." She hesitated and looked a bit distant. She saw Finlay looking at her, then she continued before he could say anything. "Don't worry, I'll catch up with you in Whistler. Ace place; I'm looking forward to spending a bit of time there." She smiled and touched his hand.

"I didn't know you were going there." He was surprised, but pleased.

"Yeah. It's to do with the sports promotion and all that. Good chance for us to get better acquainted, don't you think?" She bit her bottom lip in that Breakfast at Tiffany's sort of way. Then without warning, she stood up on tiptoe and kissed Finlay on the lips just as Monday and Wot came round the corner.

Finlay smiled at her. "See you."

"Yeah, cheerio." Roisin looked straight at Monday who did not bother trying to hide her feelings. "Bye bye," she said to her sarcastically.

Monday said nothing, at least not with her mouth. Her eyes said it all. She wasn't keen on the girl, but it pissed her off that both Finlay and Wot might think it was jealousy.

"Wow," Wot whistled through his teeth. "You've got two hot babes fighting over you."

Finlay winced. He saw the blow coming long before Wot felt Monday's fist connect with the side of his head. She had a bit of a temper on her and Wot, on this occasion, had forgotten that. In her own inimitable style, she had reminded him.

Any further discussion was put on hold with the return of a sweating Old Man carrying a big black canvas bag. He held it out to Finlay. "There you are man. When you get to Whistler, take it straight to Silver Steve's. There's a dude there named...." He reached into his pocket and came out with a small piece of paper. He unrolled it with one hand and squinted at the faint pencil lettering on it. "...Steve Vox. Just ask for him and he'll set it up for you."

Finlay paused for a second or two. He was still not sure but felt he was beginning to turn into a tight-arse. He took the bag. It felt even and weighted. He unzipped it and looked inside. There was a gleaming smooth board with a seriously fancy finish on it.

"Looks good." Finlay nodded.

"The best. Take my word for it. Once you've ridden it, you'll be smitten. You'll be wanting sponsorship from me. Bring it back to Meribel and we can talk." He patted Finlay on the back and was gone.

Finlay zipped it back up. "You OK?" he said to Wot who was nursing a sore head. Monday was sitting a small distance away not looking at either of them. Finlay put the board down and went over to her. She wasn't crying, but tears had welled up in her eyes.

"You alright?" Finlay sat down beside her.

"No, I'm not. You're not the only person here, you know, Finlay."

"What do you mean?"

She shook her head and wiped her eyes. "Forget it. I don't want to talk about it." She turned away from him.

"I'll be OK in a minute. Just leave me alone." She gave him a look which showed it was not up for discussion. Finlay nodded, stood up and went back to Wot.

Monday was always alright after a moment or two. Finlay understood that it wasn't really about Roisin and him. Monday did not get strange just because there was another girl on the scene. It was something else, more to do with her security and the tight unit which they had become. They were like a family. She didn't like to see anything threaten that and she had a point; the feelings Roisin was stirring in Finlay were more than just a passing interest.

Time for more pondering was gone as their delayed flight was finally due to depart for a slightly fog bound London. As usual, what started as a walk towards the departure gate, turned into a run. There was a further delay, as the staff would not let Finlay take the board on the plane with him, instead it was banished to the hold.

The flight was full and there were some familiar faces at the back of the airbus. Pattu, Menelik, Donny and Nyaman were spread out in their seats. They had put the arm rests up for more room and were already looking nice and relaxed. All except for Pattu, who hated flying. He didn't join in the jolly greetings which the others gave Finlay, Wot and Monday as they made their way up the plane and he reserved a special glare for Finlay who just blanked him; he was fed up with this nonsense.

# Deep Powder

Finlay sat down next to a big, heaving, sweaty bear of a man. His jacket was off but his shirt was transparent with sweat. The fear oozed off him like honey through a crack. Finlay smiled at him as he spoke.

"Not too keen on flying?"

The man tried to speak but nothing came out. His dry rasping throat was only able to send a few specks of spittle in Finlay's direction.

"Don't worry. It's nothing. Once you know a bit of technical stuff you realise how safe it is." He smiled his best re-assuring smile but he was not prepared for what he heard next.

"I know, I designed the wing of this plane," the man spluttered. The smile faded off Finlay's face. Wot and Monday looked at each other. This was going to be fun.

"Excuse me." The man grasped at the end of a flight attendant's skirt as she went past. She turned, ready to rebuff the harassment, when a look of pity spread across her face.

"Ah, Mister Bingham. It's you. Welcome aboard. Now don't worry. Everything will be alright." She patted the hand, which she had managed to remove from her clothing; a small sweat stain remained.

"Make sure the pilot sets the flaps to the correct position for take-off. This is a very sensitive wing." he panted, almost completely out of breath. She leant down and adopted a look on her face like she had just come across an injured puppy.

"Now, we've discussed this before, sir. The captain knows what he is doing." She patted his hot hairy little hand again. A few drops of moisture fell to the carpet below.

"I know, I know," he sounded genuinely apologetic but looked completely helpless.

Racked with nervous fatigue, he sat back, as the flight attendant made her way up the remainder of the aircraft checking seat belts and drinks trays as she went. The plane pushed back from the stand and made its way to the point at which it would ready itself for take-off. Finlay leaned back in his seat. Unlike his unfortunate companion, he liked flying. The flight attendants went through their routine of showing everyone where the exits were and how to operate a lifebelt in the event of having to ditch in the sea.

"It's the mountains I'm worried about," Mister Bingham whispered to himself as yet more water poured off his body. He tried to replace some from the large plastic bottle he was holding in his left hand, for just that purpose. If Finlay had expected him to relax once they had got underway, he was mistaken. After the plane was airborne Mister Bingham closed his eyes and appeared to be praying. They had a period of relative calm but then there was a terrible flash and a crack like a giant's whip. All the lights went out as the huge plane lurched to one side then another and finally slipped a few hundred feet out of the sky as it seemed to lose all power. Then, just as suddenly, it righted itself and everything seemed back to normal.

"What was that?" Even Finlay could feel himself getting a bit hot under the collar.

"Lightning," answered the well-informed Mister Bingham. He was clutching his briefcase so tight that the leather was beginning to change shape. After the captain came over the tannoy and apologised for the lightning strike, he turned to Finlay and said, "We really flapped about there. The wing can go fifteen feet one way and then fifteen feet the other."

By now Finlay could not wish the flight to be over quickly enough. This man was unsettling him with all his technical knowledge. Some drinks and light snacks were served during the flight, then not a moment too soon, it was time for the descent into Heathrow.

Mister Bingham excelled himself. "Commercial 180, Commercial 180. He's going too fast, he's going too fast." He turned to Finlay oblivious to the fact he had not asked for any clarification. "Commercial aircraft have a landing speed of one hundred and eighty miles and hour and this one is going too fast. I can tell."

Finlay was at the end of his tether now. He turned away and buried his face in the pillow and groaned. In a reversal of roles, Mister Bingham put his hand on Finlay's shoulder and said re-assuringly, "Don't worry, son. It'll be over soon."

Finlay shook his head. Eventually it *was* over and they taxied their weary way to the stand at Heathrow. Finlay did not bother saying goodbye to Mister Bingham, who would probably not have noticed. It looked like he was sending a prayer of thanks to some unseen god, for their safe delivery.

# ELEVEN

**M**onday, Finlay and Wot collected all their belongings - including the board which Old Man had given to Finlay - and headed toward the 'nothing to declare' section.

"Excuse me, sir."

Finlay looked at the Customs Officer and smiled. It was always the same. Finlay couldn't blame them. All the equipment they carried with them was usually more than they could resist. And most of the time they were just enthusiasts; they knew there was no real chance of smuggling anything. Monday and Wot were not stopped this time.

The Customs man opened Finlay's bags, then turned his attention to the board. "I won't keep you long, sir."

He unzipped the bag which made that noise which only new crisp things can produce. Reassuring and fresh. Finlay helped the Customs man take the board out, not so much because he was being helpful, but having seen the finish on it he was loath to see it chipped.

"Very nice," the Customs man said as the board came into full view.

The board caught the eye like an expensive Japanese motor bike, fast even when it wasn't moving. It was thicker than the ones Finlay was used to, but it was also sleek and smooth with an extremely fancy finish: Sunburst, like a flying V guitar. Finlay made a mental note to ask Old Man about that finish. It was unique and he had not seen one on a board before. In a museum of modern art, yes, but not on a snowboard.

They laid the out board; the Customs man turned it over. He was sweating from his exertions as he rattled the board to see if he could hear something. He peered along the line of the board but could see no seam; he turned to his fat assistant, who nodded then disappeared. The podgy sidekick returned with a black Labrador who sidled up to the bench, rose on his hind legs then farted.

"Does that mean he's found something?" Finlay asked with a wry grin.

The Customs man winced.

"No. We changed his diet. Doesn't seem to be working though. The bean counters at head-office wanted to save money and we were instructed to go down market."

"Well you managed that alright," said Finlay.

The Customs man looked at him but said nothing. Finlay held his stare for a few seconds and didn't see the two figures walk through Customs behind him. Tasty and Morsel glided through the nothing to declare section even though they had a lot to declare, an awful lot indeed.

The dog sniffed through Finlay's belongings leaving a trail of doggy snot behind it. Finlay thought he heard another fart, but he couldn't be sure. Maybe it had been the Customs man, it certainly hadn't been him. Eventually as it seemed there was nothing to be declared or discovered, Finlay was given the all clear. By then he found his humour had deflated somewhat. He was looking forward to getting back to the flat for a shower and a snooze. There wasn't that long before they were heading off for Canada. He often suffered from terrible jet lag, so he wanted to get as much sleep in as possible before he went. Walking away from the Customs desk, he paused and then turned.

"See you Windy," he said to the dog who did not respond as it was not his name.

The unsmiling Customs man stood there with his hairy hand on his over size hips. It was difficult to contain the jealousy he felt for Finlay's youth. He had been shocked at his own disappointment that the dog's search had uncovered nothing more sinister than some clothes in serious need of a session in the Zanussi.

Once through, Finlay joined Wot. Monday had gone off to search for the cab which was supposed to pick them up; it had been arranged by Finlay's sponsor's PR company. She had been disappointed not to find the cab waiting for them but then this was Heathrow. Parking wasn't that easy.

"Thought you were heading for Pentonville." Wot laughed, as Finlay struggled to stop his gear from spilling off the trolley where it had been placed a bit haphazardly. He didn't reply but tried to produce a smile, failing miserably. He was very tired. Wot realised his joke had fallen on deaf ears and changed the subject.

"Hey we just saw Mick's two boys."

"What?"

"What's their names.....um Tricky and Morsel, sorry, Tasty and Morsel."

"Oh, right." Finlay was only vaguely interested. One of the

reasons he was so tired was that he had been turning a lot of things over in his head during the flight over when Mister Bingham had allowed him the odd second to himself. He had come up with lots of questions but it seemed that all the answers lay in Meribel. Finlay felt that Canada could not come and go fast enough. Something was drawing him back to the French Alps. Something like a bottle of wine gone off. Dark, sinister and not particularly good for the health.

Monday turned up with the cab, which was actually a people carrier. The driver was a man called Rick with a rainforest of a beard like a seventies Argentinean footballer though he was completely bald on top. He had gone to the wrong terminal. Despite his mouth looking as though it had way too many teeth in it, he was a man of few words.

Wot and Finlay loaded their stuff in the back. Monday grabbed the last few bags and they all piled in. Rick, for some reason did not offer to help. Maybe it was against the driver's union or something. Their journey went smoothly until for no good reason Rick turned off the flyover towards Paddington. Monday looked at Finlay who leant forward and was about to say something when all hell broke loose. Rick slammed his foot down and the carrier leapt forward like a scalded cat. Finlay was thrown back violently as Wot and Monday ended up in a mixed up pile on the floor. Wot groaned; he had hit his head as he fell. Monday was alright as she had landed on Wot.

Finlay looked out the window, there was a big BMW with some unfriendly looking faces driving alongside them. Rick started to slow down, whilst Finlay's mind sped up. He was thinking fast. Even though he did not know what was going on, it was clear that their collective well-being was probably not uppermost in Rick's mind or that of his mates, who had now pulled in front of the carrier.

All the gear had been slung around but Finlay found his hand resting on the solid, well-balanced board which Old Man had given him. Finlay moved it with one hand. The canvas cover allowed it to glide smoothly and easily over the luggage which was underneath it.

"Oi, Fucker." It was not very original but Finlay wanted the unwelcome kidnapper to turn round. He was in luck. Finlay rammed the snowboard forward which glided like silk over oil and buried itself in Rick's face. He couldn't make a noise, he had no chance. A shower of blood and what looked like a drawer full of teeth splayed out of both sides of his mouth as he kissed the board full on. His jaw was fractured in too many places to mention and he was unconscious before Finlay had even managed to vault the seat and push him out of the van, which was had lurched to a halt.

The occupants of the BMW had exited the car and were approaching the purple people carrier when Finlay made his move. The men fell over each other as a blood soaked Rick tumbled out onto the ground just as Finlay booted the van into drive and headed for the lights of London, taking the passenger door, most of the bonnet and the front section of the Beamer with him. The heavies attempted pursuit but a fractured wheel arch meant that they only managed to drive a few yards before the car limped to a halt, steam coming out of the front like a mobile Turkish bath. The two men got out. The driver slammed the door behind him but it bounced back and hit him in the thigh. As the people carrier disappeared into the distance, a stream of vitriol left his lips. A small noise made him turn round. Rick was on all fours; the last of his liquidised teeth dribbling out of his mouth.

"What was that all about?" Monday's voice was quiet. She was easily heard as neither Finlay nor Wot were exactly bursting with conversation.

Finlay shook his head. "I don't know, I just don't know. We seem to making a lot of enemies without even trying." He was back on the dual carriageway heading for the centre of town.

Wot patted the board."Good present from Old Man."
Finlay smiled briefly and shook his head; he was kind of lost for words. He slowed down for the build up of traffic which was waiting for them as they came off the flyover and down past Lisson Grove. A few tarts crossed the road, between the cars, making their way to work in the basement brothels of Marylebone.

"I think it would be a good idea if we all stayed at my place till we get some idea of what's going on," Finlay said as the traffic started to gather speed– the filters on the right of the traffic lights easing some of the congestion.

# Deep Powder

The other two nodded.

"Should we phone the police?" Monday said quietly and without much conviction.

Finlay looked at her then at Wot. "The police weren't much use in France, I don't think they'll be much good here either. Hand me the mobile," he said to Wot who rummaged around in the mess which was all their belongings.

The car slowed. They were nearing Euston station; a small gaggle of football supporters weaved their way in and out of the cars; bottom cracks and bottles of Stella being the order of the day. Thankfully they kept moving. After the night they had just had Finlay would have run them down as soon as look them with their stupid lycra footie tops. Wot looked at one particularly large expanse of flesh bulging out of a blue Chelsea Zola top.

"Christ, the last time I saw something like that it was surrounded by Japanese ships with harpoons!" he said as Finlay punched out some numbers on the mobile.

Finlay held the mobile to his ear. A rough voice answered at the other end of the mobile. It echoed around the people carrier as Finlay drove it slowly up the Pentonville Road.

"Yeah."

"Face. It's Finlay."

The rest of the words were inaudible to the others; Finlay had put the phone closer to his ear.

"We got a few problems, need your help tonight." Finlay listened as the voice on the end of the phone responded to his request for help.

"Yeah good. See you then." He pressed the end button on the phone and tossed it back to Wot who put it back in the bag.

"Face is going to meet us at the Angel. He's bringing Tiny with him."

Monday and Wot nodded, they felt better already. Face was someone to be reckoned with on his own, but Tiny added another dimension altogether. If anyone ever qualified for the title of 'one man army,' it was him. Neither Monday or Wot were quite sure of the history but Face and Tiny would drop anything they were doing when Finlay reached out, which was not often.

Turning the motor left, Finlay passed the modern glass and iron hotel on the corner which looked like every other glass and metal thing in London and charged the same stupid prices. He then

# Deep Powder

hung a right into White Lion Street where he rented a cool flat just three floors above Pret a Manger, directly across from the Angel tube station. Wooden floors, American fridge, all the mod cons, which left little change out of some serious whack. Lucky thing was that much - though not all - of the bill was met by his sponsors. Finlay had to keep on winning or at least figure in the top three of his competitions, otherwise the good life would probably dry up quicker and sharper than a witch's chin.

He pulled the carrier over into a vacant parking space and killed the engine. They got out and began to unload the gear. Monday kissed Finlay gently on the cheek; not something she did very often. In fact, Finlay couldn't remember the last time that had happened.

"That's for saving us back there. Thanks to Old Man's heavy board as well," she added, smiling and patting the board as Finlay pulled it out from the back.

"Yeah, our friend won't be eating any toffees for a while," Finlay said as he loaded some stuff over his shoulder.

## TWELVE

Wot and Monday got the rest of the gear out of the carrier as Finlay turned and pressed the key fob; all the doors snapped shut. He didn't really know why he bothered. If the car actually belonged to the PR company then they had to come up with some answers about the less than friendly reception they had received at Heathrow. If it was Rick's property then he certainly didn't give a stuff what happened to it, that much was for sure.

He stumbled at the front door as he reached into his pocket for his door keys. The green door was the last one on the left. There were three spacious flats all owned by the same landlord, a peace loving white witch who thought the whole world would be fine if everyone would just meditate. Finlay knew this as she often came round to collect the rent in person. This, despite the fact she knew that the money was paid straight into the management's bank account by direct debit. Invariably she invited Finlay to drop in to see her African voodoo dolls. Finlay always had the feeling that she had slightly more in mind than the inspection of some souvenirs she may have picked up in Africa, or more likely from her Goth mate who worked at the sock shop in Gatwick.

Finlay took his house keys out of his pocket; holding the others in his teeth. He accidently dropped the keys on the street, the noise echoing like a bell at midnight. Wot shivered, then bent down, picked them up and opened the front door, pushing a pile of mail to one side as he did so. The other two flats were unoccupied but that didn't stop the tidal wave of paper junk coming. A big lump of useless material; double glazing and pizza delivery mainly. You could munch your giant cheesy crust as you gaze out of your thick double locking windows.

The three of them stumbled over the remains of the rain forest and climbed the narrow stairs to the top flat. Wot knew which keys were which, so he pushed past Finlay, and in order from top to bottom, opened up the three locks and let them in. He went in a bit slowly and cautiously as there were obviously people around who fancied doing all of them some serious harm.

Once in the flat, they put the lights on and wearily deposited some of the gear on the floor. Before they had a chance to sit down, a sound like an angry wasp pierced the air. It was the buzzer. Finlay dropped his stuff and picked up the speaker phone, though he was pretty sure he knew who it was. Face's voice crackled back down the disembodied phone. Finlay pressed the button to let them up.

Face was not very big but he had a strong aura about him. Coffee coloured skin, smooth hands, oiled, hairless scalp and a pair of eyes which told you everything you needed to know, which was mainly not to cross him or anyone near or dear to him. Tonight, by definition, that was Finlay. He was followed into the flat by Tiny. In contrast, his presence was all physical. Enormous, pale and with no neck, he had huge hands. Wot had met him before so he was prepared, though he'd never heard him speak. Monday had not come across him before though she'd heard a lot about him.

Tiny was a monster. A complete lack of any detectable warmth added to his 'house of horrors' look. Two marbles had crawled into his head and were masquerading as eyes. His lips were thin, his teeth even and almost pointed. The body was not natural. Possibly steroids, thought Monday, then thought again. No drugs on the market, legitimate or otherwise, could produce that.

She looked at his arms which were like metal hawsers and the things hanging on the end of them would surely not have had the cheek to present themselves as hands. More like the hods you see on a building site. Monday was suddenly aware that she was staring as was Tiny, who now smiled at her. Her blood froze on the spot. It was really a rictus grin, the kind you might see on a week old corpse.

Face sniffed. "So Finlay, what's the trouble, my man?" Finlay filled them in with most of what had happened. He left out some of the pointless detail, he was a good storyteller like that. Knew what to leave in and what to leave out. As Finlay was telling the tale. Wot started to sort out some of the gear. Monday went into girlie mode and offered tea. She expected to be rejected out of hand, but both Face and Tiny nodded as they listened intently to Finlay. By the time Monday had come out of the kitchen with two mugs of steaming hot tea, he had finished the saga. She put the milk and sugar on a small tray and left them by the side near the window. They could do that themselves; she had to draw the line somewhere.

"Ta for that. Appreciate it," a gruff Scottish voice echoed through the flat. It was Tiny.

Monday reacted like she had been slapped. A Scotsman and looking like that? No wonder he was considered to be the best minder in the business, not that Face seemed to be a slacker. What a pair.

Face nodded *his* appreciation for the tea, then turned back to Finlay. "Nice one, son. Best not to involve the dibbles less you have to. They never quite get it, do they?" Finlay grinned as he reached round and rubbed an itch on the back of his neck. "Me and Tiny will look after you for the next day or two till you leave for Canada. You sure you'll be alright over there?"

"Yeah, I can't see us getting a reception like the one tonight. Besides, like I said, it seems linked to France not Canada."

"Yeah, I can see that." Face's accent was not Scots, it was pure Delta, Thames Delta, Canvey Island– not to be confused with the Mississippi Delta of the American deep south.

Finlay got up and went into the next room. He sat down on the deep leather sofa. Outside, deep in the night, London let loose its orchestra of human noise. He picked up the phone and fished around in his breast pocket.

Monday came in and stood at the door. "He's massive. I don't think I have ever seen anyone as big as that."

Finlay laughed."You know the best bit?" He located the little card he was looking for and fished it out of his pocket.

"No, what?" her voice sounded very tired.

"He comes from a village in Scotland which I'm pretty sure has the smallest name in Britain."

"What is it?" she asked, rubbing her neck.

"I don't know how it is pronounced but it is spelt Ae."

"Is that it?"

"Yeah."

"Where is it?"

"Near Lockerbie."

Now that was a place Monday knew all about. One of her aunts had lived there when the plane had come down. She had never been the same since, nor had she ever talked about that fateful December night when death had screamed from the sky.

"If you're curious about him, just ask, he's a pussycat."

"Yeah, right and I've got a twenty foot nose." Monday was

unconvinced. She went back out to the kitchen leaving Finlay to his phone call.

∞∞∞∞

Finlay punched in the numbers for Le Blanc. It rang a few times, then a smooth French voice answered. It was female and relaxed. Finlay guessed she worked for Le Blanc, she had that tone that people had when answering the telephone for someone who paid their wages.

"Oui?"

"Mister Le Blanc." Finlay didn't bother trying to speak French. Le Blanc did not strike him as someone who would employ an individual who couldn't speak English.

After a few moments, the equally smooth voice of Le Blanc came on the line. He didn't bother with the French either.

"Yes?"

"Mister Le Blanc. It's Finlay."

"I didn't expect to hear from you."

"You said to keep in touch."

"Yes of course, I just hadn't thought it would be so soon." He had recovered his composure which had seemed momentarily absent.

Finlay described the welcome committee at the airport and termed it as a roughing up.

"That's terrible. Who would want to kill you?" Le Blanc sounded very concerned.

Finlay told him a few more details and then said he would be in touch when he got back from Canada.

Putting the phone down, Finlay pursed his lips and sat deep in thought. He had never said anything to Le Blanc about them trying to kill them. Either the long distance Frenchman was telepathic or, far more likely, he knew something which Finlay did not. This was not a settling state of affairs. He thought about it a little longer then decided what he would do. Nothing. He would wait to see what developed. He went back through to the other room where Monday was deep in conversation with Tiny who was proving to be quite an intellectual despite appearances to the contrary.

"But how can you be so sure?" Monday had obviously gotten over her initial reservations; she was sitting on the sofa next to him.

Finlay smiled at them and gestured for Face to join him by the other sofa by the window. Face took a gulp of his now lukewarm tea; he always took his time over everything, that included hurting people. He ambled slowly over to where Finlay was sitting.

"Look, do you remember the shooting down of the Iran airbus?" Tiny continued. He spoke fast, he did everything fast. He was the exact opposite of Face. People appreciated it, it also meant he hurt them fast. Got it over with, nice and quick. That was Tiny's motto: nice and quick. He could also move very quickly for a big man, a costly discovery for many fools; and he was also a speedy thinker, as Monday was finding out.

"No, what was that?" Monday changed her position in the sofa so she could see more of Tiny as she spoke.

"Exactly. The Americans shot down an Iran airbus in the Gulf. Everyone on board was killed. Hundreds. It didn't get much press in the West. Some people believe that the bombing of the Pan Am plane was in retaliation for that and that it was financed by Syria." Monday digested this. It was news to her.

"Then why did they focus on Libya and not Syria?" She felt like someone asking the questions on 'University Challenge.' She was pretty sure the presenters of that TV delicacy had probably never had a contestant like Tiny on before. But one thing was certain, he would not have finished last.

Tiny adjusted *his* position on the sofa. It felt like the whole flat had moved with his effort. He stroked one of his paws, surprisingly gently, over his brow, which was dripping with sweat despite the fact it was hot neither in the flat nor in the street outside.

"Syria gave a lot of help to the allies in the Gulf War. It surprised everyone," he had been going to say 'shocked the shit out of them' but he remembered where he was. Tiny did not swear in front of girls. His mum had brought him up properly and he'd never forgotten his lessons from his dearly departed mother. "When everything had died down it was more convenient to go after Libya for the bombing of the plane as Syria had made a really big difference to the outcome of the Gulf War. Once they decided that it was Libya, it was just a case of finding stuff to fit."

Monday nodded. She understood what he was saying but found

it really surprising that she was hearing it for the first time. She did not consider herself poorly read but he really knew his stuff.

"What do you think?"

"It doesn't matter what I think," he said with a smile.

"Of course it does. It matters what everyone thinks." Monday could hear her own voice rising. She always did that when she felt strongly about something. It was a terrible habit but she couldn't help it.

Tiny smiled at her. "Nah, that's where you're wrong, I think. It is not important what anyone thinks, I think it's important what you know. That's what matters."

"And what do you know, Tiny?" Monday said slowly.

Tiny smiled again."I know what I don't know Princess. That's what matters." He put his hand gently and warmly on hers. Although he had been born in Scotland many years south of the border had meant that he had picked up quite a few habits from that part of the world. Princess was not a term he would have used in the North, but here it seemed kind of fitting. It was not something which Monday would have let many people do but she'd warmed to this hulk of a man with his softly spoken ways.

Finlay and Face watched the exchange with some interest.

"There's not many people Monday would let do that you know," Finlay said quietly so that she couldn't hear.

"Well, you know something, Finlay. Tiny ain't many people, he's one of a kind. I'm glad he's on my side I wouldn't like to cross him." Face smiled but it lacked any warmth.

Face was a pretty solitary figure. He had few friends and almost no one he would trust. Finlay was an exception though. When Face had been down on his luck a few years ago before he'd made a name for himself amongst the tougher parts of the South London community, Finlay had helped him out with a place to stay and had put a few bob in his pocket. No favours were asked in return nor did he bring it up at every opportunity. That being the case, Face had made it clear that if Finlay was ever in any kind of bother, any kind whatsoever, he only had to pick up the blower and he would be there.

Finlay had only called on Face a couple of times before and both times Tiny had been around as well so they had gotten to know each other. This was the third time and it felt serious. From what Finlay had said, the stuff which happened in France and at the airport was not kid's play, not at all. It all sounded very grown up and not the kind of thing Finlay usually got involved in. So Face believed him when Finlay had said that he and the others had done nothing, crossed no one, to bring all this around. Finlay could testify to how Face dealt with anyone stupid enough to lie or get him involved in heavy action with only half-truths. If you liked life, you did not do that to Face. He knew Finlay and trusted him, in so far as he trusted anyone.

He'd already put a few calls out by the time he and Tiny had made their way over to Finlay's flat. No luck. All the boys who knew such things said they knew nothing related to any of this trouble. The only thing he had been told, and Face already knew this, was that there was a new operation muscling in on the heavy drugs scene though no one seemed to know who they were. That made sense, you were hardly likely to make inroads into the world of drug dealing and smuggling if you were going to print business cards and get an insert in yellow pages.

# THIRTEEN

The next day things were quiet, with everyone just hanging around the flat. Finlay made up an order from Pret a Manger which they kindly brought upstairs. They didn't seem to mind, after all they were nearly neighbours what with Finlay's flat being directly above them. A few carrot cakes, egg mayonnaise sandwiches, some lemon juice and plenty of coffees were rapidly taken care of by all and sundry.

A phone call to the public relations firm told Finlay what he had already suspected. They knew nothing of the now toothless one who had picked them up at the airport with bad things on the menu. Not surprisingly, they were taken aback with this turn of affairs. A few minutes after speaking to them Finlay got a phone call from Duncan, the head of the firm. He was pretty upset and wanted to see Finlay straight away.

Finlay showered and threw on some clothes, making sure some of them had the sponsor's logo on them. It did not look too clever to have a meeting with Duncan and not have at least something visible which related to the firm who were responsible for allowing Finlay to have so much fun. At least it used to be fun, recent events had given it all a harder edge than Finlay could have bargained for. He pulled on a fleecy top.

"You going to be long?" Monday was standing at the window with her arms crossed. She looked preoccupied.

"Not sure. Probably not; why?" Finlay asked as he stood framed in the doorway.

"Oh, nothing really. I just thought I'd give my parents a ring before we leave for Canada." She smiled a tight tense little smile. Finlay knew that it took a lot for Monday to keep in contact as her parents seriously disapproved of her lifestyle and their relations were a bit strained.

"Good luck," Finlay said as he walked backwards out of the door. He heard Monday whisper a quiet "thank-you" as he closed the door behind him.

Face was already outside warming up his Merc when Finlay

stepped out in to the fresh air. It was cold and sharp but clear and fresh too. The kind of air which made you feel like you could live forever. Finlay looked up and down White Lion Street to make sure there was no one around who might have different views about his longevity. The one-way street was deserted. Finlay opened the door of the fancy car and got in. He closed the door with an expensive sounding 'thunk.'

"Where to?" Face pressed the accelerator and the car purred forward.

"Brick Lane, the new fancy building, I can't remember the name."

"Yeah man, I know the one. No worries."

He eased the car down to the junction with Islington High Street and took a left. He was tempted to take a right, which you are not allowed to do, but the car was a recent purchase with money the tax man would have loved to know about. He had already been stopped several times by London's finest, so illegal turns made little sense. It's funny how law abiding you can become thanks to a change of circumstances. He turned right at the first legal opportunity and as the traffic was quite light they arrived there pretty quickly. The building was flash and gleaming but still managed to fit in with the rest of the architecture in Brick Lane. The planners wouldn't have had it any other way. Finlay undid his seat belt and the electrical mechanism whirred and clunked and put it back in its rightful place. He got out and looked down into the car.

"I don't know how long I'll be."

"No worries, I'll wait here and admire the view," he said with a smile as a particularly short, tight skirt glided past, powered by a pair of legs which seemed to go on forever.

Finlay closed the car door gently. He felt like patting the car on the roof, it had that kind of effect on you. He looked up at the suite of offices occupied by the PR firm. Although they had only recently moved in, the words 'Funky Vunky' were already plastered all over the windows. They liked to ensure their presence was noted. Finlay had a T-shirt on with the same words emblazoned across the front. They had done a lot of work for him securing all sorts of deals and he was grateful to them as otherwise he would have had to take some shitty job to finance his boarding. He shook his head at the thought and crossed the street.

# Deep Powder

Wafts of curry ensnared Finlay's nostrils as he stood at the plain black door and pressed the shiny buzzer. That was the great thing about Brick Lane, you could come down here hungry and broke but if you hung around a while then it felt as though you had eaten even if you hadn't. A smooth female voice poured down the intercom like syrup.

"Yes, can I help you?"

"It's Finlay. I've got an appointment to see Duncan.

"Come right up," the warm voice said.

Finlay pushed the heavy door as the buzzer sounded and he made his way into the newly painted hallway. Posters of various art festivals from all over the world adorned the walls. Subtle lighting on a fancy wall plaque highlighted the names of the companies occupying the building. Thankfully there was a lift, as Funky Vunky occupied a suite of offices on the fourth floor. He approached the lift and pressed another shiny button. The doors opened immediately and as he stepped in, the smell of country meadows assailed his nostrils courtesy of a fancy air deodorising system which was designed to do exactly that. He smiled to himself as he pressed the fourth floor button; the lift whirred into action.

On his way up, Finlay smiled as he recalled his first encounter with Duncan. Americans always have suites of offices rather than just offices, he'd said. When you write to them it is suite 203 or 204 or whatever. It always sounds grand even if it is a broken down room on the wrong side of Hell's Kitchen. Duncan loved America and everything it stood for. Finlay wondered why he didn't live on the other side of the pond, then remembered that Duncan had worked there at one time but had to leave in a hurry when a few deals went wrong. Nothing unlawful, he'd understood, just a bit close to the wind with people you don't want to stand down wind of. That had been Duncan's expression. He had a way with words, which was why he was in public relations.

Duncan and Finlay had first met on the slopes at Whistler. Finlay had been one of the few Brits to win a boarding competition there and Duncan had been the first to congratulate him after the ceremony. He represented clients looking to sponsor some hip new boarders so they could capture the youth market. Finlay had been in dire need of some fiscal bailing out at the time and it had been a good arrangement; one which Finlay hoped would continue for some time.

# Deep Powder

The lift came to a halt at the fourth floor. The doors whirred open and he stepped out into the corridor. He turned left and went into the reception area of Funky Vunky Plc.

The receptionist was very pretty and had a lilting Cornish accent. Duncan always hired pretty girls for his offices. They usually worked quite happily for him as he was a screaming queen and sexual harassment was never an issue, at least not for the girls. Finlay smiled and sat down as the receptionist buzzed through to Duncan's office.

"He'll be with you in a moment."

The Cornish lilt was really nice; Finlay made a mental note to visit that part of the country first chance he got. Any further musing was swept aside by the arrival of Duncan. Tall, tanned, with long silver hair, he was wearing probably the tightest pair of trousers Finlay had ever seen. He had a mincing kind of walk but Finlay knew that he always walked like that, so the trousers could not be blamed. Duncan saw him looking at his pants and did a twirl.

"You like them?"

"They are certainly right for you," Finlay said as honestly as he could.

Duncan stopped for a moment and held Finlay in his gaze then grabbed him by the arm and guided him into his office. "I thought for a moment there my luck was in and you had finally decided to come on over and join me."

"No, not me, Duncan," Finlay said.

Duncan looked at him intensely, as though he would suddenly change his mind, then waved him to the large leather sofa at the end of the room. He sat down behind an imposing looking desk and fixed him with two sharp, blue eyes. "Anyway, good to see you, now what's been happening? Who's been trying to hurt my little Finlay?"

Duncan put his hands behind his head, signalling Finlay to tell him all that had been going on. He did just that as Duncan listened attentively. There was a moment of silence, Duncan was deep in thought. Eventually he spoke, almost Solomon like.

"Why have you not gone to the police here?"

"I got my own protection and besides, you know I don't really trust them."

"Yeah, they could do with a little brushing up on their public
109

image." Duncan laughed as he examined his immaculate nails. Manicures were a favourite of his.

"Are you still happy to go to Whistler? You know I'd understand if you'd rather not go. I can call it all off."

"No, to be honest, I want to go and I don't think I am at any greater risk there than anywhere else, not that I know why any of this is happening in the first place."

Duncan nodded.

"Sorry, so rude of me, do you want anything to drink?"

Finlay declined, everything available to drink in Duncan's office always seemed to stink of perfume.

"Your sponsors are very happy with the way everything's going."

"So am I." Finlay could smell some of the curry wafting up from the street below. There were some serious cooks in this part of town, that was for sure.

"I was given a new board to try out by a guy in Meribel." Finlay thought it wiser to come clean, in case he got caught out and some big deal was made of it.

"What guy?"

"He's opened up a new shop. He exports boards to the North American market mainly. I've not tried it but I got a good look at it when customs pulled me over."

"You never get through with a board. Why would anyone even try to get something naughty through. No chance."

"I know." Finlay smiled.

"You going to try the board out in Whistler?"

"Yeah, thought I would."

"Well, let me know what you think. If it's any good we could always change companies."

Finlay pursed his lips. "I'm not sure. I don't know how big his operation is. It seems small at the moment."

"Well, let's see. We can always talk to him when you go back to Meribel for the end of the season."

Duncan got up. This was going to be a short meeting as he had a lot to do. He had seen for himself that Finlay was alright and there did not seem to be anything immediate to worry about, particularly if Finlay's dubious friends were looking out for his physical welfare.

Whilst Duncan liked Finlay - he represented quite a large

investment in terms of time and energy, not to mention money - he was a realist. Finlay was really an asset more than a friend of any type and he was sure Finlay understood that. He was a great exponent for extreme sports and represented many possibilities for Duncan. He was young and very marketable. If he would entertain the idea of becoming involved in some sports other than boarding, his marketability could increase ten fold. And the skills were transferable. Finlay would have to be talked to. When he came back, they'd explore this further.

"Thanks for coming in, Finlay. I hope everything sorts itself out and that you keep safe."

"Yeah, just as well, I've mates who'll look after me."

Duncan patted him on the back and opened the door.

"See you later, Finlay. Get in touch, when you get back."

"Yeah, later, Duncan."

"Oh, and Finlay...."

"Yeah."

"Keep safe and sound. You mean a lot to me."

"Thanks, Duncan."

Finlay realised that he was more to Duncan than just a good guy. And he was more than aware of the potential areas which he could develop for him. But it wasn't just about him; Monday and Wot were like family, he wouldn't do anything without seeing them right first or at least asking them what they felt about any new direction.

He smiled at the receptionist. She smiled back as he walked past the desk. It was nice for her to see someone who might be interested in women in the place. Duncan was nice and all that, but sometimes it got a bit frustrating when she couldn't use her sexuality as a tool in her day to day business. Mind you, you never know, some people change. She looked back at the tight trousered Duncan as he gently closed the door of his office and then reconsidered that thought.

Finlay went outside to find Face leaning against his Merc with a big smile on his face.

"That was quick, man."

"Yeah, there wasn't that much to talk about."

As Face leant down to open his door, Finlay saw a glint of metal under his jacket. He frowned as he got in beside Face who turned the key, pressed the pedal a bit and allowed the car to glide down the lane. He'd seen the frown.

"Something wrong, man?"

Finlay looked out of the window, deep in thought and did not answer immediately.

"I said..." Face started to repeat his question but Finlay interrupted him.

"I heard you." He lapsed into silence again.

Face drove on for a few minutes. They were quite near Angel when Finlay finally spoke.

"That was a gun I saw?"

Face reacted sharply. "You got a problem, man?"

"Well, yeah I have actually," Finlay said with an edge in his voice.

Face spun the wheel and turned the car around.

"I'm going to show you something."

"What?"

"You'll see."

∞∞∞∞

Face and Finlay rode in silence. The scenery changed a bit here and there and with all the turns and everything, Finlay was not quite sure where he was, though he knew it was South East London.

Face pulled the car over, killed the engine and sniffed as he pointed at something in the distance.

Finlay squinted, then finally focused on a Union Jack hanging out of a grubby broken window. A big white bulldog was painted on the wall underneath the window. Large men with shaved heads were sitting outside nursing pints of bitter. One of them had a Union Jack coloured into his hair. They all had big boots, tight trousers and a few had braces. If there was a sport which involved shooting skinheads then this gathering would have been considered a pot of gold. Some were deep in conversation whilst others were lost in their own thoughts.

"Take a good look, Finlay," Face said quietly then he turned the engine back on and gunned the motor. The noise drifted over to the skinheads. Some of them looked in the direction of the Mercedes. Face and Finlay looked through the windscreen as a group of them stood up. A baseball bat appeared as though from nowhere. A brick was launched into the air which fell somewhat short of the Merc. They advanced on the car, the one with the baseball bat leading the way.

They were only a few feet away when Finlay broke his silence.

"I don't know what point you're trying to make but I think we should go."

Face turned slowly to look at him. "Is that right? I've got a better idea."

The man with the bat raised it level with the windscreen. It did not take a rocket scientist to work out what he was intending to do. He smiled a malevolent, cold, smile. He had a Union Jack tooth, paid for with his job seekers allowance and family credit, though he had no family. He had neglected to clarify that point when he had applied for the mountain of benefit which kept him and his breed in a manner which others had not become accustomed.

Finlay grimaced, screwed up his eyes and waited for the sound of breaking glass and the shower of debris to cover him. There was no noise, no shattering of glass. The reason was simple, cold and immediate. Face was outside the car now as the all skinheads stood motionless, not moving a muscle. They looked like something from one of these wildlife programmes on cable tv when strange creatures suddenly stop moving and all look in the same direction apparently for no specific reason. In this case though, there was a reason, and it was specific – Face. He was pressing the muzzle of his gun into the nose of the baseball bat wielding Neo-nazi. His mouth was open but definitely not in a smile. A small drop of saliva had formed at the corner of the skinhead's dry and rasping lips, it was the only moisture visible anywhere near his sandpaper like mouth. He was not feeling very brave now.

"What do you want?" a surprisingly soft voice asked from the back.

"Nothing you got." Face pressed the gun into the pale cold flesh a little harder and licked his lips; he looked like he was enjoying himself.

A red patch was already forming around where the gun was squashed against the man's nose, though it had only been held there for a few moments. To the skinhead, these few moments felt like an eternity and he certainly did not look as confident as he had a few moments ago.

"Look, nothing personal but we don't want your type around here. Why don't you go home?" another disembodied voice suggested. The tone was surprisingly polite.

Face ran his tongue around the inside of his mouth then answered slowly. "Sounds like a good idea." He paused for a few moments before continuing. "Which way is New Cross?"

One of the skinheads pointed in a general direction away from the pub.

"Yeah, I think we'll go. Why don't you come down and see me and the brothers some day. The sisters could braid your hair and teach you to dance."

"We might just do that, but we can already dance," another voice from the crowd said.

"Good. We'll leave the dancing then. We'll just arrange for the hair. We look forward to welcoming you. See you around."

Face kept the nine millimetre trained on the face of his would-be victim and slowly stepped back into the car. The skinhead's nose looked like it had been caught in a vice and then stuck out in the sun with no sunblock on. Face gunned the engine which was still running and with one hand on the wheel, the other was holding the gun, steered them away from the hostile crowd. Finlay let out a long, deep, sigh of relief. He half expected the car to have stalled at exactly the wrong moment. It didn't.

"What was all that for?" Finlay made sure his voice was not too angry. Face was not someone he wanted to fall out with especially after what he had just been party to.

Face didn't answer immediately but drove on in silence for a few minutes, his fingers gripping the steering wheel far tighter than was necessary. After a while, he turned to look at Finlay and then his features visibly softened.

"Finlay, man. So long as there are people like that around, I will be a customer and good friend of Mister Uzi." Face spoke quietly and precisely and then looked out of the window as though he was admiring the view. Somehow the stillness and quiet in his voice and manner made him far more frightening than if he had screamed, shouted and banged his fists off the dashboard.

He looked back at Finlay. "You better know something. You can't take help from people like me and then get all edgy about how I run my business. Ya h'unerstan?"

"I understand," Finlay said quietly. And he did, probably for the very first time. You can't ask these people into your life and then expect them to modify their behaviour. There is a price to pay when it comes to having people in your life. The heavier the people, the bigger the price.

When they got back to White Lion Street Finlay waited at the door while Face located a parking space. When he joined him Finlay opened the front door for, gesturing for him to go first.

"By the way," Finlay started.

"What?" asked Face with one hand in his pocket. He never put two in at the same time; he had seen too many people regret that position when they needed their hands in a hurry.

"It wasn't an Uzi, you pulled."

They looked at each other for a moment, neither smiling. Then suddenly, without warning, Face slapped him on the back and laughed.

"My gun's the same breed. Different family but similar appetite."

Finlay smiled and followed him up the stairs to the flat. He wasn't feeling too good.

# FOURTEEN

It was decided that they'd all stay low for the couple of days till the trip to Canada. It was a dark and heavy night. The rain spattered of the windows like a metronome on a cheap four track in an urban dubber's bedroom. They had pigged out on pizza and garlic bread delivered by a psychotic looking schoolboy with a pigtail. An entertainer was on telly, trying to salvage what was left of his career after a recent sex and drugs scandal. He wasn't having much luck in front of a live audience. Sex and drugs and rock and roll are fine but it pays to make sure the rock and roll is in the heaviest percentage. People don't like to see celebrities overdoing the sex and drugs, especially if you have a small little life where even the lamp bulbs are grey.

The smell of garlic and cheese filled the flat. Wot pointed the remote control at the telly and pressed the buttons to change the channel.

"Anyone mind?" There was no reply so he continued channel surfing.

"That's a bit of fancy accent you got there," Face said as he wiped the remains of a thick and crusty cheesy special off his lips. Wot reddened slightly in the cheeks and bit his lower lip.

"It's not that fancy," he said sharply, a little too edgy for someone trying to appear cool and collected.

"Sounds fancy to me." Face winked at Finlay as he took another bite of his pizza. This could be a bit of a laugh. He was taken aback by the strength of Wot's response.

"Well, it isn't. Right." He was nearly shouting as his pizza box fell to the floor and pieces of meat and cheese slid onto the carpet in a gooey sort of pathetic way. If it was still edible, it certainly became unfit for human consumption when Wot angrily stood up and stepped in it. He sighed and then walked wearily into the kitchen and quietly closed the door behind him.

"Oops. Didn't mean to offend your bredrin," Face said to Finlay who nodded back.

"Don't matter, we all have things which we get touchy about." Finlay put his pizza to one side and walked to the kitchen door as Face shrugged his shoulders apologetically. He hadn't meant to create an atmosphere. He was used to hanging out with people in tight situations and knew the importance of keeping cool. He hadn't expected the youth to get all sensitive. He had only been having a bit of fun. God knows what would have happened if he had really got started.

Finlay knocked gently on the door. "You alright?" he asked as he opened it slowly and peered round. Wot had his back to him as he stared out of the rain streaked window at the busy Islington street below.

He took a deep breath before answering. "Just leave me alone for a while...I'll be alright." He did not turn to look at Finlay as he spoke but seemed to tighten his arms which were folded firmly in front of him.

∞∞∞∞

Face and Tiny drove them to the airport and stayed with them till they had checked in. Tiny and Monday spent a bit of time together whilst Finlay, Wot and Face had some tea and coffees in the over-priced cafeteria. Something had connected between Monday and Tiny, something spiritual rather than physical. Monday felt like the sister he'd never had. His whole life had been one which was surrounded by aggressive Scotsmen with big bellies and small necks. He was desperate to get in touch with his feminine side. He did acknowledge the contradiction which his work threw up in this matter. A fixer and sorter of problems - often in a less than savoury way - his activities did not add up to the gentler side of life.

For Monday, Tiny had hit a note. He seemed like a song bird caught in a cage of macho bullshit. That was something which she felt it was worthwhile to find a key for. They agreed that Monday would give him a call when she got back. At Departures, and in full view of the others, she gave him a very small peck on the cheek. He blushed like an over-ripe peach. Very wisely, no one cracked any smart-arse comments.

Monday, Finlay and Wot flew with Air Canada to Vancouver. Though it was twice the distance than Toronto it took only a little bit longer as the plane flies with the curve of the earth. Finlay knew it made sense when he looked at the map but he still couldn't get his head round it completely.

# Deep Powder

In Vancouver a big bus waited to drive them up to Whistler. This time they checked the credentials of the bemused driver before they stepped into the bus. They did not want a repeat of the unwelcome welcome which they had been subjected to at Heathrow. When they arrived at Whistler the air was crisp and the snow looked as inviting as a giant duvet. Finlay looked forward to doing what he did best over the next few days: riding and winning.

They were staying in a fancy, self-contained modern chalet in a complex just next to Chateau Whistler, arguably one of the best, if not *the* best, hotels in that part of the world. Finlay got a few hours sleep then he was out on the slopes. He took Old Man's board. Now was the chance to see what it was made of. He breathed the sharp air in deeply as he walked past the row of resort shops. In the distance, Blackcomb rose into the air, punching the sky. That was where he was headed. Whistler Mountain had some fine off piste powder bowls, but they could wait.

Finlay rode the lift halfway up his first run. He stretched a bit and loosened up before catching the lift to the second section of the run. He breathed in the mountain air and thought back to his childhood. A difficult one which had seen him break quite a few things, including relationships. It had been a wise outdoor person and child counsellor who had been instrumental in getting him involved in the outdoor sports. The words still rang in his ears. "Great place for angry kids. You can't break a mountain." Finlay smiled at the memory. One look at Blackcomb told him the accuracy of that statement.

With the wind whipping through his hair, he pushed off. The board was superb, it handled really well. After a while, he realised it could do with a proper waxing. No problem, he knew someone in the town who could sort that out. He stuck a few tricks to get the cobwebs out of his system falling over more than a few times. He dusted himself off then headed for the hire shop where he knew he would find Joel, who would sort out the board in no time.

Joel was a snow bum who had first come to Whistler as a student looking to make extra money while studying for a degree in philosophy. He enjoyed himself so much he had made a life there; he felt that there was nowhere better to practice philosophy than in the mountains, in the shadow of Blackcomb and Whistler. They had always given him far more useful feedback than any white-haired professor ever had.

"Yo, Finlay. Where you been man. I missed you last time you were here." He slapped Finlay on the arm as he took the board off him. He did not have to ask whether the board needed looking at, no one brought a board indoors for fun. He lay it on the table in front of him.

"I popped in but you were away," Finlay said as he sat down on a stool he pulled over from a wall covered in posters promoting all the virtues of Whistler.

Joel frowned as he looked over the board. "Yeah, my gran was ill. I had to go and spend some time with her in Vancouver." He ran his hand over the board. "This is nice, man."

"How's your granny now?"

"Good. She's like one of these cartoon grannies. Goes on forever. Gets over every ailment."

"Nice. Can you wax this for me and set it up?"

"Yeah, no problem." He turned it over and looked down the length of it. He tapped it gently on the table, then placed his ear against it as though he was listening for something. He was actually looking down it again.

"It's a nice board, but there's something strange about it."

"What?" Finlay's interest was up. He touched it as though by doing so it would tell him something.

"I don't know. Leave it with me and come back in, say a couple of hours?"

"Yeah okay. That's time enough to have some breakfast."

"See you later, Finlay." Joel picked it up and carried it to his workshop in the back.

Finlay pulled his jacket tight around him. The wind had picked up and it was biting now like a slice of ice. He hurried back to the chalet where Monday and Wot were stirring.

"Finlay, there was a telephone call for you." Monday sleepily walked into the kitchen to put the kettle on. There was a great view of the slopes from the wide panoramic windows. She stretched and then yawned as Finlay shouted into the kitchen.

"Who was it?"

"Old Man. He wants you to phone him back at the shop."

Finlay looked out of the window and saw his reflection staring back at him. There was a puzzled expression on his face. How did

Old Man get the number? He didn't know where they were staying.

"The number's on the side by the phone. On the yellow piece of paper!" Monday shouted above the sound of the kettle screaming at boiling point.

Finlay ambled over to the sideboard. Monday had been thoughtful, she'd written down the code for France so he didn't have to go searching for it. He punched in the digits which took a few seconds as there were quite a few of them. Eventually, after a few rings a voice answered.

"Old Man?"

"Yeah, who wants to know?"

"It's Finlay." Finlay couldn't get over the way Old Man had sounded like he was in the next room instead of thousands of miles away.

"Yeah, Finlay." His voice sounded a little tense.

"You got there ok?"

"Yeah, no worries, nice flight, slept most of the way."

"Have you brought the board to my man yet?"

"No, I haven't done anything with it yet."

"Well hurry up man and get it in. There's no point taking it all that way and not getting it set up properly." Old Man sounded vexed.

"Yeah, don't worry. I'll do it soon."

"Good, give me a ring when you have." There was a slight delay as the voice winged its way all the way up through France and across the Atlantic.

"Don't mean to get on your case like, but the board's worth it, you know."

"Yeah, right. Old Man?"

"What?"

"How did you know where to get hold of me?"

"There's not many places in Whistler you could be staying and I knew it wouldn't be the Chateau."

"Why not?"

"Not your style Finlay."

"Right."

"Yeah, right. All it took was a bit of detective work and now we're talking."

"Alright. I'll catch you later." Finlay didn't wait for an answer, he replaced the receiver and then stood for a moment, deep in thought. He was not sure why he been less than truthful with Old Man. Something was troubling him and Old Man being so keen about the set-up had not really put his mind at ease, quite the opposite in fact. He checked the clock. He knew that he wasn't due to go back to Joel for a while but something told him it might be a good idea to take a look at this board himself.

"Do you want some tea?" Monday shouted through from the kitchen. She did not get a reply so she went through to the lounge expecting to find Finlay. Instead what she found was a piece of paper floating in the air generated by Finlay's quick exit. She raised her eyebrows. "I'll take that as a 'no' then."

She went back to the kitchen unable to shake off the jet lag. She really did need that cup of tea. She reached into the cupboard, grabbed the tacky looking cup with a picture of a mountain on it, popped in a tea bag and poured the boiling water. As she did so, a cloud of steam rose to the ceiling and was instantly sucked into the air system and then kicked out like an unwelcome rugby fan stumbling into a society ball.

# FIFTEEN

"**S**o what do you think, Joel?" Finlay was leaning against the wall with a strained look on his face. "I don't know Finlay. It seems right and yet there's something I can't quite put my finger on." He ran his hand over the object of their attention.

"Why don't you have a look at it on the rig." Joel pointed to the workshop in the back as he went over to the coat rack and retrieved his thick down jacket and woolly hat off the peg.

"I've got to pop out for a while. I'll close the place up so you won't be disturbed. He pulled on his jacket and thrust his hat onto his head. It perched there rather uneasily, thanks to his mass of blonde curly hair.

"Thanks, Joel. I won't make a mess."

Finlay lifted up the board and carried it through to the workshop at the back. He heard Joel close the door behind him which told him that he was alone. Finlay appreciated it, he wanted to take a proper look at this piece of equipment. He locked it into place with a series of vices, carefully putting some old pieces of rag between the board and the metal so there would be no damage. Any marks not put there by the slopes were definitely unwelcome. He got down on his knees and looked along the length of the board. It was definitely a fat one, particularly in the middle where it bulged in a way that Finlay had not noticed up to now. He looked at the side, if there was a seam he could not see it. The board certainly appeared to be carved from a single piece. He slapped the board in frustration as much as anything else. He froze. He slapped it again; there was a noise had not expected to hear. The kind of noise which comes from something hollow. He did it again, this time with his ear right next to the board. It was definitely hollow.

Finlay stood back for a few moment trying to work out what to do next. His curiosity had got the better of him by now, then he spied the jigsaw, hanging on the wall. There were even a pair of thick safety goggles hanging there conveniently by the side. He hesitated, then went and put the goggles on. He wasn't sure what Old Man would say if his board came back in two pieces but he knew that somewhere in Joel's workshop there would be some extra strong industrial glue. He would try to undo anything he did, but he needed to have a look inside the board. He plugged the saw into the electrical socket in the wall by the workbench and then carefully placed it on the last section of the board where it had sounded hollow, about six inches from the tip.

He pressed the button and started to cut into the board. It slipped and nearly took his leg off. Finlay stopped and mopped his brow which was dripping with sweat. The air was thick in the workshop and the James Bond stuff was not doing his heart rate much good either. The cloak and dagger routine was not all it was cracked up to be. He got some sandpaper from a drawer which luckily was marked with its contents. Despite appearances, Joel was a tidy soul and he liked order in his work area. Finlay rubbed the veneer off the section he was to saw and blew away the dust. After a few minutes, the saw cut through to the middle of the board. Some thick brown sticky liquid squirted out and landed on his front. He ignored it and cut out another section, creating a small opening through which  a clear plastic packet with white powder in it was visible. "If this was a film, then this would be the point where I reach in and pull out some 'grade A' cocaine," Finlay said to himself, as he reached in and pulled out a packet of 'grade A' coke. He whistled to himself as he weighed it up in his hand. He knew that the rest of the board was packed with the stuff. It did not take a wizard to work out that was the reason it was so fat and wide. He thought for a few moments, then looked out of the window, working out what to do next.

It was more than an hour before Joel came back. Finlay was sitting with his feet up in the front of the shop.

"Yeah, Finlay how did you get on?"

"Chopped it up and had a look. Nothing there." Finlay said. He tried to keep his voice even so that Joel would not suspect anything untoward. Joel went back into the workshop and let out a yell.

"Finlay, you wouldn't get any prizes for finish. Man, it looks like you went to work on her with a sheath knife."

Finlay joined him in the back and surveyed his handiwork. He had to agree it would probably not have gained him automatic entry into the Royal College of Art, or anywhere near a job which required finesse. But he'd done his best and the contents were secure. That was the point though Joel obviously was not to know that.

"Anyway, thanks for your help. I'll be off now," Finlay opened up the black canvas bag and started to load the board back in.

"Here, let me help you." Joel grabbed a section of the board. Finlay could not have been less appreciative but he masked it well and there were no disasters. Finlay threw the thick strap over his shoulder and walked a little unevenly out of the shop.

"Catch you later, man."

Joel went over to the cooler, opened the door and helped himself to a cold cola. It was a bottle rather than a can. He liked things the old fashioned way. He flipped the cap and took a swig, nice and deep. He smiled as it hit the spot and watched Finlay walk out the door with about three hundred thousand dollars worth of prime cocaine. That's American dollars, not Canadian.

ooooooo

Finlay opened the door of the chalet and let the bag drop to the floor. Monday and Wot came out together to greet him.

"Hi, Finlay, Old Man phoned again. Sounded pretty edgy. Everything alright?" Wot said as he moved the bag slightly from where Finlay had dropped it as it was blocking the door.

"Yeah everything's fine," Finlay said quietly then paused before continuing, "If you consider a board stuffed full of cocaine fine, then yeah, I suppose everything's just sweet."

He walked into the front room, sat down and looked at the other two, who both stood there with their mouths open. Finlay owed them an explanation, so he filled them in as to what had transpired during the last couple of hours in which he had made his unwelcome discovery. They both sat there speechless as Finlay made a phone call. It was an important one and it was a good idea for him to make it. Afterwards he sat down.

Wot had recovered his composure. "Aren't you going to phone Old Man?"

"Yeah, good idea. Stand back; he's not going to like what I've got to say to him."

Finlay stood up, stretched his back and walked over to the phone on the sideboard. He punched in the numbers which he read from the scrap of paper then took a deep breath. This was going to be a strange call.

Old Man's voice cut through the miles. "Yeah."

"Old Man."

"Finlay." Old Man returned the recognition. There was a short silence which was broken by Finlay.

"I took a look at that board. I mean a real look." There was no answer so Finlay began his sentence again. "I said I took..." He did not get any further, Old Man's tone cut through him like a knife.

"I heard what you said. What did you find?"

"I think you know what I found."

This was the point at which Old Man would either deny any knowledge of what Finlay was talking about or would admit involvement straight away. The dangerous white powder inside the board was able to cause trouble before it even hit the streets.

"Well, well, well. I don't think you know what you're getting into Finlay. What do you want from me?"

"Maybe I want to get to know you and your business better." Finlay tried to sound as shady as possible. He thought he did quite a good job. Monday and Wot raised their respective eyebrows at this turn of events. There was a pause again before Old Man answered.

"I didn't have you down as a businessman, at least not this kind of business." Old Man sounded genuinely surprised and his tone had softened a touch.

"Look, that board was supposed to go to your man here. I'll make sure it gets there. We can talk when I return to Meribel next week, about you sponsoring me."

"Sponsoring?" Old Man spluttered.

"Yeah. Sponsor." Finlay liked his inventive use of words.

"You know where to take it?" Old Man asked.

"Give me the name and address again." Finlay gestured to Monday who brought another piece of paper and a pen over to him. He pushed the receiver to his ear with his shoulder.

"Okay, go ahead."

"Steve Vox at Silver Steve's snow equipment shop in the centre of Whistler. I'll call him and let him know you're coming."

"Ok," Finlay said quietly as he finished writing the details down.

"And one more thing," Finlay said.

"What?"

# Deep Powder

"Anything happens to me, my friends know where to come." Finlay grimaced a bit. That part sounded a little bit like something from a bad American made for tv movie.

"Nothing will happen, unless you get smart." Old Man was nothing at this point if not truthful.

"Don't worry. I want to make some serious money. I think I was born for serious money." Finlay underlined the word serious.

"We all were, Finlay, we all were." Old Man had warmed up quite a bit now.

"Cheerio."

Finlay replaced the receiver slowly and gently as though he did not want to disturb anyone who, for all he knew, had been listening to every word. No plain clothes muscle men bounded through the door, at least not yet.

"How did I sound?" Finlay looked to his resident critics. Monday smiled." Okay, a bit sleazy, but then that was probably not a bad thing.

"The important thing is, did Old Man give you the thumbs up?" Wot munched on a piece of toast which he had managed to avoid overcooking, which was some feat.

"Seems that way." Finlay seemed pensive. He was hoping that he was not biting off more than he could chew. This was not a game, at least not one which had a childish feel to it.

There was a knock at the door. Monday looked through the eyehole then turned to Finlay.

"It's that girl."

Finlay's heart leapt a beat. He jumped up and opened the door; it was pretty obvious that Monday was not going to oblige. Roisin looked even better than she did the last time he saw her. She leant forward and turned her head just as Finlay was about to plant a kiss on her cheek. Their lips brushed and she smiled at the accident. Finlay smiled back, he wasn't complaining. Wot and Monday had noticed but they did not say anything. Wot was too polite and Monday wasn't going to give Roisin the pleasure of knowing that it irritated the hell out of her. Roisin gave a little wave to them.

"Hi, you alright?"

"Yeah fine, you?" Wot answered. Monday mumbled something then disappeared into the kitchen. Roisin raised her eyebrows and Finlay smiled. There was not a lot he could say, Monday was her own person.

"Drink?" Roisin said.

"Yeah, what can I get you?" Finlay stepped back but Roisin didn't move.

"No, I meant would you like to go for one?"

"Oh, yeah. I'll just get my coat." He turned just in time to catch his coat which Monday had thrown at him, none too gently.

He smiled at Roisin then looked back at Monday with a slightly frosty look on his face. She returned the look. She wasn't bothered, she didn't like this girl and with everything going on she just felt that Finlay could be a little more thoughtful about how she was feeling. There was just something about her which Monday couldn't stand. She stood there, with her hands on her hips, looking at the door which Finlay had shut behind them as they left.

# SIXTEEN

"You OK?" Wot asked quietly.

"Yeah, do you fancy going for a ride on the slopes?" Monday said quietly.

"I'll get my stuff," replied Wot, who got up and quickly changed into his gear.

By the time he came back Monday was ready and waiting. They got the lift down to the lobby and walked out of the main door, past the ski hire section. The coffee shop just past that to the right was where Finlay and Roisin were sitting in the window, locked deep in conversation. Monday pretended not to see them. Wot pretended that he had not seen Monday pretend not to see them. They took a left and walked into the locker room where their boards were stashed. They picked them out and walked over to the chair lift.

The lift and indeed the whole resort had whirred into life. People of all shapes and sizes were buzzing about. Some of the individuals waiting for the lift looked like they had seriously over-indulged themselves at the sizzling all day breakfast bar which was set up in the cafe nearby. It was full of people who were dressed for the slopes but would probably never get any nearer to them than they actually were. It looked as though winter sports took a second to the really serious activity of eating, drinking and eating again.

Monday and Wot waited their turn at the lift. It eventually came round to them and they hopped on. The lift swayed like an old drunk, settled down and steadied itself and carried them up the mountain. Monday always enjoyed the rides on the lift, but Wot was less confident. He'd actually fallen off one a few seasons ago. He'd been so tense with worry that his body had been stiff as a board and a bit of wind had caught him and he just slipped off. The safety bar hadn't been down and the snow had been soft and deep. No poor tourists had been underneath so the only thing which had been bruised was Wot's ego– the whole thing had been the talk of the resort.

Wot remembered the whole event but for the life of him

couldn't recall the place where it had happened. It had been so traumatic for him he had developed a selective memory. Understandable, as he could have been killed. In fact, the actual boarding and skiing in these places, although quite risky, actually claimed less victims and caused less injury than the allied activities connected to them. Wot had been lost in these thoughts so he didn't hear Monday speaking at first. She nudged him.

"What is it?" He snapped back to the here and now.

She pointed at some familiar figures weaving their way down the mountain. He squinted; his eyesight wasn't much better than his memory. It was Nyaman, Menelik and the others. The air was clear and bright and Nyaman had stopped to get his breath. He looked up and saw Wot and Monday passing over him like a small aircraft. He shouted and waved, then started on his way again before they could wave back.

Monday turned and looked at their disappearing forms then a series of jolts and bumps told them that their journey on the lift was about to come to an end. It was always tricky getting off with one foot still attached to the board. Many times she had landed on her backside before she had gotten the hang of dismounting and still keeping her balance centered. Today was not one of these days, thankfully. She and Wot glided off and then stepped to one side to make sure that no one behind them bumped into them and sent them flying which was also an occupational hazard.

"Race you?" Monday shouted and laughed as she finished off strapping her trailing foot into her bindings then stood up and pushed off. Wot didn't have a chance to respond. He checked both feet were securely in place then followed Monday down the mountain. He drew level after a few minutes and gave Monday a thumbs up. She responded by crouching lower, her fingers brushing off the snow which flashed past her at a serious rate of knots as they had both picked up a lot of speed by now. They weaved, bobbed and turned, carving deep troughs in the snow. There was a time that Whistler, like many other winter sport resorts, had not been used to or indeed welcomed snowboarders but that time was long gone now. Now they were as part of the scene as a white fox in winter.

Wot pulled past Monday and then made a few mocking gestures; she just crouched lower, picked up more speed and passed him again. Wot smiled, he was not really any match for

# Deep Powder

Monday when she got going. She'd improved a lot through the seasons and Finlay had given her a lot of tips which had helped her style. He'd shown her all about where to hold her hands and how important it was to keep her head still and to carve the turns with her hips just before turning her whole body into the movement. He'd shown Wot as well, but the truth was it had sunk in a lot quicker with Monday who was always sharper on the uptake. She was well ahead now, so Wot accepted that defeat was his this time. He slowed down a little and stood up more in his turns. By the time he'd got to the bottom Monday had already stepped out of her board  and was talking to Menelik by the side of the lift queue.

"Hi Menelik."

"Yol, Wot."

"Monday was just telling me about your London adventures. Sounded a bit tasty like. What's going on?" He flicked his locks in the air and they landed behind his shoulder. He'd practised this quite a few times and had it off to a fine art now. The truth was he had never really bothered doing that kind of thing before he saw a telly programme. It was a documentary about Bob Marley and his love of football. The images of Bob and his bredrin playing footie on the beach in Jamaica and in the concrete backyard of Notting Hill had never left Menelik. The way they had tossed their locks in the air had made them look like Kings to the young Menelik, hungry like so many of his friends for images and roots which they could attach themselves to.

"Don't know to be honest. Everything seems pretty strange. I don't know what's kicking off. Can't keep up with it all," Wot said truthfully. In fact, considering they seemed to be the target for people or peoples unknown, Wot was surprisingly relaxed. He put that down to his public school upbringing. It had installed a feeling that no matter what you would always come out on top. That inner air of confidence,  even if you didn't really feel it, still came to the fore.

"Did the guy who picked you up at the airport give you any idea of what he was about?" Menelik wiped some loose snow of his trousers.

"No, it all happened so quickly." Monday had rejoined the conversation.

Menelik kissed his teeth. "Bad news," he understated. He bent down and loosened his boots. "I'm going to take a break. You want to join me for a drink?" he asked Wot and Monday.

Monday looked at Wot who shook his head.

"Nah, we'll leave it. We've only done one run so far. Bit too early."

"Catch you later, then." Menelik smiled and waved behind to them both as he made his way off to the cafe for a drink. He was thirsty and he felt like sitting down for a while.

∞∞∞

Finlay looked Roisin straight in the eyes. It was good to see her, that was for sure.

"You're looking great, Roisin."

"Thanks, Finlay. You're not so bad yourself."

"Is Rocky with you?"

"Yeah, he goes most places I go. Just the way it is. After all you won't be there to protect me all the time." She smiled and reached forward and put her hand over his. It was warm, close and very intimate. Finlay felt his heart fluttering like a butterfly in the wind.

"Always happy to protect you, you know that."

Finlay bent down to retrieve his paper napkin which had floated to the floor. If he hadn't, he would have seen the look on Roisin's face as she caught sight of Menelik and Pattu walking past the cafe window. It was strange, and cold. By the time he sat upright, Roisin was smiling; her odd expression had completely vanished.

Wisely leaving out the part about the what he had found inside the board and his new gig as a drug dealer, Finlay told her all that had happened. He then got up and paid the bill; he wanted to go back to the chalet to make some calls. Roisin walked back with him, they hadn't said anything it just went that way. He opened the door, went in and turned around to find Roisin inches away from him. She smiled, then leant forward and kissed him on the lips. He felt his body responding in all sorts of ways. He wanted this to happen so very much. They kissed for a while then Roisin took a step back, smiled, opened the door and gave him a little wave as she stepped backwards into the corridor.

Finlay was surprised and stood for a few seconds, then laughed; he should have known this was not a woman who gave anything quickly or easily. He calmed down and after his body returned to its original relaxed state, he checked the phone to see if there were any messages. The number of the chalet had been left on his answer machine back in Islington so that anyone who wanted to get in touch could do so. He always did that as he found that when he went away people from whom he wanted to hear would always try to get to get hold of him. There was, indeed, a light flashing on top of the phone. It was quite an old-fashioned looking one and was a bit out of place amongst all the other modern looking equipment in the chalet. It resembled an old bakelite phone, the kind which seemed to spend most of their time in museums or antique fairs.

He lifted the receiver and pressed the button which told him what he already knew, that he had a message waiting for him. Old Man had dropped the pretence of any smoothness now and the voice at the end of the line was as harsh as a piece of barbed wire.

"Phone me."

Finlay punched out Old Man's number on the phone. He almost knew it by heart by now. After a few rings, a voice at the end of the line.

"Yeah."

"What do you want?" Finlay tried to be as short and as gruff, but he wasn't quite so good at it yet.

"Steve Vox is waiting for you. What's the delay?" Old Man hissed.

"No delay. I had a few things to sort out. On my way now."

"Right. Oh and one more thing…" Old Man sounded like he was enjoying the role of giving out orders.

"What?" Finlay tried very hard not to sound like someone who was going to take them very easily.

"Don't forget the board."

The irony of that statement was lost on Old Man. Finlay tried hard to suppress a laugh. He failed, but it sounded quite good, kind of sinister.

"What's so funny?" Old Man hissed.

"It's just I'm hardly likely to misplace it. After all this is what its all about."

"Yeah, right. Listen Finlay, you and me can go places. You know that this is just the beginning." Old Man's tone softened a bit. Finlay smiled. That was exactly what he wanted.

"Listen, Old Man, you're pushing at an open door. Now let me go and I'll go straight to Steve's and we can get going with this business."

"Sweet." Old Man sounded a lot cheerier now.

"Catch you later, I'll phone you once I've been to Steve's," Finlay said.

He put the phone down then looked in the mirror. The face of a drug dealer stared back at him. It was not a pretty sight. He felt a warm flush come over him and he thought he was going to throw up. He headed for the bathroom and made it just before a stream of vomit exited his body and lashed the side of the toilet bowl. He was now on his hands and knees, retching for all he was worth. It was a combination of jetlag and serious tension.

Finlay looked at the contents of his stomach floating about in the toilet bowl and found himself becoming philosophical. Was that what it was all about? Puke in a toilet. People were just like that. Floating about trying to find their way but just end up wandering about seeing what was going to happen next and then getting angry because what actually happened in their lives always seemed to fail to live up to expectations. He snapped himself out of it and cleaned around his mouth with the brightly coloured towel he retrieved from the hook on the back of the door. He went back through to the kitchen and grabbed a glass of water to take the last of the taste out of his mouth, then grabbed himself a shower.

He let himself out of the chalet and stood for a moment as the door snapped behind him. There was something he'd forgotten. The board. He chuckled to himself. After what he'd said to Old Man about not leaving it behind, it was a bit rich, as that was exactly what he had done. He opened the door with the complicated looking key - it was taking a while to get used to - and picked up the board by its bag handle. Once outside, he transferred it to his shoulder. He knew that he would have to carry it by the handle again when he got in the lift but even these few yards were more comfortable with the shoulder strap; it was a serious weight. He wasn't sure what to expect but one thing was for sure, he wanted an explanation. He hoped there would be one waiting at Silver Steve's.

# SEVENTEEN

It had been half an hour since he'd spoken to Old Man. It had taken that long to clean himself up and to lose the stink of vomit from his body and his clothes. He'd even detected a whiff of it in his armpit but that was gone now thanks to the shower and some sweet smelling cream which he'd rubbed all over his body. He was also more relaxed now.

While in the shower, he'd mulled over what was happening and what he was getting himself into. It was clearer now that he was taking the right path and handling these unexpected developments in exactly the right way. He knew that everything would come right in the end. Life was never without risks and if you wanted a better life you had to take more of them. His boarding had taught him that much, if nothing else.

Outside the shop, he stopped and looked in the window. There was some serious gear there. In the window, he could see the reflections of people passing him. What about his own body language, he wondered. Did he appear shady? He felt relaxed. Making a mental note to be mindful of that, he opened the door of the shop and walked in. A big, bearded man with a pair of ripped jeans hanging from his lower half and a ragged checked shirt on his top half greeted him. Finlay couldn't make out what he said but the word 'hello' had figured in there somewhere.

"I've come to see Steve."

Finlay surveyed the immense layer of blubber cascading from ever rip and hole in the man's clothes and waited for a reply. The big man stood there for what seemed like an eternity but was in fact only a few moments. Finlay thought he may not have heard him, or properly understood his British accent, so he started to speak again. But the blubber bound one had heard him perfectly, he just always took his time in everything he did.

"Yeah, your name?" They both knew that this was unnecessary but they went through the motions anyway.

"Finlay. He's expecting me."

"Wait here, I'll see if he's free," he responded, more quickly this time. He turned and opened a door in the wooden panelling; the door snapped shut behind him.

# Deep Powder

Finlay looked around the shop. The equipment was smart and upmarket and there was a lot of variety. Some useless modern stuff which would probably fall apart the first time it was used on the mountain in anger, and some serious professional gear which proper mountain men could avail themselves of. Finlay's thoughts were interrupted by the sound of the wooden door banging shut as Steve emerged. He had a shock of silver hair so there was no need to ask where he got his name from. He was about medium build with a few muscles here and there and he was dressed in some boarding gear which was about ten years too young for him. His face was tight and two small sharp eyes told the tale of someone who liked to be aware of everything going on around him.

"Finlay?"

He did not extend an hand in greeting. He was not that kind of guy and this was not that kind of meeting.

"Yeah, Steve?" Finlay did not hold out his hand either.

Steve gestured around his shop with his left hand. There was a small oriental symbol tattooed on the flesh between his finger and thumb. "You like what you see?" His voice was a strange mixture of Canadian and French.

"Yeah, it's alright." Finlay felt like saying he was hardly there to give a critique of his shop but he knew that this was not the time or the place to get smart.

"Come into the back, where we can talk properly. Big Boy will come out and mind the shop for me, besides, I can still see what's going on." He pointed to the ceiling.

There were several video cameras with small powerful lenses and angry little lights pointing in various directions, one of them being the womens' changing rooms. Silver Steve was as interested in small lace panties as he was in not encouraging shoplifters. Truth was, there were hardly any shoplifters. The big equipment was too large to take out in a shopping bag and the small stuff wasn't worth looking at a jail sentence for.

Steve preferred to press something other than charges against the few girls he ever caught shoplifting; they usually complied. If it was a guy then a good kicking was offered. The last man they caught preferred a beating to police involvement. Probably had some skeletons he wanted kept quiet. Steve certainly didn't want any officers creeping round his shop which was why he would never have called them anyway, but the shoplifters weren't to know that.

Steve opened the door and shouted something. The barrel of lard who had gone to get him in the first place, re-appeared. Finlay did not have to ask if that was Big Boy, the answer was there, in all its corpulence. Finlay squeezed past the big guy, but only just, as the board did not leave much room. He followed Steve into the bowels of his complex.

There in the back room was a surprise. Two to be exact. Tasty and Morsel were sitting there nursing cups of coffee, one of which had a small trace of brandy in it. Tasty liked some of the strong stuff in his hot drinks while Morsel did not like alcohol of any description. There were a lot of things Morsel did not like, top of his list was women of any description. They both nodded at Finlay, who nodded back. He was surprised but then again not, they were nasty pieces of work. But he was taken aback in another way; this suggested that Mick the Trick may have a hand in here somewhere.

Steve beckoned him to sit down. Finlay did not usually sit down in a situation where his health could be at risk; he could move so much quicker from a standing start. But if anything was going to happen, it would have happened by now, he thought and so he put the board down on the floor and accepted the seat Morsel had kicked over towards him. Steve looked at him for a few seconds before he started to speak.

"Old Man tells me you're in."

That was one way of putting it. Finlay played the same trick. Looking around and thinking before answering. He looked at Tasty and Morsel. Steve gestured to them, he knew what Finlay was thinking.

"You know Morsel and Tasty."

"Yeah." Finlay tried to keep the distaste out of his mouth, with little success.

"Steve?" Tasty said quietly.

This was interesting. Neither of them looked like they were bowing to Steve. That told Finlay quite a lot.

"Yeah. What is it?" He screwed up his nasty little eyes as he spoke.

"It's the other way around." His voice was sharp like a needle.

Steve screwed up his eyes some more."What?"

"I've already told you, it's Tasty and Morsel, not the other way

136

round."

Tasty looked to Finlay as though he was expecting some contradiction. He was not going to get any. It was clear to Finlay that he was in the company of one if not more, seriously unhinged individuals.

"Tasty and Morsel, " Steve said very slowly and deliberately.

"Yeah. That's right." Tasty looked at Morsel who nodded in approval. He sniffed, his nose was running from the cold. Steve did not have the heating on.

"Whatever."

Steve was clearly irritated but he did not contradict Tasty.

"So are you in on your own or is Mick a player too?" Finlay addressed his question to Tasty though it was Morsel who answered.

"We work with Mick and for ourselves, that tells you everything you need to know. Mick's a player, always has been."

Finlay did not like the sound of the word 'always', it had a rather nasty feel to it, telling him that Mick had been bad news for a very long time. He always had Mick down as someone who sailed close to the wind, but not someone who entered hurricanes.

"What do you mean work for yourselves?"

Finlay sat forward in his seat. This was getting interesting.

"If something needs fixing, we fix it, at a price."

"Fix?"

Finlay was beginning to feel distinctly uncomfortable, he did not fancy being fixed by Tasty or Morsel, it had a very terminal and final sound to it.

"Some people seem to think it's alright to stick their noses where they shouldn't. People like that need to be fixed. In our business you can't have people running around like rats in a drainpipe, looking at everything they want."

"You need discretion," Finlay said.

"Yeah, that's right," Steve said as he bent down and picked up the board which Finlay had brought with him. Experience taught him to bend his knees to avoid back injury. He looked over at Tasty as he struggled a bit. Tasty came over to help him. Together, they carried the board to the table, whilst glancing at Finlay with a look which suggested that he was stronger than he looked if he was able to carry this thing all by himself. Finlay shrugged as he knew what they were thinking. He was used to it. Most of the boards were heavy, he had carried them long enough, though none of them, to his knowledge, had been crammed full of white powder.

As soon as he had put the board down, Tasty turned and stood with his hands on his hips. It was only now that Finlay realised that both he and Morsel were dressed in almost exactly the same way: black trousers and black rollneck jumpers, though Morsel's looked greyer than Tasty's. They looked like extras from a James Bond film.

Finlay's mouth was dry - this was no film and there was no script. And even if it was, he was certainly neither the director, producer or executive director.

"I must say," Tasty adjusted his position as he spoke, "I never had you down as someone who would get their hands dirty in this type of business." He continued looking very intensely at Finlay before continuing. "I would have thought you would have kept your nose clean." He smiled at his joke as Morsel and Steve chuckled at the thought of keeping your nose anything but clean when there was this much pure Colombian on offer at a very reasonable price.

"I am sick of doing tricks and jumping all over the place for people who don't care whether I live or die. It's about time I made some serious money," Finlay's tone was harsh and very serious. It suited the dim light in the dark and dusty back room. Steve used it to store some of his stock and, of course, to inspect his female shoplifters personally.

Tasty stood quiet and still as he listened to Finlay, digesting what he had said. He looked like he was thinking quite deeply about what he had heard.

"What about your mates?" he asked as he widened his stance a bit more. Finlay waited for the sound of material ripping. That would have given the proceedings a comical element which wouldn't at all have been in keeping with the atmosphere.

"They'll do what I tell them."

"How can you be sure?"

"That's enough." Steve stepped forward and cut through the questioning like a boxing referee. He was anxious to have a look at the merchandise and to fill Finlay in with their expectations of what he was going to do next.

"If Old Man says he's in, then he's in. That's good enough for me. Is it good enough for you?" He addressed the last part of his speech to Tasty and Morsel who just looked at each other. Then

Morsel's eyes narrowed and he answered quietly, "Yeah, course."

"One thing though." It was Tasty's turn.

"What?" Finlay's mouth was getting drier by the minute.

"Any funny business, Morsel and I will take care of them like the others. You get my drift?"

Finlay got it alright. He did not have to sit down with a computer to work out what he meant or who was referring to. He also knew that the Crossizon was fired by one of these two maniacs.

"So why exactly did you get rid of Animal and that youth?" He stood up as his back was getting stiff.

"Animal was in the wrong place at the wrong time. He was out the back at the club when Old Man was doing some business and the youth was close to him. We thought they might have been shooting their mouth off about our operation in Meribel, couldn't take the risk. The Boss doesn't like loose ends."

"Seems fair enough, and a good move if they were being nosy. The Boss?"

Though he realised that there must be more than just the people he knew about involved in all of this; he was curious to know who the Boss was. Finlay did not expect he'd find out at this stage. He was right. Tasty and Morsel just looked at him.

Undaunted, Finlay wanted to tie up another loose end. He was in for a surprise.

"Ronnie. Why did you bring his sorry little life to an end? Was that because he knew something or was it just old fashioned manners, after what he tried to do to a lady."

"I heard about that on the grapevine. I wasn't bothered, didn't affect us. He obviously had a way with the ladies which wasn't good for his health. But we weren't the doctors who handed out the final medicine," offered Tasty.

"Are you sure?" Finlay only realised how silly his question was once he'd asked it. Tasty was hardly likely to confess to two brutal murders and then deny another. There was no logic to that.

"I just thought," Finlay didn't get any further, he was cut off by Morsel.

"-Forget what you thought. Fact was, it wasn't us. Whilst we're doing twenty questions here. I heard you had a notion Animal's accident was no accident. How come?"

Finlay shrugged. "The tree which had the branch snapped off. It had been done a while before Animal had come along. I could tell from the sap that Animal hadn't broken it off so that meant," he didn't get any further.

"-We done it." Morsel smiled deeply. He must have been a foul child and one who clearly hadn't changed a bit in adulthood. It was supposed to be a joke but it lacked two essential ingredients, mirth and warmth.

"That's enough. It doesn't matter just now. Let's have a look at the stuff."

Steve opened up the bag and ran his fingers over the ridge created by Finlay's handiwork. He reached out and produced a wicked looking electric tool which was plugged into the wall. He turned it on and the noise filled the room. He adjusted the speed, then plunged it into the board opening it up as though he was filleting a fish. He reached into the bowels of the board and pulled out a bag of powder. Steve opened the bag and put some on his tongue. The glee in his face told everyone who did not already know that he was a serious user of the marching powder. He stretched his neck to look at Finlay again.

"This was the first stuff to come through like this. We just wanted to check that no one had rumbled us."

Finlay blinked as he digested this information, something else fell into place now.

"So you had something to do with the reception committee at Heathrow?" His eyes flashed; he could not conceal his anger.

"Calm down. We had to be sure that you weren't going to call the police if the action     heated up. In fact, you getting away was the best thing which could have happened. It told us you had cohones." He grabbed his balls to underline the statement which was, of course, meant to be a compliment.

"What would have happened if we had not gotten away?" Finlay calmed down. This was not the time. These were definitely not the people, nor was this the place. Steve looked directly at him but said nothing.

"Right, so it would have been me taking the fall, if not at customs then with the Anthill Mob. Thanks a lot." His eyes still blazed with fury, but he toned it down; he wasn't looking to tangle with these people.

"Relax, they couldn't have pinned anything on you. You'd have been in and out in no time."

Steve's upbeat optimism was not shared by Finlay, but he decided to leave it and refocused the discussion.

"How's the rest of the stuff going to come through?"

"Old Man'll fill you in when you go back to Meribel. He's got big plans for you."

"Is he the Boss?" Finlay probed. If the question irritated Steve he didn't show it.

"Nah, but he's a main man, so it's best not to forget that. He's going to bring some serious goods in for the North American market. Things have gotten too hot coming up from South America so now it goes directly out from Colombia to Eastern Europe, then finds its way to Old Man who prepares the way for its final journey to Canada, then the rest of North America."

He could quite easily have been a corporate fat cat talking about his latest acquisition and the merger of allied markets. All he needed was a flip chart and one of those irritating laser pointers.

"Must make some serious money."

Finlay had been paying attention to every word which was being said. Tasty and Morsel relaxed at the way Finlay was picking up on the important point of the operation.

"Buckets," Tasty answered.

"How does it get out of Colombia?" Finlay asked quietly.

"Diplomatic bag. A really big one." Tasty laughed.

Finlay nodded. "Music to my ears." His mouth was less dry now that he felt he had moved towards some kind of acceptance by the men.

"Right, I'll let Old Man know you've been by and we're all clear. When you get back to Meribel go and see Old Man straight away."

It was not a request, more like an order. Finlay did not argue. He was in too deep to start splitting hairs about tone of voice. Later on there would probably be plenty of chances for him to put Steve in check.

Finlay stood up. "Right, if it's all the same to you, I'm off, I'm bushed." He waved at them all.

"Bushed?" Steve asked.

"Sorry, a Brit saying. I'm tired, going to get my head down."

"Right." He did not sound interested in the English lesson.

"See you," Finlay said to Tasty and Morsel.

They nodded back though neither smiled. That was not their way. Steve buzzed for Big Boy to open the door and Finlay made his way through to the front of the store and out into the street.

# EIGHTEEN

Finlay took a deep breath, inhaling the fresh mountain air deep into his lungs. It felt good after the oppressive air in the shop. Slowly he walked back to the chalet, a lot of things spinning through his mind. In addition to being a fully fledged drug dealer, he now knew who had killed Le Blanc's son. It hadn't been clear whether it was Tasty or Morsel but that fine detail hardly seemed to matter. They had been the ones. That's what mattered. Before he decided what to do he would have to give it some further thought. This was a sensitive time and the wrong decision could cost him and those around him very dearly.

He pulled his coat tightly around him; he felt a lot of things just now but warm and clean was not amongst them. He kept thinking about Tasty and Morsel, about how they killed Animal. Though he knew it had been no accident, hearing it from the people responsible didn't make it any easier to stomach.

His thoughts were interrupted by a glimpse of Roisin in the distance. He was going to go over to her but then caught sight of Rocky. He was not in the mood for him; he would get to see enough of him at the competition tomorrow. With all that was going on he had almost forgotten that the real reason he had come was not to deliver drugs but to compete. There would probably be a good turn out as the event was well publicised. There were a lot of posters around the town advertising the individual sections of the competition and highlighting some of the personalities taking part. Finlay's name was there. They got the Scottish part right but there was something missing in the blurb. He was half-tempted to whip a pen out there and then and write 'drug dealer 'under his name.

He made his way back to the chalet but stopped halfway as something occurred to him: he needed a board for the competition. There were a couple with his sponsor's name on them kept in permanent store back at Joel's, so that's where he headed.

Joel was sitting there taking it easy, with his feet up reading a a New York newspaper which a newly arrived punter had brought in. It had all the usual stuff on the front about the U.S. government kicking foreign ass or not. Joel threw the informative newspaper to one side and stood up when he saw Finlay come in.

"Hey man, you alright?"

"Yeah, I just want to use one of the boards I kept from last time. Can you get it for me?"

He picked up the paper which Joel had cast aside so quickly.

"What's wrong with the cool board you had this morning?" Joel shouted over his shoulder as he went through to the back to get hold of one of the two boards kept for Finlay. The tiny storage charges were paid for by the sponsors but the truth was that Joel's bosses couldn't be bothered invoicing them in England. It was hardly worth the postage, besides it was not as though they took up much space.

"I had a proper look at it, the guts were not really up to much. I think it looked better than it really was." There was some degree of truth in that. The guts were at this very moment being inspected and most probably ingested by Steve, Big Boy and the two psychopaths with childlike names.

"Yeah, I thought it had potential to tell you the truth," Joel said as he brought a board back for Finlay. He wiped some of the dust off it with a damp cloth then wiped it dry with a soft polishing leather. He held it up.

"Nice, this should do the trick for you tomorrow. The sponsors name was sharp and clear in very big letters on both ends of the board. The letters were always oversized to cater for telly, should they be there. Sponsors felt like all their time and money was worth it when they could get some proper telly time.

Joel whistled his approval. He had always liked the sponsor's words and logo on this particular board. Big Butt. A shapely female bottom was painted on the board above the words, with a skimpy pair of pants barely covering each plump buttock. Rumour was, the model who had posed for that one had been a cross dresser from Ottawa, but it couldn't be proven.

Finlay handled the board and smiled. It felt good, and at least it was not stuffed full of cocaine. He smiled to himself at the thought of sticking a trick in the halfpipe and cocaine spilling out all over the place. No danger of that happening with this board; he stroked the buttocks like old friends.

"Did you miss them?" Joel laughed.

"Yeah, wouldn't you?" Finlay gave the board back to Joel.

"I'll pick it up tomorrow, man."

"Not riding today, Fin?"

Joel often shortened his name. He did that to everyone. There wasn't a name he couldn't shorten. He would probably have shortened Fin, if that had been his name. He could have called him 'F'. The phone rang.

"One minute, I'll be back."

Impatiently, Joel went off to the back to answer the phone. Finlay sat waiting on the ledge where the equipment was laid out for clients to examine and select from. The same area was used to measure the gear and prepare it. Punters always liked to see the prep work and there wasn't really room in the back for everyone to crowd there.

Finlay picked up Joel's discarded newspaper from where it had fallen and started to read an item on page five. It was about the rise of the far-right in Europe. Neo-nazi groups were getting funding from various legal and illegal sources. Marches and other types of visible propaganda were gaining momentum. Part of the article covered the murder of a politician in Holland who for some was considered right wing. Whether the murder was a backlash or just the work of some mad individual it made interesting reading, particularly with some of the voting strategies in Austria and France suggesting that the extreme right never seemed far off from gaining legitimate recognition for their views and approaches to social issues such as immigration. The article made interesting but frightening reading. Finlay shook his head, any further thoughts put to one side as Joel reappeared.

"I'll keep the board safe and sound for you man, what time you want to pick it up?"

Finlay put the paper down and shrugged. "Dunno, eleven ok?"

"Yeah, that's fine. See you."

Joel picked up the board and took it back to the rack in the workshop. He would have another look at it later, just to make sure it was ship-shape and ready for Finlay to strut his stuff in the competition tomorrow.

It was going to be a good one, people were coming from far and wide to compete and to spectate. There was going to be a vibe that was for sure. There was even a live band in the evening. The Electric Eels or were they called The Eels Electric? He couldn't quite remember, but they were a grunge band and a good one at that. Word was they were going to go places. A mate of Joel's had gone to college with the lead guitarist. Joel couldn't wait. It would be a gas. Word was the music critic from the *Globe and Mail* was coming. Now that was something, a National newspaper coming to cover something connected to a boarding event. Just went to show how far the activity had come since its tender beginning so many moons ago.

∞∞∞∞

The sun was high in the sky. It was a glorious day and there were people everywhere. The good weather had made sure that there was an even better turnout than could have been reasonably expected from such an event. Competitors had come from far and wide. Some Finlay knew and they knew him, but there were some who were new to the scene. One really young guy called Danny Phanni was causing a big stir and not just because of his unusual name, which you could not pronounce in any other way than it sounded, but because he had inherited stunning looks from his African American father, and mother who was of Far Eastern origin. He had a long mane of jet black hair and was powerfully built like someone who ate, slept and drank in the gym. And he was blessed with an attitude and a gentleness which brought people to him, a relaxed, flowing nature which is just good to be around. The sponsors loved him as he represented every possible market. Shame he couldn't play guitar; still, there was plenty of time.

Finlay was introduced to Danny by Joel and was immediately impressed with his air of maturity, which seemed to light up the mountainside.

"Good to meet you, man."

Danny had an accent you couldn't place; it was a kind of sing song voice which complemented everything else which was so appealing about him. He was something else alright.

"You too, Danny."

Finlay looked at him as he stepped into his bindings. He was first up today for a few practice runs. Danny had a low centre of gravity and powerful leg and thigh muscles which were heaven-sent for controlling a board at high speeds. Finlay noticed something else too, while Danny was loosening up; something which would have been missed by someone who did not appreciate such things, or who did not ride themselves. His waist was extremely flexible. Without bending his knees, he bent at the waist and lowered his torso parallel with his lower body. As he stood in the board, he twisted one way, then the other. His ankles were as supple as the rest of him; they could move with the board in every direction and follow the mountain's curve almost instinctively. He was a complete boarder, almost to computer designed standard.

Thanks to a whole flurry of competition wins, Danny was dripping with sponsorship offers but so far he had turned them all down. Even at his tender age, he had learned one thing which would never leave him. You cannot take peoples' money and think you are still your own person. It doesn't happen like that. The two do not go hand in hand, not in this or any other world.

Danny had earned enough from various summer jobs to get himself going and he knew something else. It was not the costly equipment which mattered, it was the person riding it that was the most important. It was a spirit thing. Like the California surfers who would wait, and wait, and wait some more till it came, the perfect wave. And when it came, as they knew it would, nothing else mattered. Boarding was like that, only the mountain was the wave. And like a wave, it too, was never the same one day to the next. You could ride it one day and think that you had it mastered, that you knew it like the back of your hand and the next you could come out and ride like a pussy. The mountain would upend you, almost stand over you as if to say 'Who do you think you are?'

The best, out there on the mountain, can look into someone's eyes and see things which others can't. They can tell whether a person has spirit, which is different than length of time in the sport or standard achieved. It can be easily lost. Making the wrong life choices, even the smallest of ones, can kill it.

Despite his youth, Danny knew all this. He didn't know how or why he knew, he just did. It had been like that since he had been small. He remembered when he was twelve, a bunch of kids at school running past him screaming, their eyes bulging with blood lust, as they grabbed various makeshift weapons from school satchels. Mayhem was on the cards as they looked for Romeo Titus.

Romeo was in the grade above and did ballet. His name came

from his parents and their love of Shakespeare. Their idea of a family holiday was *'The Burning Man.'* They fed their kids strange brews and weird food and drove a battered old Buick with one of the doors almost hanging off. People were jealous of them because it was obvious that they loved their kids with a passion.

The kids running down the corridor that day had never seen Romeo, in fact they didn't even know what he looked like, they just knew that he did ballet and therefore he was a faggot and needed to be beaten up. They had screamed at Danny that day. He could still remember their tight, angry little faces and the high pitched voices of the ones with balls still waiting to drop. Yeah, they had screamed.

"Come on Danny, help us beat up Romeo Titus."

"Why?" Danny had said.

"Because he does ballet and he's a faggot!" they had screamed back in a unified voice of pleasure and tension.

"Like I said, why?"

Danny had stood there, not moving a muscle. They had looked at him like he was a stranger from another planet. No one wanted to mess with Danny, their time would come another day, they thought as one. They turned and continued on their journey like a medieval monster requiring feeding. They found Romeo Titus, but no one had done their homework. He was a mountain of a boy and with self-esteem up there with the sun and he was fit and strong from lifting girls at ballet class. He wasn't going to stand there and let thin white trash pick him off.

The first two splattered noses had told them all they needed to know. They had made a mistake, big time. For many of them bullying was off the menu for good. It took too much preparation and ultimate courage when it counted, to bring something home to roost. None of them had what it took and if they did then Romeo Titus had robbed them of it that day, he and Danny. Danny had struck a blow, same as Romeo. They had not expected someone to suggest that doing ballet was not reason enough to want to hurt someone.

Danny never forgot that day. It told him more about people than he cared to know. It also told him something interesting about himself. He marched to his own drum and he could tell what was going on inside people's heads, whether their spirit was healthy or if they needed to take a long, hard look at themselves. He was a bit special alright.

# Deep Powder

Finlay stood and watched Danny ride. He was like a ghost as he came through the halfpipe and tried various tricks which, had he been twice his age, would have left people speechless. He stuck them big time too. He moved like water. Not thinking, just doing. That was the secret, if there was one. Danny had obviously taken that to a higher level. His turn was over as soon as it began and he had hardly broken sweat when he glided back off the halfpipe and came to a stop. People cheered and applauded. Finlay had never seen a reaction like that to a practice run; he was seriously impressed. Danny was the real deal. He stepped out of his bindings and moved to one side. Finlay was next. He slapped Danny on the arm as he hopped past him on his board.

"Nice one, man."

"Thanks," Danny answered. His voice was even and relaxed. Little sign of breathlessness.

Finlay bent low and went through his repertoire of tricks and moves. He was quite relaxed and felt reasonably content with his performance. When he came back to rest, Danny was looking at him very intensely.

"You're good, Finlay. One of the best I've seen."

"That's something coming from you. Thanks." Finlay was genuinely touched but he was not prepared for what the intuitive young man came up with next.

"But you're holding back, your spirit's in trouble. I can tell it in the way you move."

The tone of his voice robbed his comment of any offence. He looked genuinely concerned, as though he had known Finlay all his life rather than having just met him. Finlay was lost for words.

Danny walked quietly past him and looked him in the eye as he did so. "Sort yourself out man, you know you're tight."

With that, he was gone. Lost in the crowd of people slapping him on the back and touching him, wanting a piece of a young man they knew was going to be huge in whatever he did.

Whilst the next rider took his place at the lip of the halfpipe, Finlay walked over to the side. He was lost in thought, so he didn't see it was Rocky. Rocky noticed him though and nodded but said nothing. It was quite clear that he was not at all keen on Finlay. There could be no other reason besides Roisin, yet as far as Finlay understood it, she and Rocky were not nor had ever been

148

an item; so what was the problem?

Finlay watched Rocky perform his routine. He was good and moved very smoothly for a big man, but he didn't have the style of Danny, but that was nothing to be ashamed of. Danny was unique in his approach and execution. As he stood there, Finlay was aware of some people off to his left looking at him and giggling: two pretty young girls and a young man with piercing blue eyes. They waved at Finlay.

"You're good man." One of the girls laughed.

"We were just looking at the logo and wondering." The other girl giggled.

"What were you wondering?" Finlay pushed his hat back off his eyes. It was quite hot and the sweat was running off his brow and down into his eyes which were stinging with fatigue.

"If these were your buns." The young man pointed at the logo and all three of them laughed.

Finlay looked at the bulging buttocks on his board. He had been wondering if they were a little too obvious and needed changing. He wasn't sure but then they were preferable to a board full of cocaine on the slopes.

"Yeah, but that was before I went to the gym. They're kind of sloppy," he said with a serious look on his face.

The trio held his gaze looking uniformly serious, then they laughed. "Yeah, funny. We thought you were serious for a minute." They giggled for a bit, then one of them saw something in the distance which warranted their attention and they were off.

Finlay waited a while as the other riders took their turns one by one. Then he had another practice run. He was looser this time. Danny had been right about him being tight, though of course the child prodigy had no way of knowing the reason for Finlay being out of sorts. The sun had faded somewhat and there was more of a chill in the air so it wasn't so warm now. Some of the people on the slopes took this cue to go inside for a drink in the bar near the bottom of Whistler mountain. Finlay thought he should take another run since it was quiet, but there was something else that he needed to do.

∞∞∞∞

As he made his way back to the chalet, a lot of things ran through

Finlay's mind. He had spent all his young adult life trying to do the right thing, so this drug dealing business was a real departure. He sighed as he realised that it wasn't just his own life he was risking with all this cloak and dagger stuff, but Monday and Wot's. As he turned the corner he saw them along the walkway. They were deep in conversation and looking at something. Wot had a bundle of notes in his hands. Finlay shouted at them and walked over.

"Hiya Finlay, " Wot said as Monday grabbed him and gave a big hug.

"What was that for?" Finlay was taken aback.

"Thought you needed it. How was the practice run?" She said.

"I did a few. Not bad; got better. Watched young Danny do his stuff. He's quite something."

"Yeah we hear," Wot said as he held up the bundle of bank notes. "I think the food's on me for a while." He flicked the money like an experienced bank clerk.

"How did they know this time?"

Wot's parents always got the money to him, but they could never work out how they knew. Wot rarely told them where he was going, particularly because he did not want them to think he was looking to ponce money off them.

"I haven't a clue, man. They should work for the government, the way they track me down. They seem to know where I am going before I even get there." He gave Finlay a suspicious look. "Hey, you don't give them a detailed list of where I'm going, do you?"

Finlay held his hands up. "Don't blame me, not guilty."

"Where you off to?" Monday asked. She had a card in her hand. A post card of Whistler which was addressed to Tiny. Nothing romantic, just friendly. She would see where it went before she allowed herself to develop deep feelings."

"I'm off to have a lie down and make a call."

"Okay, see you later. We're off to spend some loot." Wot waved his cash in the air.

"Hey, careful where you flash that stuff. People will get the wrong idea."

Finlay wasn't sure what idea people would have of him if they knew what was going on. He was tired, nervous and excited; he knew what he was going to have to do tonight. Monday and Wot knew nothing, as he didn't want to cause them unnecessary worry or strife. He just hoped he was up to it after all this.

Slowly he walked back to the hotel building. He left the board in the store area and went upstairs. Once inside, he went straight over to the phone. He rummaged through some paperwork till he found what he was looking for and then dialled the number. After a bit a male voice answered.

"Yes."

"I've found out what happened to your son."

After a pause, the voice answered. "Good. I thought you would. You have not disappointed me. When you come back to France you must phone me and we will meet."

"Okay."

Finlay put the phone down a little puzzled. He had expected Le Blanc to have been a little bit more inquisitive. All of a sudden he was very tired, very tired indeed. He stretched his muscles and went through to his bedroom. He peeled off his clothes and slumped on the bed. His eyes were closed before his head hit the pillow. He slept the whole day.

Monday and Wot were in their beds after spending a little longer than intended at the bar sinking some Moosehead. They had giggled all the way home. Before they left they had tried to wake Finlay to ask if he wanted to join them but he had been dead to the world, so they had gone on their own. Now they were back and tucked up fast asleep and it was Finlay's turn to walk the night.

# NINETEEN

Finlay stretched, then opened the top drawer of his dresser. In the corner was a small leather pouch. He opened it up and checked the contents. Everything he needed was there. He showered and pulled on a black pair of trousers, a black roll neck jumper and a pair of his most comfortable shoes which still afforded him some protection from the cold. He slung on his dark parka which had a neat array of buttons on the front, went back to the bedroom, slipped the leather pouch into one of the oversized pockets on the side of the parka and quietly let himself out of the front door.

Padding down the corridor, Finlay pressed the button for the lift which stirred into action and then arrived with a whirr. The doors opened. He stepped into the bright, air conditioned lift and pressed the button for the ground floor. Finlay walked past the lobby. He noted with some satisfaction that there was no-one present at the desk. The distant sound of a television - it sounded like the Jerry Springer show - told him that the receptionist had better things to do than sit there waiting for people to come for their keys.

Finlay stepped outside. Immediately he was struck by the chill in the wind. He paused in the shadows and looked up at the building. It was impossible to tell from the outside that the floors housed complete alpine chalets which were designed to make you feel that you were actually sitting on the side of a mountain.

Walking quickly, he turned towards the covered area. Though he expected no one would pay any attention to him, he stuck to the side of the walkway, creating a kind of strobe effect as he cut through the lights streaming out of the shop windows into the night. They had all sorts of useless and expensive gear on sale and some stuff which was actually useful but way overpriced. He looked up at the mountains, their shapes quite clear even in the dark. He imagined them slowly standing up and changing position in the night. Sometimes mountains do not look the same one day to the next.

There wasn't much lighting in the next walkway, which turned into an underpass to the next section. A couple walked past arm in arm. They did not notice him as they only had eyes for each other and their minds were not on what or who was in the underpass but what they were going to get up to once they got back to the warmth and peace of their chalet. At the end of the underpass, Finlay stepped out into the section which carried on towards the shops but he stepped sideways into the darkness and leant against a tree, as much to steady his nerves as anything else.

Heart pounding and with his brow dripping with sweat, it was as though what he was into and what he was about to do had just dawned on him and his body was saying, you go on and do what you have to do, I'll stay here and wait for you; let me know when you're finished. Finlay pulled himself together and continued on. Destination: Silver Steve's shop. He knew that the back of the shop faced directly onto the unlit area just a few yards from where he was now crouching next to a tree. Patting his pocket, he checked to make sure that he still had his pouch with him. He did.

Finlay stood up, pleased to feel that the sweat had stopped pouring off his body. He walked quickly but carefully, over to the window at the back of the shop which was covered with wire mesh. The mesh was quite thin and only attached to the wall by a single small padlock. He took out his pouch, unrolled it and lay it on the ground. Unfortunate parts of his childhood had involved copious amounts of shoplifting and other types of property crime and this was going to stand him in good stead for the night's work. He lay the pouch on the crisp snow and picked the first item out. He clicked the switch on the small torch and a sharp bright beam bit into the darkness. He shone it on the padlock then back at the rest of the contents of the pouch. He picked out a thin sharp piece of metal and then placed it in the lock. After a few moments a small but audible click could be heard as it opened up in his hand. He slipped it out of the ring and placed the padlock in his pocket.

Finlay then opened up the wire mesh, swinging it towards him. He took out a glass cutter from the pouch and with the torch showing the way, traced a small circle in the glass near the catch which was clearly visible from outside, through the frost covered glass. He traced the cutter back twice, then reached back into his pouch and took out a small rubber plunger and licked it with the tip of his tongue. It took a bit of effort; his mouth was dry.

All nerves, every little sound made him jump. Somewhere off in

# Deep Powder

the distance he could hear the sound of hillbilly music coming from a drunken night-club. It cut through the air with all the subtleness of an out of tune banjo. The song was something about running after hogs, like you do in the woods when boredom sets in. The sound the band were making sounded as though some hogs had joined them on the drums. Finlay smiled to himself as he stuck the plunger to the window, held it in place with one hand and with the other reached into the pouch. He didn't look down. He didn't have to as he knew where the small diamond tipped tapper was. He took it out and steadied himself as it had nearly slipped out of his sweaty palm. Managing to stop it falling to the ground, he let out a sigh of relief. Even though the hog singers were really reaching for the high notes now, he couldn't be sure that the noise wouldn't have brought unwelcome attention.

Several times and very gently, Finlay tapped the glass just to one side of the plunger and then pulled the glass with the plunger. At first it resisted him like a petulant child but eventually it came away quietly leaving a space just big enough to get a hand in. He placed the disc of glass - with the plunger still attached to it - on the ground, reached in and slipped the catch. He slid the window up; it made a few creaky noises. But with the hog screamers now in full unbridled voice, a full squadron of special forces could probably have come parachuting in with grenades and flash flares and no one would have heard them over the boys from Dixie.

Finlay hopped in and landed gracefully on the floor. He leant back out through the window and picked up the plunger still stuck to the glass. He placed it on the floor, reached out again and picked up the rest his equipment, placed that on the floor next to the glass and quietly pulled the wire mesh back into place. He took the padlock and hooked it into the space meant for it in the mesh and closed it but did not click it all the way. To a passer-by it would seem that the padlock was locked and nothing untoward was taking place on the other side. He slid the window down, but did not put the catch back. He placed all his tools, except the torch, in their respective slots in the pouch, rolled it up and returned it to his pocket.

Turning, Finlay pointed the torch at the middle of the room. There were piles of clothing lying around wrapped in plastic, and resembling enormous chocolates waiting to be consumed by a giant with a hungry belly. The light from Finlay's torch danced around the room, reflecting off the plastic, making him feel a little uncomfortable. There was a bit too much light for his liking, he did not want to advertise his presence to that extent.

Switching off the torch, he waited a few moments until his eyes became adjusted to the dim light. Once he was sure that he could see where he was going he walked over to the only door leading to the rest of the shop. He slipped the catch and opened it slowly. It was pitch black and even with his eyes now adjusted, he could see nothing. He reached into his pocket and retrieved the torch. He flicked it on and pointed it into the room. He recognised it from before. It was where he had met with Steve, Tasty and Morsel. He walked in, closing the door slowly behind him. The wooden floorboards creaked a noisy welcome. He stopped, then started to walk more gently. Across the room there was another door with tables either side, loaded with equipment which Finlay guessed was waiting to be transferred to the main shop. He walked over and tried the thick metal handle. It was locked. He sighed and produced his pouch again. He unrolled it and picked a slim piece of metal from it. He probed the lock for a few moments. It was taking longer than the padlock had required and Finlay could feel himself sweating again. Eventually after a minute, though it felt much longer, he heard a satisfying click which told him the lock was his.

He opened the door and directed the torch. The light illuminated the very thing he was looking for. He padded up to the gunmetal wall safe and put his torch on the desk which was facing it. This gave him just enough light to do the next and trickiest bit of this night's work. Once again, he produced the pouch and unrolled it on the desk. There was a small flap on the right hand side. He flipped the top open with his thumb and pulled a small electronic device out, about the size of a very small mobile phone. It had some wires wrapped around it and some small suckers on the end of two thicker wires which were hanging loose. He stuck the two suckers on the front of the safe and put the other wires which were actually ear plugs into his ears.

Safe cracking was not a new discipline to Finlay, he had indulged in it with great enthusiasm during his wild years. Finlay smiled at his memories, and turned the switch on. A small beep emitted down his earphones, but was not audible from the machine itself.

# Deep Powder

He fiddled with the dial half expecting to get the world news or that strange voice which is the shipping news. He turned the dial one way then the next with each beep telling him that he had cracked one of the numbers. He finished after a few minutes and took the earphones out and looked down at the dial. The tiny illuminated section read 7L1R3R9L. He turned the dial seven turns to the left then one to the right. It clicked.

The sweat was running off his face like a river now. Pausing, he took a small bottle of water out of his other pocket. He flipped the cap and was about to take a drink but changed his mind. Time for that later, he didn't want to lose concentration. He put the bottle down and turned the dial on the safe three turns to the right then nine to the left. There was no click this time– he was in.

The handle turned and the safe opened with a smooth easy action. The door was surprisingly thick for such a small unit. Whatever was inside was not meant to be spirited away with any ease. There was a switch inside the door, he flicked it and light flooded the chamber. It was quite big and was stuffed with crisp one hundred dollar bills. It was impossible to say how much was crammed in there but it was a whole lot more than Finlay had ever seen in the safe of the Nice and Easy store in Nottingham where he and his crew had made several unauthorised withdrawals at the height of their Midlands crime spree.

He reached in and picked up the bundle of papers which were on the small shelf just above the cash. He pulled them out and shone his torch on them. What he saw made him gasp. In his sweaty hand was what looked like a list of every transaction and smuggling trip made so far. There was also a list of the cocaine which was due to come from Meribel. Finlay whistled softly, there was no way that amount was coming in the guts of a single snowboard. That begged the question as to exactly how was it going to come into the country. He reached down and without looking, grabbed the bottle of water. He put it to his lips, took a deep swig, then put it back on the floor. The last thing he glimpsed before his head exploded was the Evian label.

Finlay fell to one side, the bundle of papers falling out of his hand as he went completely numb. Still, he had just enough strength left to twist onto his side. He saw a pair of boots standing next to his head. One of them lifted off the floor. It did not take a whole lot to realise that the intention was to implant it somewhere in, or near, Finlay's head. He pushed himself away just as it swung into the space where his head had been. Feeling desperate, he felt power surge back into his limbs; he did not wish to die here and now.

In an instant, he sprang to his feet and stood there facing his assailant. Big Boy had a huge metal thing in his hand. Finlay couldn't make it out but it had some of his blood on it and looked like something you would dig people out with after an avalanche or use to beat their brains out.

"I thought there was something not right about you," Big Boy said with some justification and with surprising speed launched himself at Finlay.

Layers of lard rippled and changed shape as he flew through the air aiming to plant the implement in Finlay, who at just the right moment twisted, as he would on a board with a particularly difficult piece of mountain. Well, this was a mountain, a human one and made up of plenty of fat and muscle. Finlay slammed his hand into the rotund one's side. If he had been hoping to wind him he was sorely disappointed. Big Boy showed that Finlay wasn't the only one who could twist. He even added a shout of fury as he seemed to bounce off the wall and back, catching Finlay full in his face with a big hairy fist. Finlay flew back as Big Boy fell on top of him determined to finish him.

Finlay scrabbled about with his right hand which, like the rest of his body, was seriously hurting now and managed to get hold of something. Pumped up by fear, he tightened his grip and swung it into Big Boy's face with one smooth and surprisingly powerful movement. Finlay was lucky, he had grabbed a couple of crampons, one of which had sliced a piece of Big Boy's face open. The big man fell to one side, crimson liquid pouring down the side of his face. After a moment, he seemed to regain his composure. He licked the back of his hand which had some blood on it and then leered at Finlay.

This time Finlay felt the opposite effect of fear. Three quarters of his oxygen seemed to desert him as he got back unsteadily to his feet. Who knows what would have happened if the door had not swung open, taking Big Boy completely by surprise as a svelte wiry figure rolled through the door, performed a very complex looking sort of turn in mid-air and drove the heel of their hand up and into Big Boy's generous face. A few of his chins wobbled as he slumped to the floor without a sound, blood and snot making a hasty exit from his nostrils. The figure bent over the prone figure

157

and felt for a pulse. There was none as the human redwood tree
had checked out for good.

"Shit, I didn't meant to finish him."

# TWENTY

Pattu stood up and turned to face Finlay, who felt his jaw drop. This was not something he had anticipated; not this night or any other. Pattu looked at Finlay and smiled; definitely a first.

"You better sit down, mate."

He stepped over to Finlay with the same grace with which he had entered and clutched his elbow, helping him into a seat by the other side of the door. Finlay did not protest; he didn't have the strength. He felt a warm flow of liquid down the side of his face and looked down at his jacket. It was red and he was bleeding quite profusely. With one hand, Pattu gave him a cloth to stem the bleeding and with his other, took out a mobile and flipped the top. He pressed a button and the sound of speed dialling filled the quiet room.

Finlay tried to speak but no words came out. He didn't know whether it was the shock of being attacked by Big Boy or the fact he had been rescued by Pattu, whom as far as he knew, hated his guts. He could feel himself drifting into a slumber when the next thing he knew Pattu was slapping him in the face. That was more along the lines of what he had expected.

"You alright?" It was Pattu's voice but he still couldn't adjust to the caring tone. As soon as he knew he was capable of holding a proper conversation he would ask him about this new found concern for his welfare. Finlay couldn't focus properly. He really didn't feel very well.

Pattu slapped him hard in the face. That was more like it. Finlay came to full attention like a private on parade and his eyes focused on Pattu, who was speaking into the mobile. He couldn't hear exactly what he was saying, he just caught a few words here and there. Finlay rubbed his ear, beginning to worry about the possibility that Big Boy had inflicted some permanent damage. Pattu helped Finlay to his feet.

"Probably better if we walk you around a bit till we get you seen to."

Pattu put his arm around him and walked him around the room. The fact that it felt like they'd been walking for ages was due more to his screaming muscles than his conception of actual time.

# Deep Powder

He was still conscious when he and Pattu were joined by another familiar face who bounded though the door just in time to catch Finlay before he finally slumped into unconsciousness.

∞∞∞∞

Finlay flew around in the air, thousands of feet high. He saw a cloud in the distance and turned his outstretched hands slightly so they caught the wind. He increased his speed and tore through the cloud like a knife through butter. Strands of flimsy cloud stuck to his body as he turned his hands again and soared to the very edge of space, where blue becomes green. Concorde appeared from nowhere and Finlay smiled and waved in recognition. He tilted his head as the Captain waved back though slightly less assured than Finlay. The First Officer resolutely ignored Finlay as he flew level with the cockpit.

Finlay cast his memory back as he looked at the nose cone which was pointing the way to the United States. It only tilted down for landing so that the pilots could see where they were going. Concorde, if Finlay had his facts right grew in length during flight, so that a small space by the control panel became big enough to put your whole arm in. A small boy with growth problems which he had inherited thanks to an unfortunate gene, had written to British Airways to see if he could have a flight and grow in the process, thus solving his problem with being vertically challenged.

Finlay tilted his palms a bit and slowed up so that he was level with the first window. There was a small boy, with his nose pressed to the window wearing a smile which could have brightened the darkest day. He was standing on tip toe and could still only barely reach the window. Finlay smiled and knocked on the window. British Airways had obviously told the little boy that the flight would make no difference to his height but he was welcome to come and join them on one of their wonderful flights to New York. The little boy's smile grew bigger and bigger and the slipstream from the thin white metal bird grew stronger and stronger. Finlay reached out a hand and touched the fuselage. He knew that it was coated with gold to reflect the light which could damage the metal so high in the sky, but he couldn't seem to see it.

Then without any warning a thin sliver of cloud hit Finlay at one thousand miles an hour and pierced a hole in his stomach. Not very big and not very small but just enough to open up his insides. He peered down with an inquisitive look on his face to see a bright liquid spill out. It was gold. He was bleeding gold. That solved the puzzle. He had absorbed the gold coating; it was inside him, everything was inside him. He looked up to see the tail with its distinctive fin disappear in the distance. There was a small hand reaching out of the first window at the front. It waved to Finlay and then the plane, the little boy and the flashing colours of the tail, disappeared in a cloud.

Finlay spun out of control, falling down with a speed so intense he felt like he was going to explode. The pain was almost unbearable. Just as he thought his head was going to give up the struggle, land appeared from nowhere. In the middle there was a large pool of water. He fell into it with a huge splash and plunged deeper and deeper. He felt like his lungs were going to explode as it got darker and darker; then suddenly it was light and Finlay woke with a start and a gasp.

∞∞∞∞

"Sorry," the doctor said as he turned off the light he had been shining into Finlay's eyes. Finlay squinted as he adjusted his vision to take in the room. There were two figures standing behind the doctor. Finlay couldn't make out who they were as the room light behind them gave them a glowing kind of biblical image; he lay there waiting for some kind of blessing.

"How are you feeling?"

The doctor had produced his stethoscope now and gestured to Finlay to sit up in the bed. He did so slowly and painfully but eventually he succeeded.

"I feel okay," Finlay said with little conviction. His eyes were adjusting to the light and he could just make out the two figures behind the doctor, who had leant forward and placed his cold stethoscope on Finlay's chest. It was Pattu and Hugo Chirac, a very senior Canadian policeman.

Finlay winced at the coldness of the stethoscope. At least there was one consolation, Finlay thought to himself, there were plenty of other unpleasant places icy metal instruments could be placed. "Turn over," the doctor instructed. Finlay hesitated; he was aware of the fact that he might have presumed too soon that cold metal things would be kept away from his orifices. The doctor sensed his reluctance to turn over and guessed what was on Finlay's mind. "Don't' worry, I just want to check your kidneys. You took a good kicking there." Finlay nodded and turned over, as Pattu and Chirac walked around the bed so that they faced Finlay as the doctor inspected his bruised and battered body.

Finlay knew Chirac because it had been *his* idea that Finlay pretend to be a willing recruit to the drug dealing world. At this moment, listening to the policeman, did not seem like such a good idea.

"You had a close call," Chirac said as he sat uninvited on the bed. The doctor had gone over to a table where he was surveying some x-rays which Finlay presumed were his insides. Finlay propped himself up on one arm. Pain shot through his body.

"You can say that again." He looked at Pattu before continuing. "Are you going to tell me where you come in. You're the last person I expected to see coming to my rescue." He laughed and then promptly wished he hadn't as the pain shot through his side and up and across his chest. Chirac looked at the doctor who picked up some x-rays.

"Don't worry. I'll be off. I'll come back and see you later. Everything seems fine, but I want to take a closer look at these." He pointed at the x-rays he was clutching to his chest as though he had taken them himself with his pocket camera.

Chirac waited for the doctor to leave the room and checked the door was closed firmly behind him before speaking. He nodded his head at Pattu. "He works for your British special services." Finlay slumped back on his back. He had heard it all now. This was something, quite a turn up for the books.

"You make it sound like a pizza delivery job." Pattu smiled.

"Don't you do that as well?" Chirac and Pattu had a rapport which was already getting on Finlay's nerves.

"Look, I don't mean to break anything up but could you explain what all this is about?"

"Well, you remember you bravely agreed with my colleague here that you would get involved so that they thought you were a willing mule," Pattu said. His jacket fell open and Finlay saw the glint of a gun. He was dressed for action.

"Yes," Finlay said. He could hardly forget the meeting he had with Chirac. He had contacted the police once he had discovered the cocaine in the board. That had seemed to be a really good idea at the time. Now he wasn't so sure.

"Well, I was worried that you might get out of your depth and get hurt, so I kept an eye on you." Pattu's tone was matter of fact.

"You'll forgive me if I find that a bit difficult to get used to. I thought you hated my guts."

"It wasn't an act. But that was different. Once you got involved in this, it became my business," Pattu said in a colder tone Finlay was more used to. Some things wouldn't change that quickly.

"Pattu followed you, though it was against my advice. Just as well he ignored my contribution," Chirac said honestly.

"How long have you been with Mi5 then?" Finlay was curious now; he still couldn't get used to this. A thousand things were running through his mind.

"Wrong one. It's the other one." Pattu smiled as though he were talking to a small child. Finlay's brain felt slow. He knew that he had avoided serious damage in that region but at the moment, it didn't feel like it.

"Other one?"

"Yeah, all security but one's internal and the other is international."

Finlay closed his eyes. He suddenly felt very tired. The doctor had returned now and did not close the door behind him.

"I think that's enough for just now, gentlemen. A little bit of rest is in order," he said firmly.

"Fine. We'll be out here. We can talk later as there is more to cover," Chirac said as Pattu stepped through the door before him.

# TWENTY-ONE

Chirac was framed in the doorway; Pattu had already sat down outside on the chair. He was obviously going to guard the door. Finlay wasn't sure if that was supposed to make him feel better. It did and it didn't. It worried him that they felt he was still in need of protection, which suggested that none of this was over.

Finlay felt his head growing heavy and his eyelids started to feel as though they were caked in mud. He had more than his fair share of dreaming so it was something of a relief for him to be able to get a few hours of snooze in without any more glowing Technicolor images to contend with. He did dream on a fairly regular basis, but that last one had enough special effects in it for the Oscars; he could have sold tickets.

When he woke there was a buzzing noise in the room. He thought there was an insect in there with him but then he realised that it was the water cooler which Chirac had so thoughtfully arranged to be brought in. Not the Ritz, but it was a help. Finlay looked from the water cooler to the end of his bed where he found Monday and Wot. Wot was smiling but Monday had a scowl on her face. That was not surprising as she had been the least enthusiastic proponent of the scheme to transform Finlay into an international drug dealer. It had not been planned that it would come to such a violent conclusion.

Finlay was about to find out that Chirac and Pattu had further plans for him. Finlay's usefulness was not outplayed yet. If this was a game of chess then Finlay was a major player, even if he couldn't fight the feeling that he was a pawn in other peoples' dark and dangerous games. Wot reached out and touched Finlay on the leg through the blanket. Finlay smiled in response.

"Hi, mate. you've been in the wars a bit, haven't you?" He left his hand where he had placed it.

"Yeah, you could say that. I'm alive though." Finlay smiled again though this time it was more like a grimace.

Monday was not so generous. "You could have been killed, you fool." She did not reach out and touch him but folded her arms and took a step back.

"It wasn't my fault," Finlay answered though as he did so he had to admit that his argument was a touch weak. No one had forced him into this. It was Chirac who had first listened to his story about the cocaine smuggling when Finlay went to the police originally. Finlay could have refused his suggestion that he go undercover but it had seemed a good idea at the time and if he was honest with himself, Finlay liked excitement, especially if it was legitimate and was sanctioned by the authorities. Now, aching in his bed with his two friends standing vigil, none of it seemed like such a good idea.

"What's next?" Wot stood up and walked around Monday to the water cooler.

Monday's eyes looked like they were going to pop out. "Next? Are you joking? Do you want to find him on a mortuary slab? That's what's next if this carries on."

"I don't think that will happen. We'll look after him." It was Pattu who had opened the door quietly and come back into the room. He had had been standing there, with his arms folded like Monday, listening to the whole proceedings.

"Like you looked after him so well he got kicked to within an inch of his life!" Monday was in full flow now and did not appear to be in the mood for taking any prisoners.

"It isn't him who's on a slab. It's Big Boy," Pattu said with no trace of humour.

Monday looked like she was going to have a fit. What it is to have friends who care the world about you, Finlay thought to himself.

"Big Boy?" she spat the words out. The name sounded like an extra from one of the porn films on the Eurochannel, with people in cowboy hats and chaps.

"Big Boy was the guy who tried to sort Finlay," Wot explained.

"I know that, I just don't know why you have to use his nickname. What was his real name?" Monday shook her head at the offered glass of water from Wot.

"No one knows, that's the only name he's ever been known by." Pattu stepped further into the room.

"I thought you were one of these people who knew everything."

Monday hadn't bothered trying to hide the sarcasm in her voice. She had been as surprised as everyone else about Pattu's true calling in life and though she didn't know all the details, she knew he wasn't a check-out clerk for the Seven Eleven. Not unless that was something *else* he was keeping to himself to be revealed at a later date. She shook her head.

"Look, what Finlay managed to do tonight was seriously helpful. The information in these papers has gone a long way to helping us to crack this ring but we're not there yet." Pattu looked at Finlay.

"But I'm a coconut, remember?" Finlay looked directly back at Pattu who did not flinch.

"I know you are, but you did well for a coconut." He looked directly back at Finlay who did not flinch either. Eventually the silence was broken by Finlay.

"If it wasn't for you, I would be in little pieces being fed to the pigs by that human fat machine who kicked me around."

"There is that, but you don't owe me. You owe it to yourself to finish this, Finlay."

Finlay looked directly at Pattu. He knew he was right. This whole thing had gotten under his skin. He nodded.

"Tell me what I have to do."

Monday walked slowly and quietly out of the room without uttering a word.

"Don't worry, she'll be alright," Wot said with a reassuring smile.

Finlay hoped so but somehow he wasn't sure. He would have felt better if she had screamed and shouted and maybe broken something. The walking out of the room without saying a word was rather worrying; not like her. A few moments later Monday came back.

"I don't believe this." Monday sat on the bed with her head in her hands. "He's a snowboarder for Christ's sake not James Bond."

"He's the best chance we've got to bring all this to a conclusion," Pattu said quietly.

Monday stood up again sighed and walked out of the room, shutting the door slowly behind her.

"What do you want me to do?" asked Finlay for the second time.

"Nothing at the moment. But as soon as you're up to it, get back to normal and get back to Meribel. We can take it from there. Old Man is expecting you and we don't want to disappoint him."

Pattu smiled, business-like, but this was no ordinary business. The night's events had shown that it was all deadly serious. The dealers were not prone to asking questions first and listening to the answers.

"What about Big Boy's death? How can we carry on if they know he's copped it?" Finlay was sitting up in bed now, quite involved.

Chirac and Pattu had judged wisely. At the end of the day they were not exactly pushing at a closed door when it came to Finlay. He was an adventurer, a sensation seeker, a thrill junkie.

"We can make it look like Big Boy has been arrested and taken to Vancouver for questioning. We've got a friendly lawyer who will pretend he has Big Boy as a client. That will keep Tasty and Morbid quiet until we get this finished. It does mean, however, that time is not on our side. Finlay, when you get back to France you'll have to try and make sure you get as much as you can cut and dried before they eventually realise Big Boy is not just staying out for an extended lunch."

Pattu leant against the wall, evidently pleased with himself at getting so much of this organised. What could go wrong? As long as they kept Big Boy's death quiet, then Finlay would be the material witness to all the dealings when they finally round up the bad guys and take them off to court. Pattu hadn't mentioned that bit yet, but there was no hurry; they could cover that later.

"It's Morsel," Finlay said.

"Sorry?"

"Morsel, not Morbid." Finlay shifted position to his other arm as the one he had been leaning on had gone to sleep.

"What's in a name?" Pattu shrugged.


"How did you get involved in all of this spy stuff?" asked Wot pouring himself another glass of water. His throat was parched, probably with all the tension. He and Monday had been very worried when Chirac had first called them to say Finlay was laid up in hospital. That had not been part of the plan. But now he was caught up in it all. There was something right about being involved in bringing Animal's killers to justice. He may have been a rogue and not the kind of guy you would bring back to mum, but he was someone's son and would possibly have been someone's father eventually. Animal, like everyone else, had a life which deserved at least some justice. Pattu cleared his throat.

"Well, the security services have been looking to recruit people who did not necessarily come from Cambridge or Oxford– I fit the bill. Someone approached me and the rest clicked into place."

"All guns and roses then?" Wot asked, looking quite excited about the whole thing.

"Up to now, its been just going around pretty much as I used to. A lot of pen pushing and paperwork actually. But when it breaks it breaks without warning...."

"Do Nyaman and the others know what you do?"

"No. There's never been a good way to bring it up. On top of that, my employers do not encourage it. If I go around shooting my mouth off then I'll be waiting in line outside the employment office with a job seekers allowance form in one hand and a begging bowl in the other.

"Sounds to me like you've already been there, you talk with some authority on the subject." Finlay was careful to make sure there was no trace of sarcasm in his voice.

"Yeah, I've been there and I've seen some sights. Many of them to do with drugs. That's why I want to nail these flaps of skin pretending to be humans. They don't give a fuck about the peoples' lives they scum up." Pattu's eyes blazed with fury and then settled down a bit as if some long lost memory had come, and then gone in an instant.

Wot and Finlay saw this but it was Finlay who put it into words. He waited a few moments, weighing up whether he should anything at all. He came down on the side of 'yes'. After what he had been through he wasn't that worried about saying or doing the wrong thing.

"Who was it, Pattu?" Finlay spoke quietly and firmly and looked him straight in the eye.

Pattu looked at Finlay strangely, then Wot, then Finlay again before finally speaking. "My brother. He was a good kid stuck in at school and all of that...."

His words trailed off as he allowed his thoughts and his feelings to go all the say back to Peckham Rye and the life and the losses he left behind there. He could feel it and smell it like it was yesterday. He thought of the brother he had, young generous and tidy who would no more miss a day at school than go to Saturn on a motorbike. Then he thought of the thin emaciated bag of piss and shit held together with a bedraggled parka whom he had cradled in his arms.

Pattu's brother had died in a stairwell in a filthy, badly lit block of flats in a filthy, badly lit estate a tart's walk away from the Route 36 bus. With impure heroin pulsing through his body thanks to a syringe he had plunged into the last good vein he could find - in his scrotum - his brother had breathed his last. Pattu had known that day was not the end but the beginning of his personal quest to wipe out the drugs which were claiming all his brothers, not just the one related to him by birth. He had only just begun.

Finlay went out on a limb. "The dealer who was involved with your brother, mixed parentage?"

Pattu was impressed. He knew Finlay had a serious level of insight but this was almost too painful to bear. "Yeah, ran with and for some of the lowest rats you could find.

"White rats?" Finlay nailed the last piece in the puzzle.

"Yeah." Pattu sat on the chair by the door. He suddenly felt very tired. "It seems so childish when you put it like that."

"Don't worry. I knew your problem with me was deep like water, not shallow like skin. I'm on your side, mate. So's he." Finlay gestured to Wot and then to the door. "And so's she."

Pattu nodded.

"The doctor won't like it but I'll compete tomorrow," Finlay said with a determined sound in his voice.

"Are you sure?" Pattu stood up from the chair. It was a little too small for his girth.

"If I don't they're bound to know something's up particularly with the disappearance of lard man.

"Yeah, Big Boy's absence would be connected to you, if you didn't show. Well, I'll leave you to get some rest. I'll see you tomorrow. There's a uniformed guy just at the end of the corridor. Discreet but there just to make sure you're safe and well." He opened the door and was about to close it when Wot stopped him.

"Wait, I'm coming too. You're right about giving him some rest." He waved to Finlay who smiled back.

Once they were gone, Finlay turned his back and changed position; his arm was hurting. He knew the doctor would be less than impressed but he also knew that if he didn't get out there tomorrow then the whole plan would fall to pieces and he wouldn't be safe anyway. This had been started and it had to be finished one way or another. He didn't hear the door open silently and then close equally stealthily nor was he aware anyone was in the room until Monday lay on the bed beside him, put her arms around him and held him close. Her tears stained the sheet. He did not turn around but put his hands on hers and allowed himself to be gently rocked to sleep.

# TWENTY-TWO

The light on the slopes was blinding. The whole place was heaving with humanity and the atmosphere was electric. Finlay was nursing a giant headache but he had eventually persuaded the doctor, against his better judgement, to give him some powerful pain killers and allow him to get on his way. Music was pumping as Rocky, the first up on the halfpipe, stuck some tricks which even Finlay had to admit were pretty impressive.

Roisin, who was standing near to Danny Phanni, waved. Finlay smiled and waved back. He still couldn't get over the skill of the young man or his incredibly strange surname. The crowd couldn't either as they were chanting his name. "Fanny, Fanny...." They loved the double entendre of his name and they were equally in love with his skills.

Roisin made her way over to where Finlay was standing. "Hi, sweetie." She reached out and touched his face. Finlay pulled away, as his skin was tender and he was sporting a nasty purple bruise.

"Ouch." He smiled, but it was an effort.

"What happened to you?"

Finlay had already prepared his story and mapped it out in his mind so that it would sound believable.

"It was dark when I came in and one of my boards was in the front. I walked right into and took a fall at the same time."

"It looks pretty nasty. Have you had it seen to?" Her genuine concern touched him and the gentle delivery of her voice hit a nerve somewhere just above his groin and a little below his belly.

"Yeah, the doctor's had a go at it. Says I'm ok, so that's good enough for me. Look at that!" He quickly changed the subject as he pointed at Danny sticking a 560 with a tailgrab. That wasn't what was spectacular. It was his smile, as big as the Hudson, and the way he punched the air with his free hand as though he was doing nothing more than frying an omelette rather than holding a position suspended in mid-air some forty feet above everyone's' heads. He pulled a few other tricks out the bag and came away with the highest score so far– no surprise.

## Deep Powder

A few other riders made their mark one way or the other, then it was Finlay's turn. He prepared himself and looked around the crowd just before he launched himself in the halfpipe. He noticed Tasty and Morsel staring hard at him from the crowd. It was just as well he was up and about. It was pretty obvious that his absence would have led them on a trail which would have uncovered far more than Pattu, Chirac and Finlay wanted. He had a feeling that at some point in the future he was going to cross swords with Tasty and Morsel, but here was neither the time nor the place.

He concentrated hard but relaxed at the same time. After a while all thought of the pain which was coursing through his body had disappeared and was replaced by a kind of warm feeling which surged through his body. He really felt like he was flying and each trick and turn was effortless. In next to no time he had finished and was standing back on the lip, the crowd roaring his name and Danny and the others coming over to congratulate him.

That was a result. First! And he hadn't even been aware of what he'd been doing. It had been so effortless, he couldn't even remember what he'd done. Roisin came over and planted a kiss on his lips. "When I see you back in Meribel, I'll kiss you better. Well done." With that, she was gone. Finlay touched his cheek then put his finger to his mouth and tasted the sweet aroma of her perfume on his tongue.

Tasty and Morsel came up. "Well done," Morsel said with a grunt. Tasty was looking at him in a strange way and did not congratulate him on the win. When he did speak it was simply to say, "See you back in France." And they were gone.

Finlay stepped out of his board and watched the two walk away. It looked like there was a lot of loose ends to be tied up back in France.

∞∞∞∞

The travel schedule had been a long one. The three of them had flown back to Heathrow from Vancouver with just enough time to transfer to a flight to Lyon. At Lyon they picked up one of the last airport cabs available and slept all the way to Albertville where a local cab took them the last few miles to Meribel and some welcome beds. It was three in the morning by the time their heads hit the pillow. Duncan's firm had said it would pick up the bill, which was just as well as it cost quite a few Euros by the time they had finished the journey.

The plan was to go straight to Old Man, find out what he could, then step back safe and sound and let the French police - in the shape of Picot - do the rest. He was looking forward to seeing the look on the Frenchman's face once all the facts came to light. Everything seemed straight forward and simple.

Finlay, Wot and Monday relaxed on the veranda overlooking the shops next to the bars and ski hire shops below them. It was overcast and the slopes were shut; there was danger of avalanches as the temperature had risen sharply. The mountain guides had reported that there had been a lot of loose snow shifting about and they did not want to take any chances. No one wanted to breathe their last and there wasn't anyone who was in a hurry to ruin the lucrative tourist trade by losing a bunch of trippers to the cold mountain. The murders had done enough damage.

The three sat quietly watching Meribel come to life. There were big posters advertising the last of the competitions in the present series of the North American and French circuits. Finlay looked at the shop front of Old Man's place. The sign said it was closed in French and English to make sure there was no mistake. Monday wandered off and came back a few minutes later with three steaming mugs of hot chocolate she had bought from the nearby cafe.

"Thanks." Finlay took the cup of hot liquid making sure he did not spill it. He had enough injuries to last him for a while and did not want to add burns to the sorry list of ailments he was now sporting. Monday sat down next to Wot who put his hot chocolate on the table in front of them. Though it was overcast, Finlay put his sunglasses on, he liked to have his shades on; it kept him from squinting. He took another drink of his hot chocolate and then looked back at Old Man's shop. The closed sign was now gone and in its place was one which said 'open'.

Finlay swallowed his hot chocolate. It was very hot and burnt his tongue. He looked at Wot and Monday who gave him the thumbs up. It was time to play detective again. Without finishing it, he put the hot chocolate down and walked slowly over to the shop front.

# Deep Powder

As usual, the window had an impressive display of gear. There were jackets with all sorts of flaps, pockets, stripes and circles on them. The trousers had zips coming and going at all angles and there were gloves of all sizes, shapes and descriptions. Amongst the sunglasses and sunblock, there was a snowboard, with just enough room to fit. It had a smiling face on it and a sunburst finish just like the one Finlay had been charged with bringing to Canada.

Finlay slipped the catch on the door, walked in and was almost bowled over by Rocky who grunted, then kept on walking. Old Man was sitting behind the desk near the cash register. It had English and French stickers and photographs of young women in various states of undress, all over it. Old Man looked up from the glossy brochure he had been reading and turned his intense stare on Finlay, who stood there framed in the doorway, not saying anything. Eventually Old Man stood up and came towards him.

"Welcome back," the tone was friendly enough and there was nothing untoward about the way he put his arm around him and led him towards the desk.

"How was the journey?" He sat down on his stool where he had been sitting before Finlay came in and picked the brochure up again.

"Tiring, but I had some sleep so I feel okay." Finlay leant against the counter; he was trying to look casual.

"There's some nice boards here." Old Man pointed to the brochure. Finlay peered at it.

"Yeah, but they're not quite the same as the ones you put together." Finlay stopped leaning against the counter. It was giving him backache and he decided it did not feel or look particularly cool. Old Man's eyes glinted. They were quite a sight. The milk of human kindness was not oozing out of them. He was one evil bastard, Finlay thought to himself.

"Well, you know all about the ones we make now. I suppose you'll be wanting to know what your cut will be for helping to move our merchandise around." He sounded like a bank manager discussing the latest interest rates on a loan for a family car, not like a dealer in death.

"Yeah, that was something I was going to ask about. I didn't know you knew Rocky."

"I know a lot of people." He quickly changed the subject. "So you made it to Silver Steve's. Did you hear about Big Boy?"

Chirac, Pattu and Finlay had discussed at length what to say when Old Man raised this topic, as he was bound to do. They had agreed that there was no reason why Finlay would know. To admit some knowledge would probably only serve to raise his suspicions.

"No, what happened?" Finlay immediately asked. He did not want to hesitate and give Old Man any reason for sniffing a rat.

Old Man looked at him, his eyes boring holes into him as though they were searching for something which he could not see on the surface. He did not speak straight away but waited a few moments then seemed to visibly relax. It was almost as though he had been trying to make up his mind about Finlay and what he was saying.

"He got lifted. We've got some briefs on it now. We're not sure why as he hasn't been released yet. I think it might have something to do with the revenue. Big Boy is not a keen payer of tax, but we'll know very soon."

Finlay didn't like the sound of this. The way Old Man was talking made it feel that Finlay had even less time than he had imagined.

"How will you know soon?" He tried not to sound too interested nor too dismissive. He did not want to do or say anything which would bring undue attention to him or his attitude. After all, as far as Old Man was concerned he was still a trainee drug dealer.

"Well, they have to charge him with something or let him go. I don't think they suspect anything as everything is in order at the shop."

Finlay nodded. That was because Pattu had wisely put all the papers back in the safe, after he had taken photographs of them with the smallest digital camera Finlay had ever seen.

"You did well, Finlay. This is only the beginning. Come back tonight and I'll show you the rest of our operations."

Old Man stood up which told Finlay that this audience was at end.

"Tonight?" This was pissing him off. He wasn't sure how much longer he could remain convincing with the cloak and dagger stuff.

"Yeah, tonight. Is that a problem?" There was a tone in his voice which suggested that it better not be.

"No problem." Finlay quickly switched the subject.

"What was the inspiration for the sunburst finish?" he asked as he walked to the door.

"The what? Oh, you mean on the board. Well I just liked the effect it had on the old Strats in the sixties and that."

"Strats?" Finlay had opened the door now and was standing half in and half out.

"You're from a different generation. Think guitar." He spoke as though he was a lecturer on rare musical instruments. He probably could have been, if a life of crime had not beckoned when Old Man was a young one.

"Oh, yeah, like Buddy Holly, that kind of stuff."
He'd gotten the period right. Old Man beamed. Even psychos have their soft spot.

"Dead right. Holly played a sunburst Strat. How did you know that?"

"I don't know. Just some memory from my childhood. My dad was into all that. Something must have stuck."

Old Man smiled and slapped him on the back. Finlay was relieved his musical knowledge had made such an impact. It had started to feel a bit sticky in there, Old Man was not as warm towards him as he'd hoped. The business about the guitar seemed to have taken the chill off events.

"Midnight,"Old Man said and Finlay nodded as he closed the door behind him and went back to where Monday and Wot were relaxing in their seat. The clouds had parted somewhat and the sun was making an appearance.

Finlay picked up his mug of hot chocolate and put it to his lips; it was still warm. He was deep in thought. His mobile made that noise which tells you there is a text message. He checked it, flipping up the brightly coloured lid with his thumb. It was from Face, telling him to take care. He smiled ruefully. He appreciated the sentiment as he was beginning to wonder if he had bitten off more than he could chew.

Monday and Wot lay back in their chairs. They were tired after the journey. A newspaper lay on the ground. Something caught Finlay's eye. He picked it up and smoothed it out. His French was good enough to make out the general thrust of it. The front page carried a huge piece about the recent French elections. It had been a close thing with the President just scraping in by the narrowest of margins. The far right had enjoyed an unprecedented surge of support. There were many people in France who were not new recruits to the workings of the Neo-nazis and their attempt to take on a fresher and more media friendly face. As a celebration, the President was doing a walkabout in Paris the next day to meet and greet the people. A beaming President with his hands clasped together and raised in victory took up most of the page.

"You going on the slopes today?" Wot asked wearily.

"No, I'm going to get all of this over first. Pattu will have contacted Picot by now so let's hope all of this will be tied up tonight. To be honest, I can't concentrate until it's done.

"That makes sense," Monday said quietly. She was scared about all of this. She felt that in some way Finlay was being used and that his and their safety was not a high enough priority.

"I'm going to take it easy. Get some sleep." Finlay stood up and drained the last of his hot chocolate. He threw the paper back on the ground where he had picked it up from. Wot retrieved it then let it slip from his hand as he quickly lost interest. His French was not as good as Finlay's.

## TWENTY-THREE

Finlay lay in bed looking at the overcast sky from his window. The clouds had darkened and in some ways it seemed appropriate. It matched his mood. His mouth was dry and his palms sweaty. He tried to look on the bright side. As far as he understood it, all he had to do was glean the last of the information then report back to Pattu and then the cavalry were going to move in. Picot and the French intelligence services would mop it all up. That is if the French intelligence services actually dealt with drug dealers. He tried to remember who was responsible in Britain. As far as he could recall it was Customs and Excise. He didn't think it was the V.A.T. boys. As he lay there with the duvet pulled to one side Finlay smiled to himself. The value added tax boys would probably have killed the drug scene dead– in a week. They were so terrier-like in their pursuit of their prey they made News of the World reporters seem sloppy.

Finlay listened to the radio. The French voice lulled him into a slow slumber-like state, but it was not what he would call a proper sleep. He got up about seven and had something to eat, watched a bit of Eurosport, then sent a text to Face. It outlined some of what he had got himself into and what was happening tonight. It seemed wise to keep at least someone who had his interests at heart, fully informed. He didn't go into too much detail but it made him feel a bit better to keep the Face up to date.

About eleven, Finlay dressed and put his riding boots on, somehow he didn't think a pair of casual shoes were a very good idea. This decision would prove to be a pretty important one. The rest of his clothing was casual but warm. Tension had made him feel strange and his temperature was running both hot and cold.

A few minutes before twelve he let himself out of the door of the chalet and padded slowly through the snow. Something made him stop and turn. He looked up at the window on the top floor. There was a light on and Monday and Wot were staring out at him. Monday waved slowly and deliberately. It should have helped but it did not make Finlay feel any better.

The snow was crisp. There had been a fresh fall. He was careful as he walked towards Old Man's shop. A fresh dump of snow could often hide ice underneath. A loud noise in the distance made him come to a sudden stop. The slopes were all lit up and there were several big machines working, smoothing snow and firming up the loose stuff. The lights were on all the way up to a surprising height on the mountain. Finlay knew these slopes well but he had never realised that when all the lights were on, so much of the mountain would light up, like a Christmas tree.

Finlay checked his watch. It was nearly five past twelve. He was late. Some English revellers came down the street towards him, shouting and laughing with various parts of their anatomy on display. There were men and women and they looked around about the thirty plus age group, though he couldn't be sure. As they drew near someone broke wind and the whole group collapsed on the ground stricken with laughter. As Finlay side-stepped them, another one decided to lose their dinner in the snow without any warning. He made that noise which sounds like a sperm whale with a bad cough and retched the contents of his stomach up onto the virgin snow. Fondue, underdone. The smell was caught in the slight breeze and blew in Finlay's direction as he hurried on to old Man's shop. It made him retch as well as wonder about the Brits abroad. They seemed to treat everywhere they went as an extension of Palma Nova, no matter what they were doing or where they were.

The door to Old Man's shop was firmly shut and the sign, not surprisingly, said 'closed'. Finlay knocked gently a few times. Nothing happened. He turned, startled, at a sound behind him. It was some snow falling off a tree; the temperature had started to rise. He turned back to the door, there seemed no sign of life. He knocked again, this time more firmly and louder. He heard some footsteps padding towards the door, then a curtain was slowly pulled to one side. One eye peered at him. It looked familiar, as familiar as an eye can look in the night time. The owner pulled the rest of the curtain fully to the side to reveal Old Man. He was not smiling. The door was opened and Finlay stepped in. Old Man closed the door, put two locks back in place then pulled the curtain back across, blocking the lights from outside.

"You're late. His voice was cold. He gestured to Finlay to walk ahead of him. There was an old wooden door slightly ajar and he could hear some voices, one of them was familiar, very familiar and Finlay's blood ran as cold as a mountain stream as he walked slowly towards the room.

# Deep Powder

"I was held up." Finlay's voice sounded as though it was coming from another place; a kind of out of body experience. Old Man did not say anything but reached round Finlay and pushed the door open for him to step in.

Finlay knew before he was fully in the room that one of the people he would see there was Roisin. She looked stunning in a skin tight blood red one piece ski suit. Her blonde hair was scraped tightly around her head and she had a matching red headscarf keeping it all in place. She lit up when she saw Finlay and came over and hugged him in a full blown embrace. Finlay felt like he was being held by the bride of Frankenstein but he tried his very best not to let it show. His performance was worthy of an Oscar.

The explanation when it came was not something he wanted to hear.

"Finlay, sweetheart. Sorry I couldn't let you know sooner that I was part of all this, but I wasn't sure which way you were pointing, if you get my drift." She smiled and whispered in his ear. "I've been saving myself for you." She seemed more like the bride of Frankenstein, by the second. Lust was the last thing Finlay felt for her now. Funny how quickly things can change.

Finlay made sure he smiled back and looked enthusiastic at the knowledge that she was connected in some way to this crime syndicate.

"Roisin is our coordinator, you might say. She makes sure all the channels are ready for our deliveries." Old Man had walked over to the side of the room and was standing next to Tasty and Morsel and the owner of the other voice which Finlay had recognised, Mick the Trick. There had been no mistaking his mock Caribbean tones.

"And I'm her assistant." Mick came over and high fived Finlay. This was getting more and more surreal by the minute.

"Deliveries, you mean someone like me with a snowboard?" He was breathing deeply and trying not to let his emotions get away from him. He was so disappointed about Roisin.

"We operate on a bigger scale than that, my man," said Mick the Trick looking particularly pleased with himself. Like a fat cat of industry discussing expansion plans.

Tasty and Morsel walked to the window, like a pair of cats surveying their territory. Finlay thought tonight they looked even more dangerous than the last time he had seen them.

"I see your bruises have healed nicely." Roisin ran her hand over Finlay's face. A flash of jealousy spread across the Trick's face. That was all Finlay needed.

"Bruises?" Tasty sounded suspicious.

"Yeah, I had a bit of bump. Walked into a snowboard." Finlay regretted coming up with the explanation so quickly. It sounded so suspicious. He did not feel he was coping with all of this. He was out of his depth. There wasn't a person in this room who wouldn't slip a knife between his ribs as soon as look at him. He felt so alone. The sweat was streaming down his body and clinging to every orifice. He could smell something coming off him. He wasn't sure what it was at first, then it dawned on him, it was fear.

"Right let's go." It was Old Man. Finlay had not noticed that he had left the room and returned all kitted out for the slopes.

"Go, where?" Finlay could feel his blood rising and his temperature go through the roof. He was in a state of panic. This had not been part of the plan. As far as he had understood it, at some point Pattu and the swat squad would come crashing through the door. But nothing happened.

"You'll see."

Old Man started to close everything up. Now Finlay noticed that they were all dressed for the outdoors. They headed quickly for the lift at the bottom of the first run. Finlay didn't bother asking how they were going to get it going at this time of night. He did not think they were so stupid that they were not on top of that.

As though from nowhere Old Man produced a series of keys and opened up the door to the wheel house. The noise from the snow machines on the slopes was so deafening that nothing could be heard above them. The sound of the lift starting was no exception. It was only then that Finlay noticed that Tasty and Morsel were missing.

"Where's the other two?" he shouted at the Roisin, so as to he heard above the roar of the snow machines and the lift. She shrugged her shoulders and kissed him on the cheek.

"We're going to make a lovely couple." Her eyes blazed with excitement. It was only then that Finlay realised that she was barking. Completely bonkers. He smiled back and squeezed her arm. It was the best he could do under the circumstances. There was a rat the size of a cat in his heart but she did not smell it.

# Deep Powder

The first lift came and Rosin and Finlay got in. Roisin swung the bar down and twisted round to see Old Man and Mick the Trick in the one behind them. There was still no sign of Tasty and Morsel. The lift, carrying Roisin and Finlay burst out of the tunnel and rose above the slopes. The lights dazzling beneath him served to make it seem like Christmas too soon. The men working the machines paid no notice at all. It was perfectly normal for the lifts to be used by authorised personnel doing all sorts of repair work on the slopes, when they were empty. From that distance no-one could tell that the four of them were anything other than authentic work officials. On top of that it was obvious that this was not the first time Old Man and his bunch had made their midnight trips.

It all made sense. They must have done this time and time again. Perhaps it had led to Animal's death as well. They must have thought that after the rumblings at the club, he was nosing about trying to find out more when he was riding the slopes at night. Finlay shook his head. If Animal hadn't loved to ride at night, then he would probably have been alive now.

"You ok?" Roisin snuggled up to him.

"Yeah. Just taking it all in," he lied. If he thought they were going to have a short ride to their destination, he was wrong. They rode the lifts as far as they could go, then transferred to some Sno-Cats which were waiting, fuelled and ready to go.

Old Man led the way, the light from his Cat, cutting through the night like a thermal lance. He was very good, riding it like a motor bike, shifting his weight from one side then another. It was clear he knew the slopes like the bumps on his arse. He could have ridden this route with his eyes closed.

Far below Finlay could see the lights of Meribel and even further in the distance, Albertville. They were seriously high now. It would have taken at least forty minutes to ride down this on a board, presuming you were moving at top speed and not prone to falling. Finlay thought he knew the mountains but he was not familiar with the section they were in now. They took one more turn, by a big clump of pine trees and stopped outside a big wooden lodge, which had a warehouse attached to it. There were lights on inside. They brought the Sno-Cats to a halt, turned the lights out and walked inside. Finlay did not wait to be asked, but guessed correctly that he was expected to join them inside. Waiting there for him was yet another surprise.

## TWENTY-FOUR

L e Blanc was reclining in a big smoking chair, a cigar in his freshly manicured hands. He was not smiling, nor did he get up to greet them when they walked in. The lodge was immense and there was Nazi memorabilia all over the walls. Old black and white pictures of the rallies and individual portraits of the architects of that vile piece of European history. Finlay recognised Hitler and his mob though he couldn't name each one. Roisin ran her hand gently over the picture of Hitler. She looked like she was going to come in her pants. Finlay felt a wave of nausea spread over him as bile rose in his throat.

They were all standing except for Le Blanc, who eventually turned his head to look at Finlay. It reminded him of something from The Exorcist.

"Finlay," he hissed.

"Le Blanc." Finlay answered quietly.

"Do you like my little office.?" Le Blanc licked his lips and rubbed the tips of his fingers together in obvious satisfaction. "I like it. It makes me feel safe." He gestured round the room.

"Your son?" Finlay said quietly.

"Ah, yes. So good of you to be concerned. How unfortunate. He was nosy and he did not agree with my sentiments." He spread his hands around him in an open embrace of the Nazi photos on the wall.

"Unfortunately Tasty had to give him a passport to a better world. He was about to, how you English say, blow the whistle on our operation. We couldn't have that. I know he was my flesh and blood but he was not of my heart. He did not share our dreams. He had to go. Unfortunate but unavoidable."

He could have been talking about a rim of scum on the bath.

"Why did you ask me to find out?"

He looked at Finlay as though he were a disposable rubber glove. He tapped some cigar ash into a tray. It smelt expensive.

"I wanted to see if you were someone we could trust. That was all."

Le Blanc had ordered the killing of his own son, charming. He got rid of him like you would a boil, thought Finlay, standing quite still.

# Deep Powder

Le Blanc suddenly stood up. "Let me show you something." He walked through a large set of double doors and they all followed. He flicked a light switch and the massive room was illuminated. There were hundreds of snowboards, stacked in piles of ten each. Finlay could see at least fifty rows filling the whole space. Each one was exactly the same as the one he has taken to Canada. Thick and sealed and no doubt already stuffed with cocaine. There was millions of dollars worth of drugs in this one room alone.

"This is only one shipment," Le Blanc said as though he was reading Finlay's mind.

"What's it all about?" Finlay said quietly.

"Money." He spoke quietly. It gave him a serious edge of menace. Money to finance the overthrow of the French government and return us to our former glory."

He even spoke like a Nazi, Finlay thought to himself.

"The finances will help bankroll our new party."

"How are you going to get rid of the President?"

It was all fitting into place now. Finlay leant against the wall in an attempt to seem casual.

"With a bullet," Le Blanc said as though he was saying how much sugar he took in his coffee.

Finlay walked over to the stack of boards nearest to him and ran his hand over one. He imagined all the death and misery their deadly cargo would hand out to the vulnerable people who sought their solace in the mind bending powder. There were people who did it for recreation but they always ended up with their noses blown to pieces begging for mercy in the bankruptcy courts. He noticed that there were a few boards with bindings on them. No doubt, they too, were  full of cocaine. That was the beauty of it. No one would believe you could balance them with all that powder inside. They must have some of the best technicians involved. Any suspicions would be put to rest once you rode one of these monsters.

Something struck Finlay as odd. "I'm hardly your typical blue eyed wonder god. I don't think I fit into your plans, surely."

He didn't underline it too much. He didn't want them getting any ideas about getting rid of him there and then.

Roisin stepped forward. "You're different, Finlay and it's not all about colour. It's something else."

She sounded almost human. Finlay's mouth was dry. He was no

in a good situation here, debating eugenics with these nutters.

"Roisin's correct. Many people think we are just racists. We are far more subtle and forward thinking than that. It is about building a new world which has the best brains and types, people with spirit. Colour is not such an issue. It is the colour of the imagination which matters."

Finlay tried to be impressed but he was only buying time. "Who prepares the powder before it is put in the boards?" he asked.

"We have an expert in chemistry and such matters. He gets the stuff ready, here in the special room." He nodded to the closed door off to the left of the stacked snowboards. "Come, I'll show you," he offered, like a car enthusiast who had just bought himself a new vehicle and could not wait to show it off to someone. He opened the door. The sight which greeted Finlay made the whole place seem even more like Dracula's castle than before. There were tubes bubbling away and various wires connected to computers with flashing lights. He stepped forward but Le Blanc stopped him.

"That's far enough. It is very important that we maintain a constant temperature and that everything in the room is undisturbed. It is a very volatile time when the cocaine is being prepared. Our chemist uses all sorts of substances which can be very dangerous if they are unsettled. The computers keep an eye on it all.

"Don't people ever come up here?" Finlay could smell that there were all sorts of things going on in this room. It was like a regular nerve centre.

"No. We set off controlled avalanches every now and again. This is a very dangerous part of the mountain. We just make it seem more unfriendly. As far as the authorities are concerned, this area is deserted and no one comes near. Nobody wants to die under tons of snow to satisfy their curiosity."

"Yeah, I can see that. But aren't you worried that someone might stumble on it?" Finlay looked at the bindings on the board by the wall. They looked like they were tailor made for the boots he was wearing. He filed that piece of information away for the moment; it was worth knowing.

"We are due to close this down after the last shipment anyway. Tomorrow everything comes to a head and we can move our operations to another base."

"What's so special about tomorrow?" Finlay couldn't keep up

with all this, particularly the part where he was supposed to be an element in the grand plan for the future.

Le Blanc put an invisible gun up to his shoulder and took aim and then pulled an invisible trigger.

"Bang. No more President. France in chaos. We take over. The Right rises up and finishes what Hitler tried so bravely to do all these years ago. The culmination of a dream."

"I see," Finlay said quietly. "The French President gone and the start of a new Europe."

The phone rang. Le Blanc ushered Finlay out of the bubbling room. He did not lock the door, nor did he close it properly. Le Blanc picked up the receiver and put it to his ear.

"Oui?" He listened intently, his face altering into a kind of mask. He did not look like a happy individual at all. He licked the inside of his mouth, put the receiver down after muttering a few words, then walked over to the window and looked outside. It was pitch black and it was unlikely he could see anything. He snapped his fingers without looking round behind him. Old Man walked towards him then stopped and just stood there, looking at Le Blanc. It was clear they were deep in conversation despite the fact Le Blanc did not turn to look at the man.

Finlay could hear a thumping noise and tried to work out what it was. It was a few seconds before he realised that it was his own heart, pumping like a sluice gate. Something felt dreadfully wrong. The atmosphere had changed. It had been almost relaxed up until the phone call.

Old Man and Le Blanc talked at some length then Old Man turned on his heel and disappeared. Finlay was rocking from foot to foot with worry. Then suddenly he stopped rocking. The reason was simple. He couldn't move in any direction as Old Man had stuck a cold, sharp piece of metal deep into his floating rib. Finlay was no weapons expert but then he didn't have to be in this case. He knew what it was because Old Man told him.

"It's a Heckler & Koch MP5. Not the best thing to come out of West Germany, but certainly one of the best. At this range, if I let off a few rounds, your insides will travel twenty feet at least." He licked his lips.

Finlay had no desire to prove Old Man's theory.

"Look-"

Finlay got no further as Old Man raised the weapon and

slammed it into his face. He fell to the floor, blood pumping from his nose. He lay there on the ground and checked that his jaw was still intact. He looked around the room, if he was looking for some support or sympathy from Roisin or Le Blanc he was sorely disappointed. They just stood there impassively as Old Man stood over him menacingly. He really did look like he wanted to empty his gun into Finlay. This was not a good turn of events.

"Seems you are just a plant. You had no intention of helping us. You are dead meat!" Old Man screamed.

∞∞∞∞

The door swung open. A flurry of snow blew in from outside as there, framed in the doorway, stood Wot and Monday. They were not alone, as they were accompanied by Tasty, Morsel and Rocky, armed to the teeth. Finlay gasped as both Wot and Monday did not look in a very good way. Wot had clearly lost a piece of his left ear and blood was dripping down into the wooden floor, like a leaking hose pipe. He was just staring ahead, in shock. Monday had a vicious purple bruise spreading under her right eye and her jacket was ripped. She looked as though she was in shock and was shivering with cold. Rocky pushed Monday into the lodge. She fell on the floor.

"Get in, bitch." He stepped over her sprawling form. Tasty did not have to push Wot as he stepped in of his own free will. He wasn't a complete idiot, he'd already lost a piece of his ear and wasn't in a hurry to lose any more body parts. Tasty had already made it clear that he was more than happy to oblige. Blood was oozing down Wot's face and leaking into his mouth. He and Monday had been taken completely by surprise by the unwelcome trio. They had beaten Monday who had tried to resist, and had cut off a piece of Wot when his childhood stutter had returned from somewhere in his dark and distant past.

Tasty was armed with a Remington shotgun. It was the favoured weapon of the S.A.S. Tasty had always fancied himself as a member of the special forces. Since that fantasy would never become reality, he had made himself familiar with all their hardware. The first thing he had gotten his hands on was the Remington. It held a special place in his heart being the first piece of weaponry he had bought for himself.

Le Blanc smiled at Finlay. "Very bad choice to double cross us. A very bad choice indeed."

"Sorry." It was Wot. He had told them everything even through his stutter. Hardly surprising once they had started to carve him up.

Finlay raised his hand in understanding; it was hardly Wot's fault.

"This is the end of the road for you; all three of you. It's a shame you will not be around to see our brave new world." Le Blanc signalled Tasty, who then raised his Remington and aimed it at Wot, who hunched up; waiting for death.

It didn't come. Something crashed through the window; a signal for all hell to break loose.

∞∞∞∞

Had there been time for him to think before the bullet entered the left side of his head, Tasty would have appreciated the explosion from the concussion grenade. The bullet - a gift from Tiny - had spread on impact and scrambled his brains; he was dead before he hit the floor. The Remington lay uselessly by his side. Face, who was standing next to Tiny, had put a bullet clean through Roisin's face. He was not a sexist, he did not discriminate. The fact she had pulled a semi-automatic from somewhere, despite being half-blinded by the flash-bang grenade, was all the prompting he needed to dispatch her to another place.

The explosion had started a fire in the chemical factory where the drugs were made and an awful smell was now filling the place and flames were licking up the walls. Finlay was slowly regaining his sight now and he was not prepared for what he saw. Along with Tiny and Face were Pattu, Donny, Menelik and Nyaman. Pattu was not the only one who worked for the intelligence services. Donny, Menelik and Nyaman were all part of the same team. They had been tracking this bunch of Neo-nazis for some time now.

Donny shoved a thirteen round Browning semi-automatic pistol into Le Blanc's teeth, breaking an expensive crown in the process. Morsel threw down his weapon. He needed no more convincing that these men were as willing as him to use firearms to solve issues; he did not want to die. A warm prison cell was preferable.

Pattu shouted. "Everyone out!"

# Deep Powder

The place was getting seriously overheated now.

A few seconds later they were all outside as the fire blazed fiercely on and began to engulf the house. Wot had lost his stutter and had cheered up quite a bit. "I didn't know you knew each other," he said looking first at Pattu then over at Face and Tiny.

"London breeds many strange relationships," replied Pattu. He smiled at Finlay."You ok?"

"Yeah," Finlay said and went over to Monday who had been picked up and carried out cradled in Tiny's arms.

"Who did this?" Finlay asked quietly.

Monday nodded her head toward Rocky, who had appeared to lose some of his stature.

Tiny gently let Finlay take over the task of holding Monday and went over to Rocky who was flanked by Nyaman and Menelik. He towered over him and then without warning his hand snaked out and grabbed Rocky's testicles. Tiny leant forward and whispered in Rocky's ear. "Cough. Don't worry, I'm a doctor."

Rocky couldn't make a sound, as all the breath had left his body. Tiny kept squeezing. He thought one of them had popped, but he couldn't be sure. Eventually Rocky lost consciousness and then Tiny let go his grip. Rocky slid to the snow, blood coming out of his mouth where he had bitten through his own tongue. Tiny stepped back and turned away, muttering under his breath, "Why didn't you cough? I said I was a doctor."

He walked back to Monday and knelt down in the snow next to her. She would be alright; that much was obvious. Finlay looked around; someone was missing.

# TWENTY-FIVE

Old Man was now a distant form flashing down the slope through the trees. He had managed to get hold of one of the boards with bindings and was making a hasty exit. Finlay ran back into the house.

"No!" Pattu shouted but it was wasted on Finlay. He had some unfinished business. Old Man had not even said goodbye. The smoke and fumes were overwhelming but Finlay knew where he was going. He barged his way forward and then stumbled into the boards. One of them had bindings on it. He felt, rather than looked, his way back outside with the board tucked under his arm. He took the nearest exit, through the window smashed by the grenade. With one smooth movement he threw the board down on the ground, stepped into the bindings and then jump turned to face down the mountain. In a flash, he was gone. He dug low, his front hand just touching the snow. He knew he was dicing with death but he didn't care. Each time he felt the curve of the mountain change, he turned. He was riding on instinct. Every sinew and fibre of his body was stretched to breaking point. The board was surprisingly responsive.

He could see Old Man in the distance cutting through the night like an ogre on speed. Finlay crouched a few millimetres lower and felt his speed pick up. He was flying now, and riding at the very edge of his ability. One fall now and he was history. He was gaining on Old Man who, though he knew the area better than Finlay, did not have his skill or the ability to take a line which could keep him ahead of Finlay. Old Man was panicking. It was obvious as he nearly lost his balance a few times and the troughs he was carving in the snow were deep and clumsy.

By now Finlay was level with him and they were travelling at close to fifty miles an hour. They reached the illuminated area but this did not help much as the lights reflecting off the snow made it difficult to see every turn, bend and tree. Old Man looked to the side at Finlay and was about to make a gesture. It was the last thing he would ever do. He hit the tree and spun off, a bundle of limbs spraying blood, as he tumbled into the ground, the board spinning down the mountain.

Finlay slowed down and carved a turn which brought him level with Old Man's body. His neck was well and truly broken and there was a death grin on his face. Finlay did not have to check, no one could have survived that. He was gone and his sick and twisted dreams of a master race had gone with him. Finlay looked up at the tree and gasped in surprise. It was the same tree with which Tasty and Morsel had ambushed Animal. Old Man had met a poetic death, if there is a such a thing.

Suddenly, Finlay felt really tired. All the strength left his body and he sunk to the ground. He just sat there looking at the mountains. They always win.

# TWENTY-SIX

Picot sighed. His heart was heavy. He had put this off for as long as he could. He knew that he could delay no longer. His Chief had been very generous allowing him to go on this task without back-up so that he could bring the man in with the minimum of fuss and ceremony. It was a favour; Picot had asked for it. It was the last thing to be done. After this, Finlay and the others could go and he would be left behind with his pain and his anguish.

As he got in his car and started the engine he thought about recent events. He supposed that it was kind of obvious; there was only one man in the valley who had the kind of skills necessary to prepare the drugs for travel and then provide the necessary expertise to get them ready for the street. Someone who was trained in the use of pharmaceuticals. The sun was high in the sky as he slowly drove along the winding road. It was quiet at Philippe's house when Picot pulled up alongside the Mercedes. It was no surprise to Picot that the car was there. He had expected it to be, just as he expected his brother to be waiting for him.

Picot had telephoned him to say he was coming. His career was on the line. If Philippe had made a run for it then Picot would have handed in his badge. He opened the door and went through to the kitchen as he heard the kettle boiling. He was right, Philippe was waiting. He sat there in the kitchen chair, his head tilted to one side, his face a strange kind of blue, a froth gathered at his lips. Picot knew instantly that Philippe would never be going anywhere again. He couldn't be certain, but it looked like cyanide. Forensics would say for sure.

Even in his death, Philippe had been thoughtful and organised. He had used a deadly cocktail of drugs which would show on his lips, in order to warn Picot not to consider mouth to mouth. Picot turned off the kettle and sat down in the chair next to his brother. He took his cold hand in his and wept for the life they had shared as children.

END